T0267586

ONCE BITTEN, TWICE DEAD

A **MONSTER HIGH** NOVEL

TIFFANY SCHMIDT

Amulet Books
New York

PUBLISHER'S NOTE: This is a work of fiction. Names, characters, places, and incidents are either the product of the author's imagination or used fictitiously, and any resemblance to actual persons, living or dead, business establishments, events, or locales is entirely coincidental.

Cataloging-in-Publication Data has been applied for and may be obtained from the Library of Congress.

ISBN 978-1-4197-7104-0
eISBN 979-8-88707-157-2

Monster High™ and associated trademarks are owned by and used under license from Mattel. © 2024 Mattel. All Rights Reserved.

Jacket illustrations by Cristiano Spadoni
Book design by Brann Garvey

Published in 2024 by Amulet Books, an imprint of ABRAMS.
All rights reserved. No portion of this book may be reproduced, stored in a retrieval system, or transmitted in any form or by any means, mechanical, electronic, photocopying, recording, or otherwise, without written permission from the publisher.

Printed and bound in the United States
10 9 8 7 6 5 4 3 2 1

Amulet Books are available at special discounts when purchased in quantity for premiums and promotions as well as fundraising or educational use. Special editions can also be created to specification. For details, contact specialsales@abramsbooks.com or the address below.

Amulet Books® is a registered trademark of Harry N. Abrams, Inc.

ABRAMS The Art of Books
195 Broadway, New York, NY 10007
abramsbooks.com

Deadication:
To the OG fandom—welcome back to school

PROLOGUE

"It's creeperific being at Monster High when no one else is here. Don't you think?" Draculaura wasn't sure why her father, Dracula, had asked her to come along on this trip. Or, actually, why he was here, but Monster High in the summer was eerie.

The empty hallways were draped with more cobwebs than usual. She'd walked through at least three as they made their way to his office—the one designated for the head of the Monster High school board. Her heels had echoed loudly in the silent corridors while, as usual, her dad had glided noiselessly beside her. The school smelled dank, like the pool had had another toxic algae bloom or a kraken had been body surfing down the halls.

She missed the mixed aromas of the ghouls: Cleo's spicy cardamom and cinnamon perfumes and Clawdeen's pine and moonlight hair gel, the chlorine that clung to Lagoona's skin and hair, the chemicals from Ghoulia's lab, and Frankie's faintly sweet formaldehyde scent.

There were no groans, moans, or gossip. No pings of iCoffins as hexts were sent or received, no lockers slamming, no books being dropped. No other heels clicking on the marble floors or fingers drumming on the desks as she waited for her dad to stop retrieving—and rejecting—books from the shelves behind his desk and respond to her. There were still the distant echoes of whatever chaos and creepiness was happening in the catacombs, but that felt a world away from the mess her obsessively tidy dad was creating in his office.

Dracula rarely visited Monster High during the summer. He'd much rather drop by during the school year and surprise her by melting out of the shadows in the middle of Mad Science class. Last time, she'd shrieked and toppled her Bunsen burner. She was sure Mr. Hackington would've given her a detention for igniting an entire stack of lab notebooks—except her fire-elemental classmate, Heath Burns, did worse daily and her father inspired such awe and reverence from Monster High creatures that instead Mr. Hackington apologized *to her*.

"Dad?" she prompted.

"Hmm?" Dracula made a distracted sound as he finished searching the bookshelves along the office walls and turned his attention to his desk drawers. She noticed him pausing to close his eyes and rub his temples.

He was spooked by something. Dracula hated when he misplaced things. It must be burning him up—literally. Draculaura was pretty sure she saw sweat dripping off his widow's peak. She hadn't known her adoptive father *could* sweat.

"Can I help you find something?" she asked. "I'm pretty fangtastic at locating lost items. I've got lots of practice from Frankie—she's always losing her head, and her hands, and once her little toe was missing for *hours* before I spotted it by the door to the creepateria."

"It's supposed to be here." Dracula bit out the words before slamming the final drawer on his desk. Normally that would've splintered the furniture into matchsticks, so he must've restrained himself since the desk barely quivered. "I must have missed it."

She narrowed her eyes. Was he favoring his right arm? She was pretty sure he was and keeping it tucked close to his chest, hissing when he moved it.

Dracula had been oddly quiet on the trip over. He'd opted to drive—which she assumed was because she lacked the ability to phase into a bat and fly—but this time he didn't even ask her to try or insist that she *could* do it, if only she focused. Maybe he was finally giving up that battle? Realizing she'd develop her vampire powers in her own time and that pressure didn't help.

Not that she minded. At least, not usually. And when her confidence faltered, the ghouls were always there to reassure her that she was clawsome *because* of her freaky flaws. It must be so boring to be a normie-human. She knew the official reasons for keeping the monster world magically hidden from the human one was because of fear of anti-monster discrimination and attacks—but was it also because humans would be jealous if they knew monsters were real and what they could do? Hmm. Ghoulia might know.

"Draculaura?" Dracula cleared his throat, and she had the sense this wasn't the first time he'd called her name. He looked pale—well, even paler than usual. "Are you listening to me?"

He'd apparently given up his search and was leaning back in his leather desk chair. Sweat had dampened the collar of his always-immaculate shirt and darked the hair at his temples.

He'd always had a few gray streaks—you don't live for millennia without a few souvenirs—but he suddenly looked older.

Old.

The thought made Draculaura shiver.

"Of corpse, Dad." She hopped up on the side of his desk and began to rearrange his pens. He had them sorted by type—ballpoint, fountain, quill—but she liked it better when they were grouped by color. Or, actually, she just liked to see him squirm. Dracula was almost always somber—today more than usual—but she could usually tease-tempt him into smiling and flashing some fang.

"I need you to hear me," he said, pressing his left hand to his chest and clearing his throat again. "In case someday, I'm not here for you—"

"What are you talking about?" Draculaura laughed as she snuck a highlighter and a pencil among his fountain pens. "You're immortal."

He continued as if she hadn't interrupted. "And, in case I'm not here, there are some things—"

"Are you going on a trip?" Draculaura dropped the pens, surprised he didn't flinch when they landed helter-skelter on his desk. "Can I come? You're not retiring from the school board, are you? Monster High needs you."

"Draculaura, this is important." Dracula sat upright in his chair, his brows converging in an expression that would've made anyone but his daughter pee their pants. "Do you remember the end-of-the-year party at the Steins' house?"

4

She waved a quill in his direction. "Of corpse." But she wasn't sure how the two halves of that statement fit together. *She* thought parties were important, but he rarely did. And a party that had occurred a week ago? "Did something happen there?"

"Do you remember how I got sunburned?"

"Yes." She rolled her eyes. Was this going to be some sort of parental lecture after all? "But if *you* remember, I told you to put on sunscream. And I was following you around with a bottle of SPF 1000, but every time I tried to give it to you, some monster pulled you into a conversation."

Parties were *not* her dad's happy place, but it made everyone else in the monster community so happy to see him. There'd practically been a line of monsters waiting to say hi, to ask his opinion, to get just one second of his attention and acknowledgment. One second is all that most monsters could handle, since they found him utterly unnerving.

That was her dad: famous, intimidating, alluring. It had been charming to watch him try to soften his stern affect when her friend Clawdeen introduced the newest member of her family pack, or when Frankie's dad, Dr. Stein, had wanted him to admire his latest experiment in electricity generation.

Less charming had been seeing the blistered sunburn on her dad's skin later that night. She should've just interrupted, should've insisted he slather on a thick coat of sunscream or take her parasol. It might not have been a glamourous look, but it was effective.

"Ahem." Dracula cleared his throat again, then made a painful hacking sound that it took Draculaura a moment to realize was a cough. Her dad was *coughing*? Before she could process that unboolievable fact, he caught his breath and said, "Name the three ways a vampire can die."

"Die? Are you okay?" she squeaked, but when he raised an eyebrow, she hurried to add, "Sun, silver, or stake. But, Dad, you're not going to die from a sunburn." Her voice wobbled uncertainly. "It's only if you're outside so long you *literally* catch fire. And you're—you're—*you*."

"It's not the sunburn." He stood and unbuttoned the cufflink on his right sleeve, meticulously folding the starched black fabric once, then twice, to expose his arm to the elbow.

Draculaura leaned forward to see, then gave a full-body shiver and slid off the desk, wanting as much distance between herself and what he'd revealed. His skin looked thin as rice paper, cracking, peeling, and translucent. His veins were starkly visible, only they were all wrong: inflamed, pulsing, *black*. Something the color of tar was oozing from multiple abrasions, which was when she realized the fabric of his shirt was wet—not just on this arm, though certainly worst there, but the other arm too, and along his collar. The black stains blended with the black fabric, but now that she knew to look for them . . .

"What's going on?" she whispered.

"I went to the doctor to get something for the burn. You are correct, it was not fatal, just a painful inconvenience. But since my presence as head of the school board was required at the outdoor Monster High graduation ceremony the next day, I wanted something to prevent further damage."

Draculaura nodded; she was following the story so far, but none of this explained the horrifying mess of his right arm.

"There was an unfortunate mistake made at the pharmacy." He paused, and she got the sense it wasn't for dramatic effect but to collect his energy. "The pharmacist was new; he missed a warning. Every medication needs to be checked *by monster species*. The burn salve he gave me would not have harmed your sea monster friend, Lagoona, or Frankie Stein, or any of the de Nile mummies. But vampires and werewolves, we cannot have—"

"Silver," she gasped. The metal was poisonous to those species of monsters.

"Yes. A lamentable ingredient in the burn medication—silver is antimicrobial but also lethal."

"It did that?" She turned her head away before pointing at his arm. "How do they fix it?"

"Oh, my darling girl, I am sorry to say there's not much they can do. I didn't—" He faltered, then paused to collect himself. "I thought the pain was from the burn, not a reaction to the medication. By the time I realized and sought medical help, it was too late. It had entered my blood. Once in my blood—"

"Please stop saying that word—you know it makes me woozy." And combined with the visual of his arm and the mental image of what he was describing, her vision was already fading. Why did blood have to be so, so . . . red? And sticky. There was a reason she and her dad rarely ate meals together. Or why she insisted he use opaque glasses, opaque straws. Just thinking about it was enough to—well, now she was sweating too. The room was spinning.

"Draculaura, focus. I'm not trying to upset you, but there's so much I need to tell you, before—" Dracula sighed and pushed a spare chair in her direction. "Put your head down and your feet up if you need to, but we *must* talk about what's happened. Once in my blood, the silver spread to my heart—"

Her vision, which was already gray and fuzzy at the edges, faded to black, as black as the veins of his arm, as poisonous as the blood inside. Draculaura didn't feel the plush pile of the carpet when she fainted. Didn't see the concerned look on her father's unnaturally pale face. Didn't hear him struggling to breathe, or when he managed to say, "Maybe this was the wrong approach. We'll talk about this later, darling girl."

But later never came.

By midnight, when Draculaura came back to consciousness, Dracula was dead. This time, for good.

CHAPTER 1

THREE MONTHS LATER

The halls of Monster High were no longer empty. Now they were full of whispers.

They chased Draculaura as she forced herself to march through a gauntlet of pitying stares, her heels clicking unsteadily as she kept her eyes on her coffin-shaped locker and threaded through her classmates, who paused their first-day-of-school reunions to gawk and dropped their voices as she passed.

"Can you boolieve Dracula is dead?"

"I heard Draculaura was there."

"I heard she fainted and when she woke up he was dusted."

"Can you boolieve he was taken down by a sunburn?"

Sunburn. Like it had really been that simple. Like it hadn't been a combination of catastrophes. Too much sun, the wrong prescription, an inept pharmacist, stubbornly waiting too long to get help. Which of these did she blame?

And did blame even matter when she still had nightmares of waking up orphaned, beside the pile of ash that moments earlier had been her beloved father?

All she could think about—then, now, always—was one fact: *If she'd interrupted any one of his party conversations to insist he put on sunscream, he'd still be alive.*

Well, undead.

But did that mean the blame was hers?

Her dad, who'd taken in her pregnant mother after her husband (Draculaura's biological father) was struck down in battle—

Her dad, who'd saved her life by changing her into a vampire before she could succumb to the plague that had killed her mother—

Her dad, who'd been by her side for sixteen hundred years, somberly supporting her, grumpily teasing her, stoically encouraging her to try a little hard to master the vampire skills that came so easily to him—

Her *immortal* dad—

—was no longer here.

Draculaura was alone. An orphan.

She'd had all summer to digest that fact, but it still sat heavily in her stomach like an undercooked turnip. She'd rattled around the mansion for three months, alternating between craving company (beyond that of her beloved housekeeper, now legal goredian, Ms. Heaves) and dodging visits from her friends and other well-wishers, because they tried so hard to cheer her up, then looked so gravely disappointed when they failed.

Draculaura had thought today would be better. A distraction. But everyone else looked fangtastic in their new clothes.

They were excitedly swapping stories about their summer howlidays . . . or, at least they were until they saw her coming and fell dead silent, like she might find their joy offensive.

After Manny the minotaur and chaotic, fire-elemental Heath Burns dropped both their football and their gaze when she walked by, she sighed and muttered, "You don't need my permission to smile."

Even if she couldn't manage one herself—not right after passing the memorial outside Dracula's empty school board office. A mountain of blood-red flowers leaned against the black fabric someone had draped over the closed door. An *In Memoriam* plaque was mounted below a framed photo of a dark suit. Dracula's face didn't appear, of corpse, since vampires never showed up in pictures—but it was a gut-punch reminder of their family first-day-of-school tradition. Her dad hadn't been there this morning to pose her on the shady portion of their front steps, urging her to smile and "show some fang" while he snapped about a hundred pictures of a floating backpack, hair bow, her lucky safety pin earrings, and some scarefully chosen pink and black back-to-ghoul outfit that had required multiple trips to the maul to select.

Draculaura hadn't been to the maul in three months, couldn't remember what she'd grabbed from her closet to wear, or even if she'd brushed her hair this morning.

Ms. Heaves had tried to make the morning special. She'd cooked a whole plant-based breakfast feast. But Draculaura hadn't been able to choke down more than a bite of it.

She also hadn't stopped to read the inscription on the memorial plaque—there were too many other weepy monsters gathered around it.

Dr. Sanguine, the scare-apist she'd started seeing this summer, had told Draculaura that when things felt horrible or overwhelming, to focus on the present. Immortality now felt so . . . long and lonely. She should take things one day at a time. One hour. One minute.

And in this minute, she just needed to open her locker and figure out her schedule. She took a deep breath. Easy-queasy.

"There you are! We've been looking everywhere for you."

Draculaura jumped as Cleo de Nile popped around the corner, her gold highlights catching in the glow of the hallway's chandeliers as they settled against her tan shoulders and fangtastic teal jumpsuit. Cleo's boofriend, Deuce Gorgon, and the rest of their beast friends were right behind: Frankie Stein, Clawdeen Wolf, and Lagoona Blue. Their eyes were all full of pity and other heavy emotions.

At least, that's what she noticed when they met her gaze. Mostly they glanced quickly, then looked at the floor, the wall, the ceiling. It had been like this all summer—so awkward and gloomy.

"Here I am," said Draculaura, with all the forced excitement she could manage before being engulfed in a group hug.

Normally Draculaura loved hugs—she missed them. No one ever accused Dracula of being cuddly, but he'd hugged her daily—an embrace that was brief and bone-crushing. She wanted *that*—not this—too gentle, too lingering, too . . . sparky.

The ghouls jumped apart when the bolts on Frankie's neck gave them all a jolt. "Sorry!" she said, but they were used to the literal shock of their friend's emotions. Cleo was already using Deuce's mirrored sunglasses to check the static damage to her hair.

"How are you?" Lagoona asked quietly. Her blond waves dripped onto her pale cyan scales. Clearly she'd come directly from the pool, and Draculaura would much rather hear an exscreamly detailed play-by-play of swim practice than have all their scrutiny trained on her.

She shrugged stiffly. "Oh, you know. Fine."

"Truly?" Frankie's heterochromatic eyes—one blue, one green—scanned her skeptically. "Because it's okay if you're not. That's why I've been calling all week, to make sure you know I'm here. Back-to-ghoul is always stressful and without Drac—"

"Sorry I didn't answer, but I'm fine," Draculaura interrupted, her voice firm. "Toads, fine."

"Ghoul friend, I love you, but I won't lie to you. You say you're fine, but you're looking a little . . . scary. Have you seen yourself lately?" Clawdeen brushed a lock of Draculaura's hair out of the way so she could zip the last inch of her friend's dress.

"How?" Draculaura gave a tired laugh as she pulled a few random pencils and decomposition books from her locker. "No reflection, remember?"

"That's never stopped you from looking aces before." Cleo tapped a finger against her gold lipstick and tilted her head. "I always assumed it was my style sense rubbing off on you. You *need* me. Just look at your highlights—or, rather, don't look because they've faded from fuchsia to blah."

Both Clawdeen and Cleo were fashionistas—their love language was monster makeovers. But while Clawdeen aspired to create the next great werewolf fashion label—she wanted to design the fearsome clothes—Cleo just wanted to be seen in them.

"What do you need?" asked Frankie, already digging through her bag and handing things to Lagoona as she pulled them out. "Lipstick? A scarf? I think I have a headband in here somewhere. I've deathinitely got a hairbrush . . ."

That, she insisted Draculaura take, so maybe she truly had forgotten that basic grooming step this morning. At least she was pretty sure she'd brushed her fangs?

I need sleep. I need some space, thought Draculaura, but aloud she said, "Thanks, ghouls, but right now I just need to get to class."

"Hmm." Clawdeen's wolf ears perked up, like her superior hearing had caught Draculaura's inner thoughts. "Just gimme a minute to grab my books and I'll walk with you. You've got Clawculus with Lagoona and me, right?"

"We're in that too, babe," Cleo said to Deuce.

Her boofriend just grinned and clasped her hand. "If you say so. I'm just following you."

"Oh, me six!" Frankie thrust her hand up so fiercely that the stitches holding it onto her arm snapped. Luckily, Deuce caught the flying appendage before it could wander off down the hallway. He tossed it back to Frankie to reattach.

Draculaura's smile was fraying as quickly as Frankie's stitches, but she forced herself to say, "Fangtastic," and held up the ghoul's brush. "Let me just run to the bathroom and I'll meet you there."

"We'll wait here for you," said Frankie. "Unless you want company?"

"No!" Draculaura hadn't meant for the word to come out with such bite. "I don't need any help. I'll be right back." She didn't bother heading to the bathroom, just paused around the corner to lean her head against the wall, take a deep breath, and have a private panic.

Except, while she was out of eyesight, she wasn't out of earshot, because Lagoona's voice reached her loud and clear. "Do you really think she's okay?"

"Obviously not," said Cleo, not bothering to lower her voice. "We'll need to do something about that."

Draculaura grimaced. She was going to have to ask her scare-apist for strategies to deal with this. She loved her ghouls, but she was not interested in being their next project. She'd seen what Frankie could do when she started planning and had no interest in fear-up banners, being showered in shocks of confetti, or being the subject of one of Cleo's well-delegated to-do lists.

"Can Monster High even be Monster High without Dracula? It feels so eerie to know he's never going to just suddenly appear again," Frankie whispered. Well, sort of. She'd never been any good at whispering.

Clawdeen was even worse. "I know, right? And poor

Draculaura. She looks"—Clawdeen paused to search for the word—"lost."

Well, they weren't wrong. Draculaura felt lost. Monster High should be as familiar as the tips of her fangs, but it wasn't. She couldn't explain it, but it felt like the building was holding its breath—waiting. Something uneasy emanated from the floors and ancient stones of the walls. Something unsettled shivered in the cold air of the corridors.

Someone, probably Deuce, closed their locker with a bang. She heard him shout a greeting down the hall to one of his friends.

Draculaura exhaled.

Or . . . maybe the school was fine and she was just projecting? She quickly tugged the brush through her hair and rounded the corner back to the ghouls. "There. All better."

Their expressions were skeptical, but they nodded encouragingly.

Frankie hooked her elbow through Draculaura's as they started down the hall to Clawculus. The heat from her friend's mint green skin chased away the goosebumps peppering her own pale pink arm.

If only it was as easy to vanquish all her doubts and questions. Like Frankie, she didn't know how to conceive of Monster High without Dracula—but, even scarier, she didn't know who *she* was without him either.

CHAPTER 2

The ghouls—and Deuce—fanned out in front of Draculaura, creating a ca-coffin-ny of high heels on the marble floors as they strutted toward class while forming a monster shield to hide her from the gawking student body. The backs of their heads were a rainbow of highlighted hair: Cleo's brown and gold, Frankie's black and white, Lagoona's blond and blue, Clawdeen's brown and caramel. Ghoulia Yelps and Abbey Bombinable joined their flanks, adding blue-on-blue and white with pink and purple shrieks to their mix. Obviously there was no overlooking Deuce's sky-high green snake hairstyle either.

Not that she could look *over* anything. Draculaura was pretty sure that even with a new class of incoming fleshmen, she was still the shortest monster at the school.

All of her friends looked so strong—shoulders back, heads up and alert—ready to protect her. Draculaura couldn't have loved these ghouls (and Deuce!) any more . . .

Except—instead of having them walk protectively *in front* of her, she would've given most anything to have someone walk *beside* her, so she didn't feel so alone. How had nothing they'd learned in any of their classes prepared them for how to handle these feelings of grief—or how to talk about them? Draculaura made a mental note to call Dr. Sanguine as soon as she got home. She might need some extra scare-apy sessions this week.

Hopefully things would get closer to normal soon—at least with the ghouls. She missed the laughter, the makeovers, the maul trips, and the coffinchino dates to gossip and giggle until they were kicked out of the Coffin Bean for diesturbing the other customers. This whole protective act had to end, right? There was only so long that Cleo could handle being out of the spotlight, and she was welcome to it! Draculaura would be more than happy to fade back into the shadows so someone else could be the center of attention.

As if on cue, Cleo stiffened and sniffed disdainfully. Draculaura couldn't see over the taller ghouls' shoulders, but she saw when Frankie elbowed Cleo and said, "She's coming this way. Be nice."

Cleo huffed and rubbed her side. "I swear to Ra, Frankie, your elbows get pointier every year. Also, I'm *always* nice. Though I don't see why we have to be. When has *she* ever been nice to *me*?"

Draculaura was pretty sure she could guess who was approaching: Toralei Stripes.

A purred, "Hello," confirmed Draculaura's prediction, though she could only see the orange tips of the werecat's ears over Clawdeen's shoulders.

Sometimes being the shortest really bit!

"Hey there," said Clawdeen. "I see you went with the black jacket. Clawsome choice." The ghouls shifted enough that Draculaura could glimpse an unfamiliar soft smile on Toralei's face.

"Thanks. It was a *clawsome* suggestion," said Toralei softly before she narrowed her eyes at the rest of the ghouls. She flashed a sharp grin at Clawdeen. "I'll talk to *you* later."

"Fur sure." Clawdeen steered their group down the right-hand corridor, while Toralei and the other werecats, twins Meowlody and Purrsephone, turned left.

Lagoona exhaled loudly. "Toralei? That's going to take some getting used to."

But Clawdeen was too busy glancing over her shoulder to notice. From her spot in the back of the clump, Draculaura saw it all—including the matching over-the-shoulder look that Toralei aimed back at her friend. Later she'd ask what'd gone down and gripe about not knowing sooner, but right now, she just wanted all the spooky sweet details.

"Hey-ey, Clawdeen," Draculaura tried to make her voice light and teasing, and she paired it with a wink, but the ghouls turned and whipped out tissues in eerie synchronicity.

"Don't cry!" said Frankie. "Or, wait! *Do* cry if you want to. Feel your feelings! We're here for you."

Except, the only feeling they seemed to be "there for" or recognize was sadness.

"I'm not—I wasn't . . . I *winked*?" Draculaura sputtered as they entered their Clawculus classroom, but the ghouls didn't hear her. Cleo was busy ordering other students to vacate the prime front row seats. Clawdeen was lecturing their teacher, Mr. Mummy, on not calling on Draculaura, and Frankie was scooping her decomposition book from her arms.

"Don't worry about notes or homework. I'll do them for you."

Draculaura sighed. Her friends had all the best intentions, but they might just love her to death.

By the time the clock had crawled to lunch period, Draculaura was no longer wondering if her friends *might* love her to death. They absolutely would. Frankie, in particular, had barely given her room to breathe.

"You fanging in there?" asked Frankie as she tried to carry Draculaura's books and her own books and hold open the creepateria door. As expected, it resulted in Frankie's hand detaching and an avalanche of dropped school supplies.

Well, if I ever wanted to know what it felt like to cast a shadow, that mystery is solved. But instead of saying any of that aloud, Draculaura answered, "I'm truly, totally fine."

"Hmm." Frankie squinted like she didn't boolieve her. "What can I get you for lunch? Go find a seat and I'll be there in two screams."

Draculaura shook her head. "Thanks, Frankie, that's really kind of you, but I can get my own lunch." Before the other ghoul could spark a protest, she grabbed a tray and practically ran toward the lunch lady.

It's possible that she took extra-long at the salad bar, choosing her scarrots individually and studying all the plant-based protein options before settling on a scoop of gorebonzo beans. By the time she reached the table, everyone was focused on Lagoona.

Well, everyone except for Clawdeen and Toralei. The two of them were in their own private world. Draculaura could practically see the heart eekmojis in their green and amber eyes when they leaned close to each other, shoulders touching as they shared a private joke.

The rest of the ghouls were turned toward Lagoona. She waved a kelp chip as she spoke, "I just feel like, it's not that Gil was an anchor—but he's not dragging me down anymore." The light shining through the spiderweb-paned windows made Lagoona's eyes sparkle like the bluest waves of her home, the Great Scarier Reef. "I *love* being single. And I really love what being single is doing for my qualifying times. Boolympics, here I come."

"Wait. What?" Draculaura almost dropped her tray. "You and Gil Weber broke up?" This was major news! The only couple Draculaura knew who'd been together longer than Lagoona and Gil was Deuce and Cleo. Yet the other ghouls were calmly chewing their lunches like Lagoona hadn't just dropped a bombshell on the middle of their creepateria table.

"Oh, yeah." Lagoona crunched her chip and shrugged. "It happened ages ago. End of June, maybe? I was sad at first, but now I'm so much happier. My swim times are so much faster too. Coach says I'm in a fintastic position to crush the competition at Boolympic qualifiers." The blue of Lagoona's cheeks turned slightly pink as she blushed. "But, enough of that. How are you? You look a little pale. Sit. Eat."

Draculaura sank onto a chair between Cleo and Ghoulia, mindlessly chomping some scarrots. End of June . . . she'd been planning a funeral while her friend was navigating a breakup. And who knew when the Clawdeen/Toralei flirt fest had started. Normally she'd be Clawdeen's first call . . .

What else had she missed? What else hadn't they told her? Logically, she knew their lives hadn't been on pause just because her world had stopped, but she hadn't considered what could've happened to them in the three months since they'd last all been in this building, in these seats.

She swallowed a jagged bite of scarrot and said, "The Boolympics? That's scary cool. And are you okay? With Gil? Is that why we haven't seen him around all morning?"

Lagoona waved off the question. "It's not all that finteresting, nothing fishy. It sounds a bit like what you and Clawd went through when you broke up. He's not a bad guy, but we'd grown apart, you know? Anyway, he enrolled in another school. We haven't really talked; we're respecting each other's space." She frowned at Draculaura's mostly full plate. "Coach says that lunch is the most important meal of the day. Are you feeling okay, mate?

Truthfully, she wasn't. And it wasn't the mention of her ex-boofriend that had her reeling—that was ancient news.

Draculaura had been having these periods of wooziness and tunnel vision, sometimes accompanied by nausea or exscream fatigue. Dr. Sanguine had told her grief took a toll on the body and urged her to take more time for self-care: sleep, food, and since she didn't drink blood, making sure to swallow her daily iron supplements.

None of that seemed to be helping, but nothing was going to be accomplished by repeating any of her complaints to Lagoona and the ghouls. It would just give them another excuse to fuss—another reason not to update her on the major events of their lives.

"I'm fine," she repeated for the eight hundredth time.

Maybe if she said it often enough, she'd start to boolieve it.

Cleo pressed her lips together like she might protest, but her attention was snagged by something over Draculaura's shoulder. "Daddy?" she gasped. "Nefera? What are you two doing here?"

Draculaura turned to see Cleo's father and older sister strolling across the creepateria toward their table. The Mummy was as intimidating as always; his haughty eyes and smug smile radiated through his ancient burial wrappings. She avoided Ramses de Nile whenever possible and trusted Nefera about as much as an angry asp. The fact that Nefera's signature teal lipstick was curved into a smile only made Draculaura more wary.

But . . . on the other hand, she was willing to overlook a lot—even one of Nefera's meddlesome schemes—if it meant the attention was off her for a bit.

"Daughter," bellowed Ramses. This wasn't abnormal, his voice *only* functioned at bellowing levels. "How has your first day of school gone?"

"Oh my Ra, did you come here to check on me?" Those same words, coming from most any other monster in this room, would sound petulant, but Cleo was dielighted! She pressed her hand to her heart—or, rather to the large gold necklace that covered it. "After all these years, I didn't sphinx you still got excited about first days and all that."

"Yes, yes," said Ramses. "Why wouldn't I come check on my princess?"

Cleo preened under his attention, flipping her hair and smiling like she was posing for a photo shoot. "Oh, Daddy."

"But now that I've seen you, I need you and Draculaura to come with me." He snapped his fingers, creating a soft shower of sand that coated Draculaura's salad. "Right now."

Cleo stood immediately, abandoning her half-eaten lunch.

Draculaura frowned and stayed seated. "You need me?" She wasn't a fan of Cleo's father. Or it was probably more accurate to say that she wasn't a fan of the traits he brought out in Cleo when he tried to get her to participate in his ambition agendas.

Deuce, she noticed, was staying far, far away, ducking down in his seat at his table with a group of mansters. She didn't blame him. Ramses was forever telling Cleo that Medusa Gorgon's son wasn't nearly good enough for the daughter of Egyptian royalty.

If *she* were Deuce . . . well, Draculaura wasn't saying she deathinitely would've taken off her sunglasses and turned Cleo's dad to stone, but she would've highly considered it.

"Yes, you." Ramses's loafer tapped an impatient beat on the creepateria floor. "Sometime this dynasty would be nice."

"I swear to Ra, we've built pyramids faster than this," griped Nefera.

Draculaura wasn't sure if Cleo's sister meant stone structures or towers of fearleaders, but either way, insults weren't going to make her move any faster. She took another bite of scarrot.

"Mr. de Nile, sir," Frankie began, her voice going squeaky. "Draculaura's just lost her father, and—"

"I'm aware," said The Mummy. "Three months later and the whole monster world still seems unable to talk of anything else."

Draculaura's eyebrows went up. Well, at least someone was capable of acting like she wasn't breakable.

Toralei turned, appearing to tune into the conversation for the first time. She smiled up at Cleo's dad, but it was sharp and toothy as she purred, "That's a funny way of saying, '*I'm sorry for your loss.*'"

Clawdeen beamed at Toralei and clasped her hand before adding, "Yeah. What my ghoulfriend is saying is: Where she goes, we go."

Nefera frowned, and Ramses made a sound that was a mix between a growl and shifting sand. It set Draculaura's fangs on edge, and she stood quickly. "Thanks, ghouls, but it's fine. I'm happy to help with whatever Mr. de Nile needs."

The bandages on his face split to reveal a smile as he turned and began to strut out of the creepateria. "I was hoping you'd say that."

Draculaura hadn't meant it when she said she was "happy" to help him, but she was curious. And thankful that the ghouls had decided to follow along. Especially once they rounded a corner and she realized where Ramses was leading them.

Her feet faltered. "That's my dad's office."

"Correction," said Ramses as he continued toward the door. "It's the office of the head of the school board. That position is vacant. The room needs emptying too."

Draculaura's steps felt unsteady as she approached the office. For the first time that day, she was grateful that Frankie was sticking to her like her nonexistent shadow, because it meant she was *right there* to lean on. Well, as long as she didn't lean too hard and tear the other ghoul's stitches.

"I got you, boo." Frankie's bolts sparked as she gripped Draculaura's shoulder tighter.

The mound of flowers in front of the door had been pushed to the side. The black cloth was taken down, the door opened. Draculaura was entirely unprepared for the flood of memories that washed through it.

She took a step inside, expecting to still see writing utensils scattered across the desk where she'd dropped them. To see a scorched mound of ashes on her father's chair. Instead there were boxes. The shelves along the back wall were already bare. There were piles of items scattered across the carpet where she'd lain unconscious while her father died.

"That's—that's my mother's diary." She pulled away from Frankie to dash across the room and pluck a well-worn book from a stack in the corner. It was tucked below a ceramic coffin she'd made in arts and bats class when she was just a few hundred years old, and above a framed photo of a kite being flown between two empty outfits on one of the full moon midnights when her dad woke her up for an impromptu adventure. She set these carefully aside. "Why is my mother's diary on the floor?"

"It was in one of the drawers." Ramses gestured toward the desk. The drawers were all pulled open. All empty.

She stood, hugging the ancient and priceless book to her chest. "What are you doing with my father's things?"

"I'm having Dracula's personal effects boxed. One of my ushabtis will deliver them to your house." He pointed to one of his jackal-headed servants waiting silently in the corner.

Clawdeen stepped forward, her claws flexed as she growled, "Who gave you permission to go in Dracula's office?"

Toralei stepped forward too. "Fur real. I mean, let the body get cold before you start staking your claim." She paused and tilted her head. "Wait, bad word choice with the 'staking' and I guess vampires are already cold-blooded. *Still.*"

Clawdeen raised an eyebrow as she turned to her . . . her *ghoulfriend*—that was the word *she* had used to describe Toralei in the creepateria, so Draculaura was going to use it too. And grill her friend about it. She wanted all the dire details . . . later.

Because right now she was confused, anxious.

"Kitten, we talked about this," said Clawdeen. "Pause, paws, *then* claws. Remember?"

Toralei rolled her eyes. "Everyone's always so sensitive."

"You don't like it, then go away," said Cleo. "This is more of a family meeting anyway."

"The rest of the family already knows," sniped Nefera. She made a show of examining her manicure and looking bored. "As usual, we're just waiting for you to catch up."

Draculaura tuned out the de Niles' sister squabbles and studied the other items on the floor. One of the jackal-headed servants was dutifully packing them into boxes. Her dad's lucky Magic-8 Bat, the stress ball shaped like a bulb of garlic she'd given him as a joke last April Ghoul's Day.

When the ushabtis brought the boxes to her house, she'd have Ms. Heaves put them in Dracula's home office or his bedroom. It really didn't matter. She wouldn't open them. Just like she hadn't opened the doors to either of those rooms. If she kept them shut, she could pretend her dad was busy working. He was in a meeting. He was taking a nap. Or a trip.

The illusion lasted only as long as she could make excuses. If she had to come fang-to-fang with his absence, it would shatter.

Draculaura turned away from her dad's personal effects, from the pens she'd teased him with that last night, which were being dumped into boxes. She headed out of the office. She didn't need to see this, didn't want to know whatever Nefera was taunting Cleo about.

Ramses followed her into the hall. He smiled approvingly at the crowd that had gathered, drawn in by the raised voices and promises of drama. Spectra Vondergeist hovered front and center, her iCoffin pointed toward them, already recording. The violet-haired ghost ran the *Gory Gazette*, a gossip blog that was the main source of news for the student body and most of the monster world.

Ramses turned toward Spectra and cleared his throat. "Some monsters are meant to lead—this is a burden I gladly shoulder for the monster community. As long as there has been a record of time, there have been de Niles in powerful positions. Today I find that there is a new role, a new responsibility, that requires my skills—heading up the Monster High school board."

Draculaura whispered, "What?" but her voice was lost among so many others.

The Mummy paused to let the commotion die down. If he was expecting gasps or applause, he was probably disappointed that the reaction was a mix of *"What does the school board even do?"* and *"Should we care about this?"*

There was one other monster in the crowd who was having a personal reaction. Cleo had gasped and clutched her necklace. Not that Ramses noticed. He was too busy posturing and arguing that *yes*, the students need to care. "This position is important and powerful. I'll be deciding the policies that run your school."

"Oh, so, like better food in the creepateria," said Manny. The minotaur nodded his bull head slowly.

"No, not like—"

The Mummy launched into another speech, ignoring or too self-focused to notice Cleo tugging on the sleeve of his blazer and asking, "So, you're not here to see me? This was never about my first-day-of-ghoul?"

Deuce put an arm around her. "Sorry, babe. That sucks rocks."

"But *why*?" Cleo asked her father. "Why would you want a *job*?"

"Typical Cleo," scoffed Nefera. "Needing to be told that power is power. Why wouldn't we want it?" She stepped between Cleo and Spectra's camera—as always, making sure the spotlight was more clearly on her.

Draculaura tried to shuffle backward and out of view. Not that she'd show up on the iCoffin's recording, but still, she wanted nothing to do with this. It had nothing to do with her.

Two jackal-headed servants materialized to block her path. Before she could pivot and find another way to escape, The Mummy strode through the crowd to stand beside her.

He made his voice sticky sweet as he said, "I know Dracula was a beloved leader—he did much to keep this school safe for hundreds of years"—Ramses shuffled forward, practically pushing Draculaura ahead of him as he continued—"but the de Nile family is even older and more powerful than he was. Our family line extends past the sands of time. And in uncertain days like these, we need to lean on tradition, wisdom, experience."

"Un-uncertain times?" asked Jackson Jekyll. He was the cautious human personality of a monster-hybrid. Holt Hyde, his monster alter-ego, lived for causing chaos. While Holt would've been cheering, Jackson looked like he wanted to hide in the closest locker.

Ramses nodded somberly. "I've heard rumblings of a 'threat' to the school. Disquiet among certain pockets of normies—"

"Are we safe?" called out Spectra as she floated higher to film from a different angle.

Ramses's bandages split to reveal a smarmy grin. "With my family in charge, certainly."

"But . . . you're not in charge," said Clawdeen.

"Not yet." Somehow The Mummy made those two words sound like a warning. He'd accompanied them with a pat to Draculaura's head. She ducked away from his grip as he looked directly into Spectra's phone camera and said, "But I will be as soon as I'm appointed."

"Who says you *will* be appointed?" growled Clawdeen.

"I'm saying it, right now." Ramses was clearly losing patience with the ghoul.

And when she followed up with, "But based on whose authority?" he ignored her entirely.

"What is this threat?" demanded Abbey Bominable. "And are we safe *now*?"

Ramses gave a stoic shrug. Draculaura got the sense that he was thrilled by the panic he was causing—that this interaction was going exactly as he'd planned.

Spectra certainly looked defrighted by the footage she was recording. Draculaura wished, not for the first time, that she could appear in pictures or videos. If only so that her expression would make it clear she didn't agree with Mr. de Nile.

She exhaled in relief when she caught sight of Headmistress Bloodgood. The school leader was astride her magical blue horse, and the crowd quickly parted to avoid getting trampled by Nightmare's hooves or singed by her fire breath.

With a final throat clearing, the students in the front of the crowd shifted to let the headless headmistress through. Right now, her head was cradled in her arms, but she set it back on her neck before turning to The Mummy.

"Ramses de Nile." Her school-leader voice made all the students take a step backward. "Shame on you for spreading fear and hysteria in these hallways. How dare you tell the students they're unsafe."

"Are you saying I should've told their parents first?" he asked, his bandaged mouth curved up in a sneer. "Because, in my opinion, the students deserve the respect of being informed, since *they're* the ones in the school."

A few monsters shouted their agreement before Headmistress Bloodgood quelled the cheering with a single look. "I'm worried less about the protocol of who is informed first and more about you spreading unsubstantiated rumors to the student body."

She paused to peer at the students over her glasses. "The same student body that is supposed to be in class right now. Unless they'd like their teachers to start filling out detention slips. There's a recently unsealed room in the catacombs that needs cleaning . . ."

Draculaura had to jump to the side to avoid being crushed by the hastily dispersing crowd. Catacomb-cleaning wasn't a threat that anyone took lightly. Even Spectra stopped recording and took a ghostly through-the-walls shortcut to her next class.

Ramses frowned at the headmistress before turning his back on her to face his daughters: Cleo pouting, Nefera preening. His voice was a low rumble that Draculaura couldn't hear over the departing students, but whatever he said made both de Nile daughters beam and embrace him.

Jealousy over that father-daughter hug made her knees weak, made bile rise in her throat. And that was before Ramses met her eyes over Cleo's head and said, "You and I, we need to talk soon."

CHAPTER 3

"Draculaura, a moment."

She'd hesitated too long, not fled with the rest of the crowd, and now it was too late to pretend she hadn't heard the headless head-of-school say her name. Especially since the decapitated woman was pointing her face directly at Draculaura, her dark eyebrows arched in a way that dared you to ignore her at your own academic peril.

Draculaura sighed. "Yes, Headmistress Bloodgood?"

Everything about the headmistress was stiff—the gel that held her black hair up in a bun, the pointed collars of her purple frock coat and white frilled shirt, and her sense of right and wrong. Normally the school's leader also had a wicked sense of humor—but there was no trace of that as she pointed to a side corridor, indicating that they should step out of the way for some privacy.

The headmistress looked especially imposing as she stared down at Draculaura from the added height of Nightmare's back and said, "I've been trying to get in touch with you. I've left several messages at your house."

"Oh, Ms. Heaves must've forgotten to give them to me."

Draculaura had barely swallowed down her guilt about lying *and* blaming her goredian, when the headmistress arched an eyebrow and added, "I've also left several voicemails on your iCoffin."

Right. She didn't have an excuse for not returning those. And didn't want to explain the truth: that she deleted all messages unheard. She couldn't add other people's sympathy, concern, and grief to the emotions already weighing her down. "I'm sorry?" she said.

Headmistress Bloodgood waved her off. "Never mind all that right now. I have a question to ask you." She paused to glare at a spot near the ceiling. "Shouldn't you be in class, Miss Vondergeist?"

Spectra materialized with a shrug. "You caught me, but you can't *blame* me, can you? Everyone at Monster High is just dying to know if our favorite vamp is fanging in there."

Headmistress Bloodgood tsked and waited for the ghoul to float down the hallway before she continued. "Draculaura, the inspectors handling your father's death need to know: Would you like to press charges against the pharmacist?"

"What?" She'd been expecting a question about if she was ready to be back in class, or an offer of support.

"From what I understand, the charges would be negligence or involuntary vamp-slaughter. I can look into it and report back. The investigators would want to ask you some questions. It's possible you'd be asked to testify."

Draculaura shook her head. "I—I . . ." She took a step backward. "They fired the employee who filled the prescription, right? And it was an accident? I don't want to testify."

She shut her eyes, trying to slow the pounding in her

temples. What could she possibly say? Would she have to tell the world about how in her dad's final hours, she'd been the worst listener, the worst daughter? That she'd passed out while he was trying to pass on some important secret? And now she'd never know what he'd wanted to tell her. These thoughts already kept her awake—they would haunt her forever if everyone knew.

"Then I'll let them know. The last thing anyone wants is for you to have to keep resurrecting the events of that night," Headmistress Bloodgood said softly. "But I wanted to make sure you have all the closure you need. And support. I've instructed your teachers to offer whatever accommodations you may need this fall."

"Thank you," said Draculaura, then she jumped as Frankie appeared at her left. Frankly, it was shocking she'd left Draculaura unattended for so long.

"Hey! What're you ghouls chatting about? Can I help?"

Headmistress Bloodgood smiled before turning Nightmare back toward her office. "Looks like I'm leaving you in good hands," she told Draculaura. "Now, both of you should get to class."

Frankie nodded but stayed where she was, putting an arm around Draculaura in a sideways hug. "This whole stitchuation must be exhausting."

Draculaura nodded. Right now, her whole afterlife felt like a bad dream she couldn't wake up from.

Frankie squeezed her again. "Why don't we have a creepover at my house tonight? I hate the idea of you all alone in your big, spooky mansion, and I already asked the other ghouls. Cleo, Lagoona, and Clawdeen are all in."

Draculaura could picture it: more of Lagoona's "advice," which was just her swim coach's words repurposed; Clawdeen would tell funny stories to distract her; Frankie would cling tighter than Cleo's bandages. And Cleo . . . she actually wasn't sure what she'd do. Likely obsess about Ramses and the school board.

Draculaura loved these ghouls, but she couldn't handle that. "I can't tonight. Ms. Heaves is expecting me." Not that her housekeeper/goredian *expected* her to do more than come home and poke at her dinner before shutting herself up in her room. "And I think I'll be too tired after my first day back. Another time."

"Oh, come on, it'll be fun," insisted Frankie. "We can make smoothies and do facials and watch that new movie with Jenna Goretega."

"I can't." Draculaura felt her patience thinning. She fought to keep her voice from going as sharp as her fangs. Everyone stared at her, but no one listened. Maybe she deserved that for not listening to Dracula when he was sitting in the office across the hall, at the desk that Ramses was now trying out. Her stomach clenched. "I—I'm late for something. Sorry."

Draculaura fled down the hallway, ignoring Frankie's protests. Anyone chasing her would've thought she was taking turns at random, but she knew exactly where she was headed. There were so many nights when Draculaura had had free run of the halls while her father and the other school board members met. While they'd debated curriculums and field trips and other Monster High policies, she'd explored the school. Well, at least parts of it. Dracula had always told her the catacombs required a bloody system; she wasn't allowed to wander there alone.

But right now, she wasn't taking the secret passage to the pantry for a snack. Or creeping in the hidden hallway behind the faculty lounge to see if any creatures were talking about pop quizzes. She was looking for a secret doorway in the hall past the clawditorium.

This particular doorway led outside. Not just outside the main building into the courtyard, athletic fields, the garden, the swamp, or the grounds. This door led to an underground corridor that opened to the world outside the gates. The world that was off-limits. The world that belonged to the normies.

Dracula had been the one to show her this escape route. After some particularly exhausting school board meeting, he'd clasped her hand, led her down this seemingly dead-end hallway, and pressed on the middle head of the hydra statue, causing it to slide to the side. He'd led her down the tunnel that was revealed and out into the night.

She followed the same trail now that he'd brought her down then. A path they'd walked through so many evenings, her father's stern voice lecturing on vampire history or school board politics, or other issues of balance and fairness in the monster world. His tone would soften when he asked for her opinion, guiding and helping her find her own beliefs and positions.

Those memories swirled around her like lies.

As always, the path ended at a cemetery. It was a *human* cemetery, technically outside their world and its protections, which meant it was strictly off-limits to monsters. But did "off-limits" really apply to Dracula? Besides, as he'd once told her, "No normie is in a cemetery late at night for anything but nefarious purposes. Midnights should belong to monsters. To us."

But it was a gloomy mid-afternoon, not midnight. And she was alone.

Vampires didn't cast shadows, but she and Dracula had walked among those of the gravestones. Here, he taught her the skills of their kind. Or at least he tried to. While Dracula levitated with eerie grace, she'd managed little more than a shaky hover. He could transform into a bat and take off into the night, soaring and diving in circles around her. Draculaura never got further than making her ears pointier and her arms fuzzy. Mind control and charismatic charms were skills that they'd only discussed as theoretical, since Dracula refused to demonstrate his mastery on her, and she couldn't even mentally persuade him to push back her curfew five minutes.

Now she walked the same paths without him. She had no desire to go back to school, with the ghouls' suffocating concern and the de Niles' power plays and Bloodgood's question about pressing charges.

But she didn't want to play hooky and go home either. Her housekeeper/legal goredian, Ms. Heaves, would ask questions.

She knew Frankie meant well planning a creepover, but she couldn't. At least not tonight. Did that make her a bad friend?

Maybe it was because she'd been an only child for sixteen hundred years. Maybe it was a vampire's solitary nature. Unlike Clawdeen and her pack of siblings, or Cleo and her intense—and intensely loud—sibling rivalry, Draculaura had spent most of her childhood alone.

She was used to the quiet and the darkness. But her *alone* had never been lonely. She'd always had Dracula. He might not be her father by birth, but he was the only dad she'd ever known. And his blood *did* technically flow through her veins—since he was the one who'd changed her into a vampire more than a millennium ago.

Being human—those years felt more like a fever dream than actual memory. She remembered her mother's laughter, flowers, running barefoot through the warm dirt of Dracula's estate. She remembered sunlight being cozy, not scary, and feeling like she couldn't wait to grow up and see why humans made such a fuss about being an adult.

Almost sixteen hundred years later, she had more questions than answers. Dracula had changed her to save her. She'd been on death's door when he'd drained her blood and helped her sip some of his. And when she'd reawakened as a vampire, he'd been there to guide her.

Everything about her life right now felt like learning how to breathe again.

Dracula wasn't here to arch an eyebrow at her outfits or pretend not to understand the slang she and the ghouls used as they chatted. He wasn't around to threaten to take her iCoffin if she spent too much time on the MonsterWeb.

But without him telling her *not* to stay up all night watching BooTube makeup tutorials, she didn't want to do it anymore.

She was going to have to learn this new normal, how to be an orphan after sixteen hundred years of having him always hovering—sometimes *literally* hovering in bat form—but she couldn't do that with an audience.

Not even an audience composed of her best friends.

The last time she'd had a transition this major—the last time she'd mourned—had been when her mom died. Back then, there hadn't been social medea—there hadn't even been indoor plumbing or electricity.

Dracula hadn't been the playdate type, so back then, there also hadn't been other mini-monsters around to watch her stumble through learning to use her fangs while she learned to let go of her mom.

She'd thought the summer would be enough to mourn her dad. And maybe it should've been. Maybe she *should* be fine by now.

But she wasn't.

She sniffled, felt her lip quiver, and, after looking around to make sure she was truly alone, she let herself cry.

Gracefulness was another one of those vampire skills Draculaura had never quite mastered. When her friend Elissabat cried, it was delicate and dignified. When other vampires walked, they glided.

Draculaura was a wheezing, snorting, sobbing mess—and that was *before* she tripped over a gravestone and nearly bit it.

She should've fallen headfirst into a headstone—but instead, a strong arm shot out from behind a neighboring monument, clasped her wrist, and caught her.

"Whoa. Are you okay? I've got you."

"Yes—I . . ." She trailed off. The arm was attached to a shoulder, a torso, a neck, a head—they were crouched over a grave so recent it was covered in a bright green rectangle of sod that hadn't merged with the rest of the cemetery grass.

For a second, she thought this guy was some sort of fresh zombie rising from the grave—but when he stood and straightened, he looked so . . . *human.*

There was always a vulnerability about mortals that made them easy to pick out. It was the way they stood, protecting their fragile organs, and in the reveals of their skin—it shouted their emotions in flushes and blushes and under-eye circles.

This guy's face was blotchy, and when he let go of her arm to swipe at his cheeks, it was clear he'd been crying too.

Draculaura tucked her fangs behind her lips and wiped her own face, hoping the tell-tale red of vampire tears wasn't visible in the gloomy afternoon light, because this was a human—a normie—and he'd probably wet his pants if he realized he was alone in a cemetery with a vampire.

"Oh, sorry, I—"

"I'm sorry—"

They laughed at their overlapping apologies, but just as abruptly, both choked to a stop. Draculaura wasn't sure of *his* motivation, but as for her own—how was she laughing? In a graveyard? While crying over her dead dad?

That just sounded . . . *wrong*.

"I didn't know anyone else was here," he said, tugging up the collar of his T-shirt and using the inside to give his face another wipe. The motion pulled the fabric tight around his broad shoulders and rumpled the already rumpled blond curls that spilled across his forehead in a tangle. He gave a sheepish shrug. "You scared me. You almost looked like a ghost, just appearing from the shadows."

"Except ghosts aren't so clumsy," Draculaura answered self-consciously before cringing. Had she really just brought up *ghosts* with a normie?

"Yeah, I guess I've never seen a movie where the ghost trips and falls." His mouth twitched at the corner, like it wanted to smile but couldn't quite pull it off.

Ghost—*movie*? Draculaura gulped. Any second now this normie was going to realize what she really was and run away screaming. And, judging by his tears, he'd already been through enough.

This was why monsters were not supposed to leave the protective boundaries of their parts of the world. Their schools, their towns, their neighborhoods. It wasn't safe for normies to know they existed. But there was nowhere in the monster world that Draculaura could exist without the weight of everyone's expectations.

"I can go," she offered. "I didn't mean to disturb you."

"No, you don't have to go. I can." His reddened blue eyes drifted down to the new plot. A mason jar of wildflowers sat against the base of it. "I was just visiting my mom."

"*Oh*. No. Stay." She had no right to chase this guy away from his mom's grave. Especially since she wasn't even supposed to be here. "My dad's not buried here." When vampires died, they turned to dust. This fact was common knowledge, but, like vampire death, witnessing it was exscreamly rare. Not that she had witnessed anything. She'd been useless. Passed out while he passed away. Unable to offer him support, say goodbye, tell him she loved him.

And when she'd awoken—orphaned beside his ashes—she'd screamed so loud that all manner of creatures and ghosts rose from the catacombs to witness the spectacle.

Draculaura blinked away the memory and finished her explanation, "But since my dad doesn't have a grave, this is the closest place to visit." Dracula's ashes had been sent to his birthplace in what was now Romania.

The guy winced. "Recent?"

"Three months," she said. "You?"

"Two."

She gave him a sad smile, making sure to keep her fangs tucked behind her lips. "Worst summer break ever, huh?"

"Yeah." He raked a hand through his blond curls. Some fell haphazardly and some stuck straight up. "Though today's first day of school might've been worse."

"Tell me about it." Draculaura sat down on the ground beside him without thinking, but once she *did* stop and consider it, she didn't want to move. She'd never spent time with any human—except maybe Jackson Jekyll, but he didn't count. This was very much against the rules. Forbitten. Still, she'd meant what she said; she wanted him to tell her about *his* day, so she knew her own wasn't uniquely awful.

"I don't know about your friends, but mine had tissues ready before they even said *hello*." She could only see the side of his expression, because they were doing that thing where they talked parallel instead of facing each other. It made conversation easier, pretending to talk to grass or trees or headstones instead of faces. "And the guys on my soccer team—they barely covered me during yesterday's scrimmage, like somehow grief would mean I couldn't kick a ball. That was after they'd looked shocked that I'd shown up at practice. So today . . . I didn't. I'm here instead."

She nodded. "All any of my friends want to do—all anyone at school wants to do—is talk about my father. But not about *him*, just about the fact that he's dead. And it's like they're standing around, just waiting for me to cry. . . which might be why I had to play hooky to come *here* and do it."

He palmed the back of his neck. "I get that. I *so* get that. At home, I feel like I can only cry in the shower or if my dad's out running errands. I can't if he might hear me."

She wanted to ask about his dad, but it felt too soon. And she had a bigger question rolling around in her mind as she stared down at the dust collecting on the wedge heels of her sandals. "Is it strange I don't know how to cry with my best friends, but I'll pour my heart out to a stranger?"

"Stranger?" He clasped a hand to his chest in feigned hurt. "I prefer co-commiserater. Or comrade-in-grief."

"Kindred spirits?" Draculaura suggested, though she doubted he thought of ghosts when he heard the term.

"Pity partner," he offered, then leaned back on one elbow so he could see her more fully. "I'm Poe."

In books about normies, they always held out a hand to shake when they introduced themselves. He didn't do that. He just looked at her with those sad blue eyes that made her lose her thoughts for a second.

"I'm—" She paused. This guy had no idea who she was, *what* she was. And while it was unlikely her name would trigger a million previous impressions like it would in the monster world, where her dad's identity meant she was famous by association, she knew enough about normies to know he'd find *Draculaura* to be a *very* unusual name. He'd probably ask some stupid question about the stupid book named after her dad.

And if that happened, she'd have to hate him. She really, really didn't want to hate him.

"I'm Laura," she said finally.

He gave her a shy smile. The action drew her eyes to a freckle above the left side of his lip. It wasn't his only freckle; there were a sprinkle across his nose, one above his right eyebrow, and two on his neck that could almost be fang marks if she squinted.

She stopped squinting and focused on what he was saying: "Is it weird to say that it's nice to meet you? That I really *needed* to meet you—meet someone who gets what I'm going through?"

She smiled and decided *she* would be the one to hold out her hand for a shake. Her eyes went wide and her voice got squeaky at the feel of his fingers against hers. Warm and steady. "If you're weird, then so am I, because I needed to meet you too."

CHAPTER 4

Draculaura had already missed fourth period and most of fifth. She didn't even know what class she was supposed to be in right then: Home Eek? Study Howl? It didn't matter. Frankie had been over-eager to take notes for her anyway, and this felt like where she was supposed to be: sitting beside Poe on his mom's grave, staring out over the other plots, and truly feeling *seen* for the first time in months.

"The other day I chuckled at a stupid meme someone sent to a group text. and my dad looked horrified. Like I'd committed some sort of crime by laughing. It's like I need permission to be anything but *his* version of depressed." Poe twisted a blade of grass around his finger. "Worse, the friend who sent the text messaged me privately to apologize for being 'insensitive' and including me in the group."

"Right?" Draculaura felt herself nodding frantically. "I miss my dad, but I still want the hex—*texts* and to know about my friends' breakups and new crushes. Him being gone isn't going to change. I'll *always* miss him, just like I've spent centuries missing my mom."

Poe snorted. "Centuries? Man, it feels that way, doesn't it? The past two months have lasted a decade at least."

Whoops. She was grateful that he'd assumed she was exaggerating, when in reality her mom had been gone more than a millennium. Talking to a normie was like navigating a booby-trapped room in the catacombs.

But then Poe's forehead scrunched. "Wait. Your words just clicked—does that mean your mom died too?" He looked down at the new grass beneath his feet and cursed softly. "I'm sorry—that's . . . that's . . ."

Draculaura shut her eyes, hoping she still liked him after however he ended that sentence. There weren't many who were orphaned in the immortal monster world, and others' reactions to that had ranged from treating her like she was irreparably broken to avoiding her like she was recklessly dangerous, like somehow parent-death might be contagious.

Pain flared in her head, pounding at her temples as she waited for Poe to speak.

"I don't have a word for what that is—" he said. "And you don't need *me* to label your lived experience anyway. But I'm sorry."

She opened her eyes and blinked up at him. "My scare-apist always says 'grief isn't an identity.'" Draculaura left off the second part of Dr. Sanguine's oft-repeated motto: *Afterlife is for the living . . . er, undead.*

"Scare-apist?" Poe chuckled. "I like that. It fits. When my mom first got sick, she kept trying to convince me to go see a therapist, but I guess I was too scared. After . . . well, my dad doesn't believe in that stuff." He scratched his neck again. "I did go to a grief group at the hospital once. But it seemed like the opposite of what yours told you—like they *wanted* grief to be our whole identity."

She wrinkled her nose. "Yeah, I'd pass on that too. Little did they know, your true identity was graveyard superhero, waiting to catch clumsy grievers."

He gave a slight bow. "It was my pleasure, but I still need to get a spandex costume and to figure out some sort of superhero name. Captain Cemetery?"

She groaned. "Keep thinking. Maybe your grief group pals can help you brainstorm."

He grinned. "The worst thing about grief group was it didn't even have good snacks. They served stale pretzels and fruit punch. Like, the only thing a group like that would have going for it was doughnuts or some good cookies, you know?"

She giggled—and knowing that Poe *wouldn't* judge her for daring to laugh, she let it linger an extra beat. "Yeah, the bright spot of mourning is the non-stop deliveries of baked good to my door." Of corpse, most of the monster world assumed she ate a more traditional vampire's diet, so Ms. Heaves had to taste test all deliveries to make sure they didn't include blood. There'd been a close call with a cake she'd *thought* was red velvet. The memory made her shudder.

Though, food being bloodless didn't necessarily mean it was edible—while Deuce's angel food cake would've made actual angels sing, Cleo's pound cake could've doubled as a stone from a pyramid. She pulled a disgusted face. "But you learn real quick which of your neighbors can't bake."

Poe's laughter made her cheeks heat—not unpleasantly, not

like when she woke in the night feeling feverish, stomach churning, head spinning.

Except her head was spinning now too. And what started as a swoony, giddy feeling was changing to something more disconcerting. Maybe Lagoona's swim coach was right about nutrition and the importance of lunch. Maybe all these strange symptoms were related to that. It wasn't like she'd been super focused on eating lately. Or it was possible she'd missed a day or two of the iron supplements she had to take to replace the lack of b-word in her diet.

But, yeah, those were problems for a different time. A time when she wasn't sharing a shady graveyard with Poe, a guy who felt like a map and a trap. Someone whose grief experiences could help her navigate her own, but also—she could get lost in his eyes, his sadness, the chaos of his curls, the shadows of his cheeks and collarbones.

Collarbones? Had she ever noticed a guy's collarbones before? But the ridges of Poe's, the hollows beneath them, called to her. Her eyes traced the cord of muscle running from his shoulder up his neck to where those twin freckles teased. She frowned when she realized she was running her tongue over the tip of one of her fangs.

"Are you okay?" Poe shook his head. "Stupid question—and if you're like me, one that makes you want to scream because it's all anyone is asking."

"They mean well," Draculaura said distractedly.

"Yeah, but—*are* you? Your eyes got a little unfocused there for a second and they looked a little"—he shrugged—"they kinda turned red."

Draculaura stiffened. Red? Like a hungry vamp? She scooted backward, putting extra inches between herself and his collarbones and freckles.

Poe frowned. "Not in like, a weird way. Of course, your eyes are red. Mine are too. We've been crying. They're pretty. I mean, you might have the prettiest eyes I've ever seen."

And while his clumsy compliment was endearing, it was the "We've been crying" that she latched onto. Like there was a *we*. Like they were a grief group of two.

Like she wasn't alone.

"Thank you."

Poe exhaled his relief. "And they're all purple now—no red to be seen. I think you might be the first person I've ever met with purple eyes."

Except, she *wasn't* a person, and that was a good reminder of why she shouldn't be getting so comfortable, so cozy, so . . . hungry around Poe.

Draculaura stood and brushed off her dress. "I just have a headache. I should get back to school."

Poe stood too, and she was pleased to realize he was taller than her—which wasn't exactly hard—but not absurdly so. He didn't tower over her like Manny, Deuce, or the other mansters.

"What school do you go to?" Poe asked. "I've never seen you in the halls of New Salem High, and I'm a hundred percent positive I would've noticed you."

"No, it's a . . ." She looked down at her sandals. Her toe-nail polish was a chipped mess of whatever had hung on since her last pedicure three months ago. She hadn't noticed, hadn't cared, before now. "I go to a private school."

"Right, well . . ." He gulped in a breath and pulled a phone from his pocket. "What about your number? Could I . . . would it be okay if I got it?"

No. He couldn't. Like, it was literally impossible for him to call her. iCoffins and human phones worked on different frequencies. Just like the internet and the MonsterWeb. She'd heard there were technologies that crossed the divide, and ways to communicate with the few humans who did know about monsters, but those were more friend-of-a-friend stories than anything she'd seen. She'd certainly never needed to use them.

Poe's expression shuttered as he read her hesitation as rejec-tion. "Sorry. I didn't mean to overstep." He took an actual step backward, like she might welcome the space.

"No. No, you didn't." Draculaura tried to figure out a way to explain that she wanted to but *couldn't*. Also, shouldn't. What would happen if she did?

Frankie's parents would ground her circuits so quickly if they ever found out she chatted with a normie. Clawdeen's would stick her on permanent cub-sitting duty.

But Draculaura didn't have a parent to punish her . . . or to rescue her if things blew up in her face. She rubbed her hands on her dress. "There's just so much—"

"It's okay," Poe said quickly. "I get it. I don't know what

I was thinking. We're both so . . . I mean, it's not like either of us has the emotional energy for new people right now. Well, besides my bestie grief groupies." His attempt at a smile fell flat.

He was letting her off a hook she wished she could be caught on. Her head started to pound again, and her voice was quiet when she said, "But I really liked talking to you."

"Yeah. Me too." He shoved his phone in his pocket and pulled out a crumpled gas station receipt and a pen. "How about this? I'll give you *my* number. No pressure. If you want to call, if you ever need to talk about this"—he gestured to the cemetery around them—"with someone who gets it, hit me up. Any time, day or night. It's not like I sleep anymore."

"That's so nice, but—" She didn't want to give him false hope or convince herself this might be possible.

"It's okay if you don't call." He placed the receipt in her hand and closed her fingers around it. For that brief moment, her headache paused, the pain replaced by a wave of sparks. These were nothing like the kind she got from Frankie when her bolts backfired.

Then he let go.

The pounding came roaring back to her temples. "I need to go," she managed. "Bye, Poe."

"Bye, Laura."

As she hurried out of the cemetery, she found herself glancing back over her shoulder at the tousled-haired normie who *saw* her but whom she could never see again.

He was looking back over his shoulder at her too.

And for an instant, their bloodshot eyes locked, and she imagined a whole future where this wasn't another ending, another loss to mourn.

Then a stab of pain at her temples made her flinch and blink. The connection between them was broken. She turned back toward her school, back to the protections and boundaries of her world, where she belonged.

As she trudged through the woodsy path toward Monster High, Draculaura slid Poe's number into her pocket, her fingers grazing the leather cover of her mother's diary. It had been in there throughout . . . whatever that whole thing with Poe had been. The idea that her mom was with her during a freaktasically, awkwardly agoreable encounter with a boy helped.

Now if only her mom could somehow give her advice.

Draculaura and her dad had often traded the diary back and forth—the ancient book was almost all they'd had left of her mother, Camilla, who Dracula had unabashedly called "the love of my afterlife."

Draculaura had been too young and naïve to realize how rare and special that was. A monster in love with a human, inviting that human into the monster world. Not that Dracula had loved Camilla when he first offered her protection and a place to stay. He hadn't even known her. But her mom's husband, Gaius, had been killed in battle, leaving her pregnant and alone.

Dracula had always claimed he'd reached out because he'd been army friends with Trajan—her bio dad's great-great-grandfather—but Draculaura always suspected it was more than that.

Now she wished she'd asked—wished she'd lobbed her suspicions at him and seen how Dracula responded to the words *love at first sight*. He'd often liked to tease her that *she* was the romantic, not him.

But for someone who "wasn't a romantic"—it was fangtastically sweet that he'd still treasured and reread her mother's diary. Was that what he'd been looking for in his office the night he died? The item he'd been so desperate to find? The thing he'd wanted to tell her?

She sighed. But, no, it couldn't have been. Not if it was at the top of the pile of items from his desk drawers.

Draculaura could really use a little parental insight today, so she closed her eyes, took a deep breath, and gently opened the diary to a random page, her brain automatically translating the words from her first language, Latin:

5 Augustus 409

My little family—it does not look as I expected, but it fills me with joy. They make quite the pair—boisterous little girl and reserved monster. Though I confess, it pains me to use that word to describe a man I hold in such esteem. She smiles without ceasing whenever she spends time with Dracula, and he—he smiles when he thinks she is not looking.

It is an unusual life we have built in the foothills of Dacia. Dracula's castle and lifestyle are more lavish than anything I could have dreamt for us. He worries that we are lonely and isolated, but I have never felt that way.

My world may be small, but it is full of love. Unusual, "unnatural," or not, I am quite content with the life I have chosen. I hope that someday Draculaura finds as much satisfaction in her own choices.

The choices she'd made today? Draculaura wasn't sure her mother would approve of her skipping school and dabbling in the human world, but she didn't regret it either. And with all the pity being thrown her way, she doubted she'd get in trouble for missing her afternoon classes.

It was later than she'd realized when she reached the boundary between the worlds. There was nothing physical to signify it, but humans crossing past this point would feel vaguely anxious and uncomfortable until they'd crossed back into their own portion of the woods. The sensation would grow stronger the closer they got to any monster structures. The monster neighborhoods were all gated and warded, as were their cities and towns—and Monster High the most protected of all. They were safe, and humans were . . . oblivious that they even existed. But, as her dad had often told her, it was *because* humans were oblivious that they were safe.

Draculaura reached campus right around the time the final bell rang—which felt perfect, since she could slip back into the crowds as everyone was released from class. No one would ever have to know she'd spent the afternoon in the human world with a normie.

But it wasn't the sound of the final bell that split the air.

Even before she could see the Monster High gates, Draculaura could hear the screams.

CHAPTER 5

Draculaura froze on the path, her breath hitching as the echoes of the screams faded, leaving behind a dead silent forest. She stayed still, uncertain, until the rapid approach of footsteps and voices had her diving into the brush to hide behind a tree.

A group of a half dozen human teens in workout gear sprinted past her, their voices overlapping in a hyper-panicked blur.

"*Did you see that?*"

"*It can't be real.*"

"*That kid had claws.*"

"*There was one with fangs.*"

"*And fur.*"

"*—snakes for hair.*"

"*This has got to be some sort of group hallucination. What did Coach put in the team water bottles?*"

But it was the last comment that haunted her most: "*It's real—I got it on video.*"

Draculaura craned her neck to catch a glimpse of a skinny redhead holding up a phone just like Poe's before the group disappeared from view.

She waited until she could no longer hear them, then counted an extra sixty seconds before emerging from the woods and running toward the school.

Her head was spinning as she dashed through the Monster High gates. The semi-circular drive in front of the school was packed with students. It usually was after dismissal, but this wasn't the casual chatter of monsters headed to the parking lot or off to sports practice or clubs; their voices were frantic, frenzied.

Draculaura picked her way through the crowd to where Clawdeen stood beside the building's main stairs. She was breathless and woozy as she latched onto her friend's arm and gasped, "What's going on?"

"Ghoul, where have you been?" Clawdeen scanned her head to toe and grimaced, then began leading her up the stairs. "We'd better find Frankie. She's about to blow a circuit because she couldn't find you. Especially now that—"

"But what happened?" Draculaura interrupted, stumbling on a step as she tried to keep up with her less-winded, longer-legged friend. She steadied herself on one of the gargoyles and looked up to see Ramses de Nile stepping through the massive double doors at the top of the steps.

He paused beneath the center arch of the portico and his voice rang out across the crowded lawn as he answered her question. "What happened? Exactly what I predicted would happen: The school was attacked. Humans got onto campus. They've filmed us."

"But that is not possible," called Abbey Bominable from where she was seated on the edge of the fountain in the center of the drive. There were ice crystals forming along the surface of the water near her clenched hands.

Draculaura nodded her head along with most of the students. Humans couldn't get on campus. Monster High was the most protected place in the monster world. Its protections ensured that even if normies somehow got near the campus, they would stroll right past the school and never even see it.

"It shouldn't be possible," agreed Ramses. "And yet, it happened. This is why Monster High needs strong leadership. I warned you all, you need me to keep you all safe. This is just the start. The threat on the school is only going to escalate. After millennia of maintaining secrecy, who knows what will happen now that humans have proof that we exist?"

"Wait. You're saying we're not *safe*?" Heath Burns's hair flamed and voice cracked on the final word, a reflection of the panic that seemed to be fracturing the student body. Their voices rose in other questions, some directed at classmates, some at The Mummy, some into their iCoffins as they called home.

Ramses chuckled. "As I told you earlier—you *will* be safe, once I've been appointed to the school board."

"Students. *Students!*" Headmistress Bloodgood emerged from the building and pushed past Ramses at the top of the stairs. She had to hold up her head as high as her arms could reach in order to be heard over the crowd. "Students! I beg you all to take a breath. We will get to the bottom of why those teens were able to see our school and figure out the ramifications of the exposure. But in the meantime, I would like you to gather your materials and depart for your homes. Our first day of school is over—and this . . . this *interruption*, whatever the cause, is no excuse for not completing your homework assignments."

The collective panic turned to groans as the ghosts floated, the zombies shambled, and all the other monsters flew, oozed, rolled, or trudged off to their lockers. Draculaura could tell Abbey was still feeling stressed, because the yeti left an accidental trail of ice—and slipping students—in her wake.

But there was one ghoul pushing against the flow of students—Frankie nearly detached her shoulder fighting through the crowd. "There you are!" She practically knocked Clawdeen off the steps to reach Draculaura. "I was looking everywhere for you. Are you okay?"

"Of corpse," said Draculaura. She wished Poe were here so they could share an eyeroll at the question. And for a moment she actually wanted to go to Frankie's creepover, so that she could gush and giggle about the cute boy she'd met . . .

"Stupid normies. They'd better not come back here if they know what's good for them." A passing swamp manster punctuated his statement with a flexing of his claws. His buddy stomped a hoof in agreement.

Draculaura flinched. Yeah, so probably not the right time to tell her friends she'd gone all swoony for a normie. Especially when they were already exchanging glances and looking at her like she was batty.

"It's okay to tell us you've been crying . . ." Clawdeen said gently.

"Next time, just let me know if you need to skip class to have a good cry. I'll happily come with you. Well, not *happily*, but you know what I mean. I can bring the tissues!" said Frankie, her bolts sparking slightly.

"I'm fine," said Draculaura. The whole reason she'd left campus was to cry in peace. Not that she could tell them that. "I wasn't crying."

"Really?" Frankie raised an incredulous eyebrow. "Then why is there makeup all over your face?"

Draculaura's hands shot to her cheeks—and Frankie wasn't lying. Her fingers came away smudged with mascara. "Stupid lack of reflection," she muttered. Not that it would've helped her, since it's not like she had a mirror in the cemetery. She scrunched her eyes shut in embarrassment—this meant that when she'd met Poe, she'd been a melted makeup mess. Well, that was just fangtastic.

Frankie and Clawdeen were still watching her, so she sighed and said, "Maybe I had a teensy moment, but I'm fine now."

"You know you don't have to be fine," said Clawdeen. "We're not going to judge you for being sad."

They might not, but it's not like she could just spend all her time breaking down, and sometimes when she let herself cry—it felt like she'd never be able to stop.

"Thanks," she told them. "I need to go get my stuff. You?"

Before she could slink off into the shadows or work up a full mortification about Poe and the makeup, Ramses's voice boomed: "Draculaura, a word."

He managed to make it a demand, not a request, and he didn't seem to care that their interaction had an audience. "We'll be expecting your support when I take control of the school board," he told her. "We'll get it, won't we? Perhaps you'd even like to go on record and nominate me to replace your father."

He'd slung an arm around Cleo's shoulders as he spoke, making his daughter beam. "Oh my Ra, Daddy. Of corpse she'll support you." Cleo was blinking at her expectantly too. "Right?"

"Er. Um—" Draculaura knew one thing for certain: Her dad never felt that he "controlled" the school board. He'd *led* it, and he'd always said that a leader's job wasn't to decide or demand but to empower others to make good decisions. Then again, her dad also valued loyalty—and Cleo was one of her best friends.

Draculaura didn't know everything the school board did, but she knew enough to recognize it was a huge responsibility. Her dad had talked often about the burdensome privilege of the role. It was the school board that established policy—they'd been the ones to decide that Monster High would be diverse and inclusive of all types of monsters, not be species specific like the vampire school, Belfry Prep; or the werewolf-only Crescent Moon Academy; or the freshwater monster school that Lagoona's ex-boofriend, Gil Weber, had transferred to.

Her dad had attended endless meetings to select curriculum, approve creature hirings, establish foreign exchange programs, and balance the budget. It had been a lot of work, without a lot of recognition.

Which, come to think of it, was the exact reverse of what Ramses de Nile valued, so why would he even want the role?

"Well?" Ramses prompted. He dropped his volume, his voice rasping like sandpaper. "Think of how it will look if you *don't*. I don't *need* your endorsement, of corpse, but it's the appearance of things. Your father would want this for me."

Would he? She wasn't so sure.

"Um," Draculaura looked around for an excuse and found one above her. The sun had burst through the clouds for the first time all day. She didn't have to fake the tremor in her voice as she pointed to it. "Sorry, I've got to go. Vampire skin and UV rays don't . . ." She trailed off and dashed into the building, her breath coming fast and fearful.

Except, when she paused inside the doors and pressed on the exposed skin of her forearm, then face—they didn't hurt. Which was odd, since she hadn't reapplied SPF 1000 since this morning. How could she have been so foolish? She blinked her eyes, trying to clear the mental image of her dad's charred arm. Maybe the UV index was lower than it looked?

"We'll talk more soon," Ramses called after her. "You can count on that."

And maybe the words should've raised goosebumps across her skin, except, no need—they were already there. She shivered from the combination of air conditioning and the memory of The Mummy's words from earlier: *This is just the start. The threat on the school is only going to escalate. After millennia of maintaining secrecy, who knows what will happen now that humans have proof that we exist?*

CHAPTER 6

Draculaura slept better that night than she had in three months. She attributed it to the emotional exhaustion of going back to school and being around other monsters after so long spent solo. Or maybe it was Cleo's dad's fault? Or her own dad's for dying and leaving her. But the dreams—she blamed those solely on Poe, because she'd dreamed of the normie all night.

Only, in her dreams he *wasn't* a normie. He was the one hiding in the shade while she frolicked in the sunlight. He stared into a puddle with only his empty sweatshirt reflected back at him, while beside him, her happy grin beamed up from the water's surface.

It was eerie and unsettling. But when she'd walked into Monster High the next morning—after Ms. Heaves nodded approvingly at every bite of toast with booberry jam she'd eaten—it was even eerier how *calm* things seemed. She'd been expecting a huge uproar over the normie-runners' video—but there'd been almost no mention of it on Critter or EekTok or any other social medea. In the halls, monsters chattered quietly, smiled tentatively. It was like everyone was waiting for the other shoe to drop.

"My father says it's only a matter of time," Cleo was explaining when Draculaura approached the ghouls at their lockers. "According to his sources, the video *is* up on the normies' web, it just hasn't been discovered yet."

"Maybe it won't?" suggested Lagoona. "Lots of things that *should* go viral, don't. And lots of things that *shouldn't*, do."

"Ugh." Clawdeen shuddered. "Remember this summer when the trend was putting ectoplasm on everything and eating it?"

No. Draculaura didn't remember this trend at all. At least there was one part of their summer plans she was grateful to have missed.

Frankie nodded. "Eggs with ectoplasm, eye scream with ectoplasm. Muffins, cobwebs, and smoothies with ectoplasm."

"I had *one* sip of a smoothie, and it took me a week to claw the taste out of my mouth," growled Clawdeen.

"You should've listened to me," Toralei purred, embracing Clawdeen from behind and pressing a kiss to her cheek. "I told you it was gross."

"Actually, I think what you said was, 'There's no way you're really going to drink that,'" said Clawdeen, spinning to face Toralei and resting her arms on the other ghoul's shoulders. "And I don't know about you, but that sounds like a dare to me, which you know I can't resist."

"In that case," said Toralei, "I dare you to kiss me."

Cleo cleared her throat. "Are you two done trying to be cute? Because no one out-cutes Deuce and me."

Clawdeen laughed, and Toralei muttered something that

sounded like, "Now *that* sounds like a dare to me," which made Clawdeen laugh even louder and nuzzle her cheek.

"Anyway," said Cleo, "my father says that no one should get too comfortable, because people *will* watch the video. And once the news hits, it's going to be bigger than the pyramids. Just wait and see."

"Can't we at least *hope* he's wrong?" suggested Frankie.

"What? No. Wait. Yes? I don't know!" Cleo threw up her hands, clearly flummoxed. "Ugh, it doesn't matter what *you* hope. It's happening."

Draculaura exchanged a look with Ghoulia, unable to keep the grin off her face. She wasn't smiling because of monument-sized problems but because, for once, the attention wasn't all on her. It was a defrightful way to start the morning.

Or at least it was until a stab of pain sliced through her forehead, making her stagger into her locker door—which closed with an attention-grabbing slam. Through blurry eyes she watched Ghoulia's face droop in concern.

"Are you alright, mate?" asked Lagoona, her fins drawn in tight with apprehension.

Well, the reprieve from that question had been fun while it lasted. She gave a tight nod, but even that small movement made her vision spin. "Headache."

"I'll take you to the nurse!" volunteered Frankie, her hand shooting up so fast, the stitches at her wrist strained.

"I'll be okay. I just need a second." *And an explanation . . .* but she wasn't saying that part out loud. Seriously, though, she'd

67

slept well *and* eaten a good breakfast, dutifully swallowing her iron supplements. What more did she need to do?

"Hey, babe," Deuce grinned at Cleo and nodded to the rest of the ghouls as he approached from his own locker.

Cleo glanced at Clawdeen and Toralei's clasped hands, then trotted to meet Deuce halfway, throwing her arms around his shoulders and launching herself into a kiss that wasn't strictly school-hallway-appropriate. If Deuce was caught off guard, he reacted quickly—returning the kiss while picking her up and swinging her around. Once he'd set her back on her heels, he grinned. "That was quite the good morning."

"Exactly," said Cleo, turning to look at the other duo. "And *that* is why Deuce and I will always be Monster High's cutest couple. Got it?"

Draculaura was pretty sure she saw Clawdeen squeeze Toralei's hand before she wrestled the smirk off her face. She didn't quite manage to erase all the laughter from her voice before she told Cleo, "Deathinitely. Fur real, no way we could compete with that."

"I'd think not," said Cleo, before adding with a magnanimous hand wave that fluttered her bandages. "But you two can be a close second."

"If you want me to keep our *no-scratching-her-eyes-out* rules, then I've got to go," Toralei hissed at Clawdeen, who only laughed and said, "I'll see you at lunch, kitten."

Toralei smoothed the orange and black streaks in her red bob and spun on her heels. "Later, ghouls."

If Deuce was bothered by being excluded from that farewell, he didn't show it. Though, actually, as the sole remaining manster in their group—now that Gil was gone—he was probably used to it. "Babe," he said, "you'll never guess what everyone was saying on the casketball court this morning."

"Is that why you're all sweaty?" Cleo wrinkled her nose. "I thought practice was after school."

"It is. This was just a pickup game. Anyway, Slo Mo's all, 'We should get someone to hack the human web and spread rumors and discredit the video as fake.'" Deuce actually did a pretty good zombie accent. Even Ghoulia nodded approvingly at his impression of her sometimes hookup. Or maybe she was agreeing with Slo Mo's idea? Draculaura wasn't sure. "And then," Deuce continued, "Holt was all, 'I think we should just tell everyone. Be like, monsters do exist, deal with it.'"

That got a bigger reaction—Lagoona gasped, Clawdeen said, "No creepin' way," and Frankie's eyes popped out of her head (the left one, literally, but Deuce rebounded it to her without pausing his story). "And Clawd was like, 'No, we just need to ignore it. Only conspiracy theorists are going to boolieve it.'"

"My big brother, he sheds everywhere and leaves the toilet seat up, but at least he's occasionally the voice of reason," said Clawdeen.

"Reason?" scoffed Cleo. "If you sphinx this is going away, you're dead wrong."

"Well, *you* seem scary invested in things going poorly," retorted Clawdeen. Draculaura was glad that Toralei had left, because now that Clawdeen had her own claws out, she doubted her ghoulfriend would decide to play nice. "Or are you just repeating what your *daddy* says in the hopes he pays attention to you?"

"What did you just say?" Cleo snapped, and Deuce had to band his arms around her waist to keep her from lunging. Cleo might not have claws, but she had long, pointy, perfectly manicured nails.

"Um, ghouls, let's all take a nice, deep breath," said Lagoona. "There's no need for—"

All the lockers in the hallway swung open and banged shut. The sound was thunderous and either drowned out Lagoona's words or shocked her into silence.

Draculaura held up her hands. "Okay, that time it wasn't me."

"Whoa." Deuce let go of Cleo to give her locker an experimental try. The door seemed fine now—it swung freely on its hinges, and the lock engaged when he spun the dial. "That was freaky."

"I've heard the school is being *weird*." Frankie leaned in and used her gossip-voice. "Operetta told me she heard from her dad that there are all sorts of new tunnels appearing in the catacombs. Some of the Phantom's night music students got lost on the way to his class. And I overheard the creatures talking about lights turning on and off all over the school."

"And don't forget the whole normies-on-campus thing! That was proof that we need strong leadership." Cleo flipped her hair and added, "Like my father."

Clawdeen sucked in a loud breath and let it out slowly before growling, "And, on that note—let's get to class."

Draculaura reached for her locker to grab her books when Frankie put a hand on her arm, "Unless—if you're not feeling up for class, I'll walk you to the nurse."

She shook her head. "I'm fine. Promise."

And she wasn't even lying, she felt fine—then.

She felt less fine a few hours later when they walked past her dad's school board office on the way to lunch. Though the twisting in her gut was the ordinary, anxiety kind—inspired by the sight of the de Niles' servants carrying boxes down the hall.

At first she thought the ushabtis held more of Dracula's stuff—she pulled out her phone to hext Ms. Heaves a heads-up about more deliveries—but then she realized the boxes were being carried *into* the office, where Nefera waited to direct them.

The third jackal-headed servant to pass them was carrying a set of gilded canopic jars and an onyx and gold obelisk. Flashy had never been her dad's style, but it was very much Ramses's.

"Are they—" Frankie pointed to the ushabtis. One had paused to affix a nameplate to the door. It was written in hieroglyphics, so Draculaura couldn't be completely sure what it said, but she had a good guess. Then the servant added a second name plate beneath it. This one read: Ramses de Nile, Pharaoh. Frankie sucked in a breath. "Yup, they are."

"That's a little presumptuous, don't you think?" Clawdeen asked. "Doesn't he have to run or something? He doesn't get to just move in and declare himself the leader."

"One would think." Draculaura tried to keep her voice light.

"How did your dad get the job?" asked Lagoona. "Was he elected? Appointed? Was there some sort of bat signal?"

"I don't know," Draculaura said honestly. "Even Head-mistress Bloodgood can't remember how it was decided. She says she is looking into it, trying to find a record of the procedure. But as long as there's been a school, my dad was head of the school board. No one thought to write a protocol for if he wasn't here to lead it anymore."

Because why would they? Immortal was supposed to mean forever.

"Yes, take down the blackout curtains," Nefera was ordering. "I want to feel the sun! In fact, everything in this blah office has got to go."

Draculaura was scary glad that Cleo wasn't walking with them to the creepateria. She was going to need every remaining step between here and their lunch table to get her game face on before she saw the other ghoul.

The PA system squealed loudly, interrupting a lunch table conversation about all the odd things that had happened at school that morning. But when nothing followed, the ghouls went back to swapping stories.

"Manny swore he was late to class because the hallways moved," gushed Lagoona. "He said it was like a maze."

"The temperature dropped to teeth-chattering levels in the middle of Mr. Hackington's Mad Science lecture," added Clawdeen.

"The fountain out front—instead of spewing water, it was totally spitting out bl—" Frankie glanced at Draculaura and decided not to finish her story. "Anyway, they drained and refilled it. It seems fine now."

Cleo was doing a good job of *not* making the conversation about her father, and even Frankie hadn't gone into fix-it panic mode when Draculaura contributed to the conversation: "When I was in the bathroom, there were these weird, shadowy smudges following me in the mirror."

"Was it—" Ghoulia's question was cut off by a second burst of static from the PA system, this time followed by a deep throat clearing.

Cleo sat up straight. "Daddy?"

"Hello, Monster High students—" The disembodied voice of Ramses de Nile cast a spell on the creepateria. Not a *literal* spell. At least, Draculaura didn't think so, though the family had been known to dabble in ancient curse magic. But the student body remained eerily silent as The Mummy continued, "I deeply regret that it is my responsibility to inform you that all sports and clubs will be suspending their after-school practices. This policy is effective immediately and indeathinitely—"

"*Excuse me!*" A new voice rang out over the PA, and Draculaura almost didn't recognize Headmistress Bloodgood, because she'd never heard the unflappable head of school sound so . . . *flapped*. "Ramses, what are you doing in my office? Who gave you permission to make decisions about school activities? And while we're talking, who gave you permission to move into the school board office? Wait, are you still broadcasting? Turn that off!"

"Monster High gave me permission." Ramses, on the other hand, was cool as Nile water—and twice as toxic. Maybe three times. Draculaura would have to ask Lagoona if the pollution problem in that river had improved. Could be four times. "I've heard about the problems you've been having at the school. Ogrethor got locked out of his custodian's closet. Students getting lost. Hypothermia in the class—"

"I wouldn't exactly call it hypothermia—just some mild frostbite," muttered Clawdeen, while elsewhere in the creepateria, Abbey was saying, "I knew that ice was not my fault. I am not even in that class." And at another table, Venus McFlytrap called out, "See, my locker really did eat my homework! Does that count as recycling?"

Ghoulia rubbed her eyes and mumbled something in Zombie. Draculaura was pretty sure she'd said, "Something is scary wrong with the school," but she couldn't be positive, because Ramses was orating again.

"Since the school allowed me access to the school board office, it seems obvious that Monster High *wants* me to head the school board. Just like it wanted me in *your* office to make this announcement. Why, it practically threw open the doors for me. So why don't we go ahead and make the title official: Ramses de Nile, Pharoah and Supreme Leader of the School Board."

"Or, perhaps, the doors were simply unlocked," countered Headmistress Bloodgood. "I won't be making that mistake again. Are you *still* broadcasting?" She sighed into the microphone before adding, "Students, I do not want to cause you undue alarm. At this point, no *official* decisions about school clubs and sports have been made."

That statement was met with a whole spectrum of reactions around the creepateria. Hex, even everyone at their table was processing it differently. Frankie's bolts were sparking, Clawdeen's hackles were up, Toralei's eyes were wide and delighted as she ate a bowl of fried anchovies like it was popcorn and she was watching some fabulously gripping movie. Cleo was trying to project confidence, but her eyes were darting around the room, watching everyone's reactions. Most were . . . not good. Even Deuce's snakes were frowning, though Lagoona was the one who looked closest to tears as she stared down at the training schedule on her iCoffin.

And Ghoulia . . . well, it was always hard to read her expression, but she'd pushed her tray down the table and had her laptop out instead. The screen was facing away, so Draculaura couldn't see what she was researching, but she hoped their smartest classmate was finding answers, because she had none.

"Oh, my mistake," said Ramses, who clearly still had control of the PA system. "I presumed that you—like me—would care about the safety and well-being of our students. It's alarming to me that you do *not*."

"Why I never—I certainly—" Headmistress Bloodgood

sputtered. "Turn that *off*. Let's have this discussion as adults, *then* pass the decision on to the students."

"I boolieve in keeping them informed," countered Ramses. "And until we can ascertain that this campus is secure and the human threat has been eliminated, students should not be at Monster High beyond the school day. Unless you're saying you can *one hundred percent* guarantee their safety? That humans won't film or attack them while they're at their most vulnerable—their focus on a harmless game of maceball or casketball—so they're defenseless when some human sneaks up and—"

The sound of the headmistress's horse, Nightmare, rearing and whinnying cut him off.

"That's enough!" Headmistress Bloodgood announced. "Students, we will institute a *temporary* pause on all extracurricular activities while we consider the situation."

Either Ramses was satisfied with that response or she finally managed to wrestle the broadcast button from his hand, because the PA system fell silent . . . only for the creepateria to explode in chaotic conversations.

"Good going, Cleo," Toralei purred. "What's next? Is your daddy going to ban desserts? Implement mandatory pop quizzes? Forbit fun in general?"

Cleo lifted her chin. "He'll do whatever he has to do to keep the school safe. You should be thanking him."

"Thanking him?" Clawdeen shook her head. "I don't understand why *he* thinks he can do anything. How is this fair? What authority does he have?"

Cleo scoffed and adjusted her massive gold necklace. "Besides being a pharaoh for more than five thousand years? How about the fact that he's the only one with the vision and courage to get the job done. Real leaders don't wait for permission to lead."

"He's not the *real* anything," said Toralei. "Him saying he's on the school board doesn't mean he is. He might as well *say* he's the tooth fairy. And the fact that he's not approaching this like a fair election makes me think he's scared he wouldn't win if there was a vote."

"My father isn't scared of anything or anyone!" Cleo screeched. "And if he *wanted* to be the tooth fairy—he'd be good at that too."

But Toralei just arched an eyebrow and left the table.

Clawdeen paused to add, "I don't know, Cleo, he seems awfully scared of a few normie boys, if you ask me," before she followed Toralei out of the room.

"Well, that was just ridiculous." Cleo's attempt to laugh sounded more like a cough as she tried to dismiss the fight with a wave of her hand—but her hand was shaking, making her bandages flutter erratically. "Some people just don't get it."

Draculaura noticed she wasn't the only one at the table avoiding eye contact. Ghoulia was attempting to hide behind her computer screen. Lagoona was sending panicked hexts about the canceled swim practice to either her coach or her parents. Frankie was picking at the stitches on her wrist.

They were all playing a classic game of not-it, because none of them wanted to be the one to tell Cleo she was wrong. Where was Abbey when they needed her? She never hesitated to deliver the iciest truths.

Deuce cleared his throat. "I know I'm not the smartest monster—but, Cleo, I don't get it. This feels wrong. Your dad is making all these decisions—and even if he *was* actually on the school board, there are other monsters on it too. He wouldn't get to just dictate everything. He's not even asking Bloodgood."

"Babe, you have to understand, this is my family's destiny." Cleo paired this over-the-top statement with an equally over-the-top gesture, both hands flung in the air, her bandages fluttering around her wrists like pom-poms.

Normally, Draculaura would've met Frankie's eyes and tried not to giggle, but this time it just didn't feel funny.

"Actually, I don't have to understand," replied Deuce. His snake hair was standing at attention and rattling. A clear warning he was fearious. "And I don't. All I understand is that I no longer have casketball practice or baking club because your dad bullied Bloodgood into canceling everything so he'd look more powerful."

Cleo laughed and propped a hand on her hip. "Babe, you're being absurd. Really, are you *this* upset because you can't play your silly sport? Gather your fiends and come over to the mansion, I'm sure there's a room somewhere where you all can bounce your little ball. As for cooking—there are kitchens everywhere. I don't understand why you're making this into such an issue. Everyone else agrees with me, right?"

Draculaura turned away before Cleo could try and snare her into a shared eye roll.

"I don't know what I think," said Frankie. "But fearleading, casketball, and all the other clubs and activities—they're not silly. And I know *you* don't think they're silly. Remember how hard we worked at fearleading Monster Nationals last year? For some monsters, those sports and clubs are the only reason they want to come to school. Taking all that away when we don't know if there's actually a threat or if it was just some fluke . . . that's a big deal, Cleo."

She sniffed. "Well, excuse me and my dad for wanting to keep everyone safe."

"It's not just that," said Lagoona softly. "It's how he's going about doing it. Cornering Draculaura to demand her support, clearing out Dracula's office and moving in, telling the student body we're all in danger. Just announcing he wants the job and expecting to be given it. Shouldn't there be a vote? There's got to be procedures for filling a vacancy—why shouldn't he follow them?"

"You all just don't get it!" Cleo stood. "You don't know what it takes to be a *real* leader, because none of you are. My dad—"

"Cleo, babe." Deuce tried to put a hand on her shoulder, but she shook him off. "Stop and think. You're hurting your friends; you're turning your back on your school. Why? Do you even boolieve what you're saying? Or are you just repeating what he tells you?"

"Of corpse I boolieve it! My dad has a dynastic vision for the school. He says he's going to let *me* help him plan it. You're not saying *I'm* wrong, right?" She batted her eyelashes in a way that felt like both a flirt and a threat. "In fact, I *was* going to invite you over to help make posters for him, but with *that* attitude, and, well . . . you know you and Daddy never get along. I'll just let you help hang them up when they're done."

The snakes on Deuce's head hissed their disapproval, but Cleo was too busy scoping places around the room for future postures to register how red her boofriend's face had turned.

"You'll *let* me? You sure your dad will be okay with my non-royal scales touching his 'dynastic' posters?"

"Well, that's just silly," Cleo said with a laugh. "Who's going to tell him?" It wasn't until one of Deuce's snakes snapped at the air that she registered Deuce's frown and pouted. Propping her hands on her hips, she asked, "Are you feariously saying you won't help me?"

"It's not *you*. It's your dad. It's the fact that you're falling for his scams, *again*, when you promised me after his last power scheme that you were done being manipulated by him."

Cleo stomped her foot, her cheeks turning the color of the Red Pyramid. "You're wrong. I'm not doing *exactly* what he wants, because if I was, I'd be breaking up with you."

"You don't have to bother," Deuce said. His face had gone stony, his snakes rearing back and hissing. "I'll save you the effort and do it myself. Get someone else to hang your doom posters! I'm through watching your dad control you like some toy. We're done."

"What?" Cleo chuckled, but Deuce's face only went stonier before he turned and stormed away from the table. Cleo called after him, "No. Deuce? Babe?"

He didn't turn around. Draculaura kept waiting for him to pause and let Cleo apologize so he could forgive her. But he didn't. He hesitated only slightly at the creepateria door, his fingers curling tightly around the frame. But then he pushed off it and left.

Not even the snakes on his head had turned to give Cleo a last look.

CHAPTER 7

Draculaura's stomach twisted—not that that was new. She was going to have to buy stock in whatever company made Tombs, because she'd been double-fisting those chalky antacids lately.

Only, when she looked down at her creepateria tray, Draculaura realized that Tombs was going to be no help preventing what was about to happen. There was no stomach medication that could.

The noodles on her tray—the ones she'd been distractedly forking into her mouth while Cleo and Deuce imploded—were sitting in a pool of tomato sauce. And floating in what remained of that sauce were large chunks of *garlic*.

She wasn't sure how she hadn't noticed earlier, because now that she was paying attention, she felt the burn all the way down her throat. Things were about to get ugly—in more than one way.

First, garlic made vampires break out in horrible acne. Second, it caused them to vomit—creeptacular amounts of vomit.

She needed to get out of this room. Now. And there was zero chance she was telling the ghouls why. Who would she even tell? Clawdeen had stormed off. Cleo was crying on Ghoulia's shoulder. Lagoona was panicking about canceled swim practices, and

Frankie was so torn about who she should comfort that she looked like she was about to split at her seams.

Not that Frankie wouldn't drop everything to rush her to the nurse, but Draculaura didn't need the nurse or an audience for this—she covered her mouth as the first of the garlic burps started—she just needed to get through it.

While they were distracted, she stood and mumbled, "Bathroom break." But instead of heading to the bathroom, she turned down the hallway to the secret exit she'd taken yesterday and headed outside.

If she threw up in a bathroom, she was sure Frankie would hear about it, track her down, and make it a whole thing. But if she threw up outside, maybe nobody would have to know?

Once she was free of the campus, she stood in the shade at the edge of the woods and waited for the nausea to start.

And waited.

And waited some more.

Her iCoffin buzzed with hexts from Frankie:

We're in Phys Dead—where are you?

Do you need me?

Tell me where you are, stay put, I'll come to you.

Oh, no thank you. Draculaura typed out a quick hext: Feeling crummy, decided to head home. Then she began to hurry down the path.

But even practically jogging didn't trigger the pukes. In fact, her stomach didn't *hurt* anymore. Maybe there hadn't been that much garlic after all?

And even though it was bright out, the sun barely stung her skin. Though, she could thank SPF 1000 for that one.

All in all, it was shaping up to be a much better afternoon than she'd anticipated back when she'd been staring down at her gastrointestinal foe. Not that she was going to Phys Dead class. Coach liked burpees and pull-ups a little too much—there was no way she was chancing those leading to *burping* and *puke-ups*.

But if she wasn't going back to class and there was no practice after school . . . what should she do?

Draculaura had told herself she wouldn't return to the cemetery. She *couldn't* call Poe—and the reasons for that were a perfect explanation for why she shouldn't be walking down this path in the hopes of seeing him again. His phone and hers couldn't connect—their worlds shouldn't mix. And if he knew what she was? He'd be just as terrified and disgusted as the guys who'd run by her—the ones who'd posted their video.

Also, why did she even *want* to see him? Deuce and Cleo had just broken up, Lagoona and Gil too. It's not like anything *lasted*. Not couples you thought were forever, not fathers who were supposed to be immortal.

What could a human boy—the very definition of a fragile, temporary being—possibly offer her?

And why, knowing all of this, could she not stop herself from creeping into the cemetery and heading directly to the grave where they'd met? She paused and gave a silent moment of reflection in front of his mom's headstone. It was small, simple.

Julia Beissen: Beloved Wife & Mother was inscribed above a set of dates that encompassed a pitifully short life.

How could humans handle walking around knowing their time was so brief? That they were so frail?

Poe was nowhere in sight, but he'd been here recently. There were new flowers on the grave—white ones that hadn't yet wilted despite the baking sun that was making Draculaura second-guess her sunscream.

Maybe it was for the best he wasn't here. She probably looked a fright. Though, when she rubbed her hands over her cheeks expecting to feel the telltale bumps of a garlic-zit invasion, her skin felt smooth. Tacky with sunscream, but unexplainably smooth. She bent and placed the fuchsia and black flowers she'd picked on her walk down beside Poe's.

It's not that she expected him to guess they were from her, but hopefully when he came back and saw them, he'd feel comfort knowing someone else was thinking of his mom too.

The hallways were empty by the time Draculaura returned to Monster High. It was weird not to have fearleading practice or to hear the echoes of the debate team's arguments, the rebounds of casketballs, or the noises of any other clubs and sports. It felt like spooky déjà vu—a callback to the quiet of the last night she and Dracula had been here.

Draculaura crept down the hall on tiptoe. She wanted to get

her books and get out as soon as possible—preferably without running into any of her creatures, or worse, Ramses de Nile. She knew he was somewhere on campus, because she could hear his raised voice echoing down the hall, demanding . . . *something*.

She didn't really care what, so long as she didn't get cornered by him again.

Draculaura knew her locker's reputation. She wasn't exactly what other monsters might call "orderly" and she'd yet to find any sort of organizer or system she couldn't overwhelm or bury beneath all of the academic, fashion, and beauty supplies she needed to keep in there.

That being said, it was only the second day of class. She hadn't yet had enough time to cover the floor of her locker with notes, or snack wrappers, or accessories she'd worn to school then changed her mind about.

And even if she had, the ancient, dusty book propped in the bottom of her locker was impossible to ignore. For one, it had that musty, old-book smell that made her sneeze. For another, it was mammoth. No way any of her current creatures assigned a textbook that enormous. It wouldn't be worth the student complaints about lugging it back and forth.

But if it wasn't a schoolbook, how had it gotten in her locker? And who had left it? And why? If it was from one of the ghouls, why wouldn't they have left a note, or told her?

Frankie loved to say, "I've left you a surprise," but if it was from her, it would be covered in sparkles, like her shoes or her phone case. Clawdeen gave great presents, but only on *occasions*, and Draculaura's birthday wasn't until February fourteenth. Lagoona wrapped everything in seaweed or other biodegradable materials, and Cleo's gifts were always delivered via jackal-headed ushabtis.

Draculaura shrugged and flipped open the book's creased red leather cover. The language and letters were old-fashioned. The kind where an *F* looks more like a *Z*. It was so old that the word *vampire* was spelled with a y: *Vampyre*.

There was a page marked with a thin strip of plain white paper. Draculaura turned to it and blinked at the heading: *Human Reversion Azter Creator Death*—or, rather, *Human Reversion After Creator Death*.

A shudder ran through her as she began to read the essay: *The vampyre has bountiful powers and strengths—including the gift of eternal unlife. Yet these dwellers-of-night are immortal, not invulnerable. The application of sunlight, stakes, and elemental silver will prove fatal—*

It was a fact that Draculaura knew all too well, one she had no desire to read, but as she skimmed ahead, it became clear that wasn't the essay's point.

Furthermore, the implications of the demise of a vampyre extend beyond their own being to those they have created. The undead scions of a vampyre shall not join their sire in disintegration. Instead—Draculaura paused here, her hands trembling with dread over what would come next—*following the demise of a creator, their line shall revert to the state from which they originated. Those who were depleted of their human blood, then given to drink from the vein of a vampyre, shall find themselves regressing back to which they were.*

The text made her blood run cold. *Her blood*—Draculaura almost laughed at the thought, because wasn't that what the passage was about? The very blood that flowed in her veins and how it was "regressing."

But her throat was too dry, her mouth too bitter for anything resembling laughter. The message of the essay was as clear as it was devastating: She was turning human. Except, that wasn't possible. Was it?

The sound of a locker closing reverberated down the hall, and Draculaura looked up from the book to scan the corridor around her. It was empty. It could've been the school playing tricks again. Or it could've been someone watching her. Had whoever put this book inside her locker stuck around to see her find it?

She needed to read the article again slowly, carefully. To take notes on what to expect and what it all meant. See if she could find a flaw or loophole, because if this were as true and straightforward as it seemed . . .

Human?

But first, she had to get out of here. The fact that this was left for her—page marked—meant someone else knew what was happening to her. They'd known before she did.

Draculaura shivered again as she slipped the book into her backpack and jogged toward the exit. From cold? Fear? Or was it a symptom of her de-transformation?

Regardless, without knowing who this book was from, she wasn't sure if it was meant to be interpreted as helpful . . . or a threat.

CHAPTER 8

"**D**raculaura? *Draculaura?*"

She ducked into a small doorway as Cleo's voice chased her down the hall. Draculaura was turning human. *Human.* She hadn't been human in almost sixteen centuries.

Even after tossing and turning over that fact all night, it was no closer to making sense. Not even after she'd memorized everything the book said about the process. There was a line that read: *Those who act with haste shall be able to forestall this transformation.* But forestall *how?* The book gave no insight into what, specifically, could be done to slow, stall, prevent, or reverse the change.

At two a.m. she'd even gotten out of her coffin and gone through the two boxes from Dracula's office that the de Niles' ushabtis had delivered to her house. But all they'd contained were heartache in the form of personal items that reminded her of her dad. To-do lists in his precise, spindly script, arts-and-bats projects she'd made him over the years. His favorite cobweb-scented lip balm and fancy hair pomade—though he'd defiantly deny using either. There were agendas and address books—Dracula hadn't exactly been a techie—and she'd poured over the contents of both looking for any clues but come up empty-handed. There'd been bundles of letters and tokens of appreciation from so many other monsters. He'd been so loved. She missed him so much.

And she was fangry at herself for being fangry with him. He'd left her alone without a roadmap to navigate what was happening.

Draculaura tugged on her hair in frustration. If Cleo found her right now, she'd take one look at her face and know something was wrong.

Actually, maybe that wasn't true. Cleo would deathinitely notice that she looked a fright but was way less likely to ask about her emotions than her appearance. Style, loyalty, cunning—these were skills Cleo had wrapped up, but *empathy* . . . not exactly her friend's strength.

Down the hallway, she heard Cleo groan. "Where did that ghoul go? Ugh. How am I supposed to keep her company if I can't even find her? You'll tell Frankie I tried, right, Lagoona?"

"Huh? What? Oh, sure thing, mate."

If Draculaura had to bet, she'd say that Lagoona was distracted by some training plan or coach's feedback on her iCoffin. Or she was watching a video of the last Boolympics. The ghoul was losing it without her daily swims.

So clearly Frankie had organized some sort of ghoul-sitting schedule. She'd actually assigned shifts to make sure Draculaura always had company. Thoughtful . . . and suffocating. The very thought made her shudder.

All three ghoul's phones chimed in stereo. Draculaura's volume was set way too loud to be overlooked. And since she was busted, she slunk out of the doorway to join them, but Cleo barely glanced at her other than to say, "There you are," before pointing back at her phone. "That's Ghoulia—she needs us in the library." She snapped her fingers when the ghouls didn't react fast enough. "What? Are you stuck in quicksand? Let's go."

Ghoulia was seated at a computer in the corner of the library when Draculaura, Cleo, and Lagoona arrived. Ghoulia had chosen the one with the largest monitor, and the rest of the ghouls had formed a semicircle behind her. Their eyes were all transfixed by the BooTube video on the screen. The play count at the bottom already hovered around a million, and the number was climbing fast.

"See, I told you it would go viral," said Cleo. "And this is just the MonsterWeb version. The normies have watched it way, way more times."

"This is the video those invaders took?" asked Lagoona. The screen showed a shaky video that had been filmed through the gates of Monster High. The students caught on camera were being totally normal—walking between buildings, sitting on the school steps, gossiping by the fountain—but the humans behind the phone's camera were hyperventilating.

"What is this place?" one of them cried.

Another screamed—and that's when the Monster High students turned and saw the normies. That's when pandemonium erupted on both sides of the camera. The monsters standing up, saying, "Who's over there?" and the normies yelling, "Run! They're coming to get us!"

They fled as the first Monster High student—Manny—took a step in their direction. He was probably just trying to see what was going on—but on camera, it looked like he was gearing up to charge.

Ghoulia hit replay on the video, and Draculaura cleared her throat. "I don't think we should call them invaders—I'm pretty sure they were just runners."

"Hey, ghoul. When'd you get here?" asked Clawdeen.

"A couple—" Draculaura's words were choked off—literally—by one of Frankie's voltageous hugs. Well, that shock certainly wouldn't do anything to tame her hair.

"Draculaura! We were looking for you." Frankie squeezed her again before her heterochromatic eyes shot to Cleo. "*Someone* was supposed to be with you."

Cleo shrugged. "There's a reason I don't babysit. Some were born to rule . . . and others to clean up drool."

Draculaura took a deep breath and counted to ten, deciding to let that comment pass *only* because Cleo had gone through a horrific breakup less than twenty-four hours ago.

At least she'd been *planning* to let it go, before Cleo said, "Besides, clearly she's fine"—then looked up from examining her nails and did a double-take at Draculaura—"er, or maybe she *isn't* . . . Ghoul, I'm booking us a spa day. Those pores and that hair need some serious damage control."

Draculaura ground her fangs. "I do not need a babysitter. I deathinitely do not drool. And my hair and pores are both fine."

"Hmm. They've looked better," admitted Clawdeen.

"Wait! Just a wait a minute, mate. You've all missed something fishy. Draculaura, how do you know those fellows were runners?" asked Lagoona. "But, also, maybe just put on a pair of sunnies to hide those eye bags."

The sea monster handed her the pair of sunglasses perched on her own head, and Draculaura started to protest. *Vampires don't get undereye bags* . . . except, humans did. Maybe she did now too . . .

She swallowed and focused on the other question. "I saw the runners right when they left campus. And honestly—they were far more scared of what they saw—us—than we should be of them."

"You *saw* the normies and you waited two days to tell us?" demanded Clawdeen, as Lagoona asked, "Why were you off campus?"

Frankie's bolts sparked so fiercely that Ghoulia told her to take an extra step away from the computers. "What if something had happened to you?" she asked. "The normies could've vamp-napped you! See, *this* is why we should be using the bloody system."

Draculaura forced her jaw to unclench; if she kept grinding her fangs in frustration, she'd look human even faster! "I *need* you to hear me when I say this: Being sad doesn't mean I'm stupid or that I need to be treated like a tiny ankle-biter."

"Well, you *were* off campus and apparently ran into the attackers," grumbled Cleo.

"They weren't *attackers*!" said Draculaura. "There's deathinitely something freaky going on with the school—with it being able to be seen by normies, and the lockers and the lights and all the rest acting creepy—but it was surprised normie teens at sports practice who filmed that! They didn't have a big, evil agenda."

Ghoulia said something in Zombie, but Draculaura was so fangry that it took her brain a second to translate: "*Those* normies didn't have one—but there's plenty of other humans with scary opinions." She was pointing at the computer where another video was playing—this one had a split screen, with the original on the left and a greasy-haired teen on the right. Between pops of a massive wad of chewing gum, the teen said, "This is so clearly fake. Or, like, leaked from a music video or something."

Ghoulia clicked again. Another split screen. This time an angry human with a buzz cut and cheeks that grew increasingly red as his volume grew increasingly loud. "Of course it's real. Just like aliens are real. It's a government school. Who knows what else they're hiding in the woods. They're probably breeding them as the ultimate weapon."

"As if *I* would ever fight for normies," sniffed Cleo.

Another click. This time it was a tall woman in business attire. "I just saw the video. I've seen everyone reacting to the videos. They all seem so *certain*. I just don't know what to believe, but my husband has joined the neighborhood patrol, and I'm not sure if I should let my kids ride their bikes in my driveway with those . . . those monsters out there."

"What does she think we're going to do with their bikes?" asked Lagoona. "*Or* her kids?"

"The humans are really in a tailspin over this," said Clawdeen.

"They should be. *We* should be—shouldn't we? I mean, isn't the whole point of all the rules and protections on our world to *not* let them know we exist?" asked Frankie.

Ghoulia wasn't the speediest, but that never slowed her down when it came to expressing herself. She snapped her fingers and pointed to the screen, where a new video was playing.

"That's my dad—" said Cleo.

"And that's *my* dad's office," said Draculaura.

Cleo frowned as Nefera appeared behind Ramses on the screen. "What's she doing there? He didn't tell me about this."

"When is this from?" Clawdeen growled, though the answer was right there at the top of the video.

A banner reading LIVE cut across the corner of the screen, and Ramses was saying, "As you know, I'm planning to take over as head of the Monster High school board—"

"Someone teach this guy that just because he *says* something, doesn't make it true," muttered Clawdeen, but the ghouls shushed her. They could—*would*—criticize later, listen now.

"Some of you have asked if there'll be an election or how you can support me—but there's no time for the formalities of campaigns and elections, not when our very way of life is under attack. I appreciate that you all *want* to vote for me, and I'm sure some of you have already made campaign signs for me—when all of this is over, I can sign them for you. Perhaps we can even do a special exhibit at the Museum of Monster History? But right now the school *needs* me to be appointed in this role without delay. It's obvious the students and school are upset by the destabilization caused by a loss of leadership."

Draculaura bared her fangs at this screen. Ramses was using a whole lot of words to avoid saying her father's name.

"Just this morning, a gargoyle statue crumbled off the school and fell *on* a student. Poor"—Ramses glanced down at a sheet of paper—"Danny Taur is currently in the infirmary with a cracked horn."

"Does he mean *Manny*?" asked Lagoona as Frankie gasped, "I passed by those gargoyles this morning too. We all did!"

"But the injury could've been far worse, and it's abundantly clear the school is dissatisfied with our failure to act—to institute a new leader. *Me*." Ramses smoothed down the front of his blazer and smiled at the camera. "By now you've all seen the normie videos. You've heard the humans are organizing patrols. We need to do that too."

"Patrols to watch the humans? Doesn't that sound dangerous?" asked Lagoona.

"And counterproductive if we want to *avoid* being spotted," added Clawdeen.

Draculaura shushed them both. All this anti-human talk was making her chest feel tight.

"Now is not the time for complacency," Ramses was saying, slamming a hand on her father's desk. Behind him, Nefera clapped, but her face sobered when he added, "We all must be on guard. I've experienced firsthand what happens when you're attacked by a mob of angry humans. No monster should go through what my family has endured."

Draculaura heard a sniffle and reached back and offered Cleo her hand. The other ghoul clasped it tightly.

"We must be proactive. My daughter Nefera and I will be reaching out to all the families at Monster High within the day and letting you know what you can do to support us in supporting our school."

"Wait, what about me?" asked Cleo in a soggy, indignant voice.

Ramses frowned and leaned closer to the camera. "An attack on this school is an attack on our very way of life. We cannot let it stand."

Draculaura frowned too. It hadn't been an attack—she wasn't sure why that was the word Ramses was using. Well, actually, she *was* sure. He was doing the same thing those normie reaction videos had done—stirring up panic. Using monsters' fear to fuel his own agenda.

Which begged the question—what did the humans in the incendiary videos hope to accomplish?

The ghouls were silent after the broadcast ended. They were officially late for first period, but no one seemed to care.

Frankie spoke first, "I haven't been around as long as any of you, but—I've heard the stories about humans from Hisstory class. And maybe Cleo's dad is right. Maybe we do need patrols and stuff to keep us safe."

"Of corpse he is!" said Cleo. "I'm the oldest of you all, and some things never change—like humans hating monsters. And some things *shouldn't* change, like those who lead." She paused to point to herself, in case they'd missed her subtle claim to power. "Humans and monsters—we don't mix. We can't trust them, we don't need them, we don't want them."

"Geez, don't let Jackson Jekyll or any of the other hybrids hear you say that." Clawdeen shook her head in disgust.

"That's different," said Cleo.

Draculaura slumped lower in her seat. She wondered where the distinction lay. If Cleo found Jackson acceptable because he spent half his time as his monster ego, Holt Hyde, would *she* be accepted once she became human, because she *used* to be a vampire?

Or a much better idea: She needed to figure out a way to *not become a human.*

"Humans," groaned Lagoona. "They just think everything is theirs to destroy. The oceans, the land, the air. Pollution is practically their favorite pastime. I don't even want to know what they'd do to monsters if they knew we existed."

"It would be horrible." Cleo placed the back of her hand to her forehead. "They chased my family down and trapped us in a *pyramid*. Do you know how dark it was in there? How hard those thousand years were? If we hadn't had magical bandages, we would've died. And sometimes, with only my dad and Nefera for company, that didn't sound like the worst outcome. Humans are *awful*. None of you can understand what they're capable of."

Draculaura tilted her head. Really? Because she was pretty sure she'd been chased out of her childhood home by a mob with stakes, pitchforks, and torches after some villagers had gravely misinterpreted an incident that involved her and some messy tomato eating.

"Yeah, but the pyramid was *so* long ago," she said, thinking of the sad-eyed guy in the graveyard. Would Poe come hunting for her with a pitchfork and a torch if he knew what she was? "Maybe times have changed?"

"Um, I've heard my parents' stories," said Frankie. "They had to flee for their lives because some normies got it in their heads that monsters are murderous."

"And have you *seen* how werewolves are depicted by Hollywood?" asked Clawdeen. "There's not a stylish one in the bunch. Humans think my kind are bloodthirsty animals."

Ghoulia grunted and made a slashing gesture at her neck to show how zombies were treated in movies. And once decapitation was on the table, Lagoona decided to rattle off her favorite pollution statistics, and Cleo launched into a description of the interior of the pyramid where her family had been imprisoned. "It only had eight chambers. Can you even imagine? The square footage was embarrassing."

Draculaura slipped out while they were still fighting over which of them had been treated *worst* by humans. She thought of the last normie she'd met, the one who'd been so kind. The one who'd made her feel seen and understood. The one it wasn't safe to go see again, since it sounded like the woods were full of humans hunting for their school.

She shook her head. She couldn't go back to the cemetery. She had to stay on campus.

Stay safe.

Except, school itself no longer felt safe. Everywhere Draculaura went, monsters were talking about the dangers and evils of humans. She couldn't tell if her heart was racing out of stress at their constant condemnation of what she was becoming, *or* if a racing heart was a symptom of the transformation. The dusty old book hadn't exactly been clear on the process, and it wasn't like she could look up "symptoms of turning human" on *CobWebMD.monster.*

But the sudden sweat and hot flashes—those had to be because of the human-thing. Vampires were notoriously cold. She had a sudden pang of missing her dad's reminders to *Bring a sweater, you know you'll be chilly*, or welcoming her home with a mug of warm tea. Though the thought of either of those things made her even sweatier. She wished she could ask Abbey to dowse her with a quick arctic blast, but that would be utterly suspicious.

Plus, after an unintentional icicle incident in the creepateria, where instead of cooling Operetta's soup, she'd almost impaled the ghoul, Abbey was scared to use her powers. Everyone with magic was, now that the school was behaving so wonky.

And Manny wasn't the only Monster High student who'd been injured. The school nurse was working double-time trying to take care of the students who were coming in with bruises (after the main stairs had turned into a greased ramp between second and third period), cuts (after the nightshade the Biteology class had been pruning suddenly grew thorns five times larger than usual), and burns (after all of the Bunsen burners in Mad Science class ignited with wild flames in the middle of a test).

Draculaura had cowered under her desk, shaking as others put out the fire. Lagoona summoned water from the sinks, and Frankie and others used ordinary—but effective—extinguishers. If anyone knew *why* she was hiding instead of helping, they didn't say so. Clawdeen had crouched and said in a voice so gentle it sounded unfamiliar, "Hey ghoul, it's safe to come out now."

And with their tests reduced to smoldering, soggy ruins, Mr. Hackington had scowled and pointed a finger at Heath Burns. "What have I told you about using your powers to avoid examinations? Detention! Double detention!"

The fire elemental's cheeks had burned hot as he stammered. "What? I wasn't even *in* here when they ignited! I was in the bathroom."

Clawdeen had stood, ready to fight for the underdog. "It's true. Heath wasn't in here."

Mr. Hackington had looked skeptical. "He asked for the pass *ten minutes* ago. He had to be back."

"Right, but funny thing is—the bathroom, um, it wouldn't let me leave." Heath shrugged, warming up to the attention. "No, really, the door locked from the outside and I was just stuck in there . . . alone with my thoughts and the smells."

While some of the other students snickered, Mr. Hackington hadn't thought this was so funny. He'd promised the makeup test would be twice as hard.

This hadn't helped Draculaura's headache, but even if she *had* wanted to go to the nurse and ask for something for it or her stomachache or sweats—she couldn't. The sight of Twyla and Skelita walking down the hall with freshly applied burn cream made her want to scream, or cry, or hide. For once she was incredibly grateful that Frankie was always by her side. She'd needed to squeeze her best friend's hand and lean on her a little—even if she didn't have the words to explain her distress or share why she was struggling.

But maybe she didn't need to. Frankie squeezed her hand back. "I'm here, boo. I've got you."

And for a moment, Draculaura exhaled. But only until Frankie added, "Those normies don't stand a chance against our ghoul squad."

Everywhere, all day, us against them. Except, unless she could find a cure—quick—Draculaura was no longer going to be an *us* and would instead be a *them*.

Things were even worse at Monster High the next day when a gaggle of scargoyles attacked before first period. These flying, red-eyed squid-like creatures looked like they'd escaped from someone's nightmares. Which was not that far from the truth—they'd somehow escaped from the wilds of the catacombs to swarm through the hallways, diving down to slash at students and smash lockers, then swooping out of reach.

It had been chaos. Clawdeen had looped an elbow through Draculaura's, her other hand clasped tightly to Toralei's as they ducked, dodged, and weaved their way to where Frankie was holding the door to the ghoul's bathroom. They'd cowered together against the door, Frankie glued to her iCoffin, her seams straining as her fingers flew across the screen.

"Who are you hexting and are they coming to rescue us first?" Toralei kept extending and retracting her claws, practically daring anyone to call her a scaredy-cat.

"The other ghouls," Frankie said, without looking up from her screen. "I'm checking where they are."

Draculaura read their responses over her shoulder.

Cleo wasn't at school yet: Running late, nail screamergency.

We're locked down in the pool. All's good, Coach is tough as scales. Draculaura decided it wasn't the time to mention that Lagoona's practices were supposed to be canceled.

From Ghoulia: Library. Safe.

"Library?" Toralei crinkled her nose. "It's the first week of school. That ghoul is an ogre-achiever."

"She's just deadicated," said Clawdeen.

It was Frankie who said what they were all thinking: "Thank ghoulness they're all safe." But were they? Were any of them? Draculaura tried to pay attention to the funny story Clawdeen was sharing about the smallest cubs in her pack, but she could barely hear her over the pounding in her ears.

By the time Mr. Rotter, Headmistress Bloodgood, and Coach Igor had managed to capture all the scargoyles, nineteen students had needed to be sent home to either mentally or physically recuperate, or for changes of clothing—mostly because they'd been shredded by the scargoyles' claws, but Toralei swore that Jackson Jekyll had peed his pants.

If so, Draculaura didn't blame him. She'd seen a lot of freaky things at Monster High, but this was the first time it had felt *scary*.

Some of the students heading home were vowing they wouldn't come back. She heard Gory Fangtell say she'd already filled out the paperwork to transfer back to the vampires-only school she'd previously attended.

"Sure, Belfry Prep might not have all the same opportunities as Monster High, but at least no one's getting killed," Gory sobbed as she headed out the door with her shoulder covered in bandages.

Not that anyone had been killed . . .

Yet.

CHAPTER 9

Draculaura was hiding in the library to avoid a cat fight. Well, technically it was a were-cat versus mummy fight—Toralei and Cleo were going at it in the hallway, arguing about Cleo's father. Draculaura was pretty sure that Toralei didn't truly care about the school board, she just didn't want to see the de Niles win.

And, honestly, Cleo didn't care about the school board either—she just cared about winning.

The library served another purpose beyond being a hiding place that neither ghoul would willingly visit and away from the visible reminders of yesterday morning's scargoyle attack—Draculaura was looking for Ghoulia. She had exhausted all the places she knew to search for information and needed help on her vampire-reversion research. There was no one at Monster High who was smarter than her friend—plus she had permissions in databases and libraries that Draculaura barely knew existed—but Ghoulia moved at her own zombie-speed, and Draculaura was worried she was running out of time.

Unfortunately, when she found Ghoulia lurching her way between two library shelves, the other ghoul was already working on a different project: star charts for Cleo and Seth Ptolemy, the son of the second-most powerful Egyptian family—and the monster that Ramses de Nile most desperately wanted Cleo to date—or as he put it "form an alliance with."

"Is she really considering it?" Draculaura asked. "This breakup with Deuce, do you think it's for real?" Because until this moment, she hadn't.

Ghoulia groaned and rolled her eyes.

"Yeah, I know what you mean," said Draculaura. "Everything about school this year feels hexed." She hesitated, then whispered, "Can I ask you to keep a secret?"

Ghoulia looked insulted.

"Right. Of corpse I know I can trust you. It's just . . ." Draculaura took a few steadying breaths, "it's about *humans*."

Ghoulia raised an eyebrow but moaned and motioned for Draculaura to continue.

Draculaura inhaled, then poured out the story of her symptoms, the book in her locker, and what it revealed. When she was finished, the zombie stood there, mouth agape.

Draculaura twisted a strand of pink and black hair around her finger and waited for the rest of Ghoulia's reaction.

And waited.

And waited.

Just when she thought she might explode from stress, Ghoulia blinked behind her red glasses and said one word (in Zombie). "No."

"No?" asked Draculaura. "No, you can't or won't help?"

"No, you're not losing your vampirism. That's not happening." Ghoulia reached past Draculaura for her notepad. After being motionless for so long, her fingers practically flew as she jotted down a list of topics to research, calling directions to Draculaura in Zombie as she wrote. "I'll need to see the book. And I need a list of your symptoms, when they started, how they're changing."

"Okay, I can do that," said Draculaura. "But . . . aren't you disgusted by me? Turning normie?"

Ghoulia grumbled in Zombie without looking up from her notepad. "You *won't* turn normie, if I have my way."

"You really think you can find a cure or solution or something?" Hope fluttered like bat wings in Draculaura's chest.

Ghoulia waved off these comments with an irritated moan, which Draculaura was choosing to interpret as: *Have we met? Have I ever met a research project I couldn't solve?*

If anyone could find an answer, it was Ghoulia. The zombie practically oozed brains. She could read a half-dozen dead languages and was so creeptacular at research that the teachers often went to *her* for help instead of the other way around.

"What about Cleo's star chart?"

Ghoulia rolled her eyes and mumbled in Zombie, "I'll just give her the same one I do every time her dad starts this nonsense. They're *not* compatible." Her fingers were still a blur, filling page after page with indecipherable scrawls of probably brilliant theories. Even squinting and tilting her head, Draculaura couldn't make out more than a few random words. Ghoulia stopped writing just long enough to give Draculaura a why-are-you-still-standing-here? look.

"Okay, I'll just . . ." Draculaura scanned the library. "Go and see if I can find anything." She headed to the dustiest shelves in the back. Old books meant old answers, right? And the book that had been left in her locker was ancient. There hadn't been anything nearly as old in the boxes from her dad's office. She'd gone through them twice already. But she'd check them again. Or help however Ghoulia instructed her.

Draculaura swallowed down the pang that came from thinking about how somehow, all her dad's time on the school board, all he'd done for Monster High, had fit into two cardboard boxes.

If he were still here, he'd have answers for what to do about the attacks, for how to stop her transformation.

But then again, if he were still here, she wouldn't be transforming.

That must have been what he'd wanted to tell her that last night—if only she'd listened.

She grabbed a book from the shelves and blew the dust off the cover: *Ghastly Gripes and Grievances—Volume 1.* Glancing inside the cover, she saw the book had been published centuries ago. It might be nice to get lost in problems from another era, since the ones in her own life felt too pressing.

As if everything else wasn't falling apart, at lunch Lagoona had shared that she was considering leaving Monster High. "I just can't take the chance with my training. It's too important to me—I shouldn't have to choose between safety and my dreams. If I transfer to another school, I might not have to."

Draculaura wasn't so sure about that. If Monster High was exposed, what were the chances the other schools of the monster world would stay hidden? But just the possibility of Lagoona leaving had thrown Frankie's voltage off-kilter. She was sparking at the bolts trying to come up with ways to convince the sea monster to stay.

Miraculously, this new catastrophe seemed to have lessened Frankie's ability to micromanage Draculaura's grief. She'd even given her a task: "Do you think you could ask Ms. Heaves to bake those kelp cupcakes Lagoona loves for ghouls' night? It's okay to say no if that feels like too much."

And somehow, even more miraculously, Frankie had boolieved her when she'd said that asking her housekeeper a question was *not* too much of a burden.

Draculaura had just decided the book she'd selected was a bust—at least for her research, though Spectra might like it since *Ghastly Gripes and Grievances* was pretty much a first-century version of the ghost's news and gossip blog, the *Gory Gazette*—when she began to cough.

The air around her had filled with dust, like a thousand neglected book covers had been simultaneously blown off by a thousand invisible readers. The motes swirled in the air, faster and faster. They formed into a dust cyclone, the force of it rattling the pages of the book in her hand and pushing her forward.

Dropping *Ghastly Gripes and Grievances*, Draculaura grabbed onto a shelf to anchor herself. It was hard to see through the tempest; the urge to shut her eyes was almost irresistible. Even braced against the shelf, her feet were sliding forward from the force of the wind.

And then the first book struck her.

"Oof." She couldn't be sure which shelf the book had come off, but it was large and hardback and knocked the wind out of her before being flung away by her own personal maelstrom. The second book hit the back of her knee. The third, her arm, just above the elbow. It made her hand go numb, making it harder to hold on to the shelf.

The next two tomes hit her head, and Draculaura decided she'd rather this tornado push her wherever it clearly wanted her to go than end up concussed—or worse, bleeding. She released the shelf and covered her head. Instantly the aisle stopped raining books on her, but the dust storm didn't subside. It propelled her down the aisle toward the main part of the library, pushing her all the way across the open space until she was only a few feet from the far wall, standing just in front of a life-sized painting of the school's founding back in 1814.

Then the wind . . . stopped. Not a single page on any of the study tables was fluttering. And while her hair was a storm of snarls, no one else seemed to have a strand out of place. They were all looking at her. Staring, really. Draculaura hoped they'd been able to see her own cyclone, that it hadn't looked like she was going batty or battling invisible demons.

It *hadn't* just been in her head, had it? She gulped at the thought and straightened the skirt of her black and pink dress. The box pleats were hopelessly ruffled—and her hair . . . she gave up trying to smooth it and hoped it looked "windblown chic."

"What was that?" demanded Mr. Hackington.

Phew. So, the creature had seen it too. And judging by the fact that he was grumping toward her, his frown even more pronounced than usual, he either didn't understand what he'd seen, or he blamed her for it.

Draculaura opened her mouth to say, *I don't know*, but her answer was interrupted by a loud *crack*.

The massive painting on the wall—the one that showed the thirteen most revered monster families coming together to sign the charter for Monster High—was tilting like it had been shoved from behind by invisible hands. Headmistress Bloodgood was in the painting. As was Dracula; he was smack in the center; his arms held wide in a gesture that was supposed to symbolize the school's embrace of *all* sorts of monsters. Monster High had been the first school of its kind—one that accepted every monster, regardless of their parentage or abilities. It was disappointing to realize that more than two hundred years later, Monster High was *still* the only inclusive school in their world.

It had always made her laugh that they'd chosen her dad—who was *so* not a hugger—to place in that pose. She'd like to tease him that his fashion sense hadn't changed much since the nineteenth century either. He still favored black slacks and frock coats.

Or . . . at least, he *had*.

But now she watched in horror as the painting fell from the wall, the frame cracking, the canvas tearing, and the glass shattering in a tsunami of shards. They coated the floor, the tables, the books.

But somehow spared her.

There wasn't a single glass splinter in her hair, not a fragment on her shoes or dress. There was a perfect circle around her feet that was free of debris. A glassless oasis amid the chaos, as everyone else began to scream and freak out. Those who hadn't tuned in while she was a vampire windstorm now rushed out of study rooms and dark aisles to see what was going on.

"I'm okay," she said, holding up her unmarked hands to reassure the crowd of creatures and students that had formed behind her. Everyone was staying back at least ten feet, past the boundary drawn by the broken glass.

"No, look," said Ghoulia in Zombie, pointing past Draculaura at the newly blank wall where the painting had hung.

Except, it wasn't blank.

The writing started with faint stains emerging through the white paint, but they soon erupted with violence, lines blooming, forming letters that dripped down in crimson smears.

Draculaura gave a full-body shudder. Her head started to spin.

"Is that—" asked Purrsephone. She had Meowlody's paw clasped tightly in her own.

"Well, it's not ketchup," said Mr. Hackington.

"Blood," whispered Draculaura.

She wasn't answering the werecats; she was reading. But as the second word was appearing, her own vision started to fade.

"What language is that?" Spectra floated above the broken glass, daring to get slightly closer to Draculaura and the writing.

"Latin." The answer was automatic, as was translating it to English. Latin, her first language, the one of her childhood and her mother's journal, was now considered a "dead language." The perfect language for the undead.

Perfect for a bleeding wall.

"What does it say?"

She wasn't sure who'd asked. Their voice sounded far away and distorted. Draculaura was lightheaded, struggling to breathe, to stay standing, to stay conscious. She knew she *had* to read the message—just like she knew the message was meant *for* her.

"Blood," she whispered again, then cleared her throat and spoke louder; as loud as she could with the room swaying around her. "Sanguis requiritur. *Blood is required.*"

As soon as she spoke the words, they vanished.

The crowd was left gasping and staring at the blank wall, at the smashed painting, at the wave of glass that had miraculously missed her.

But Draculaura could still picture the words, the sticky scarlet drips rolling down from uneven letters.

Sanguis requiritur.

Blood is required.

But whose? Why? And How?

Draculaura was one hundred percent certain she didn't want to know.

CHAPTER 10

This was the last time. Draculaura knew this even as she jogged down the path. It wouldn't be safe to keep coming here. There were too many risks. More now than there'd been a few days ago. But she was proud of herself for not fainting in the library, and since that epic accomplishment had used *all* her self-control, she had none left to prevent her fleeing feet from leading her here. Honestly, she hadn't even hesitated, though the journey through the woods had been an exercise in evasion. She'd had to dodge both a monster-parent patrol *and* a normie-led monster search party. She was pretty sure she'd be picking leaves and moss out of her hair for a week, but she'd managed to duck into the underbrush without getting caught.

Also, it was Friday. She'd made it through her first week of school, and—she couldn't emphasize this accomplishment enough—*not passed out* in the library when the wall began to *bleed* with messages about *blood*. She deserved a reward. Even if she had skipped a truly scary number of classes this week . . .

Dracula would not have been pleased.

Not that she had high hopes for what she'd find in the cemetery. There were fourteen hundred and forty minutes in a day— even *if* Poe was planning to visit his mother's grave, what were the chance he'd choose the same minutes she had?

It was just that—she'd spent the whole school day listening to all her classmates and all her creatures talk about how awful humans were. How no one could trust a normie.

And she was becoming one . . .

Blood is required. What did that even mean? Just thinking about it gave her the shivers, even while dashing across the part of the path with the least shade. Which made her shiver in a whole new way. She froze at the edge of the shadows. The entrance to the cemetery was right across the street, but both lanes were in full, bright sunlight.

Was she wearing enough sunscream? Sunburns used to be scary annoying, but now they were just scary. If only she'd dared to be rude at the end of the school year party and interrupted Dracula during one of the conversations with his many, many fans to *insist* he slather on SPF.

If only he hadn't been burned, he wouldn't have gone to get the ointment.

If only the pharmacist had done his job correctly, he wouldn't have been given the silver ointment.

If only he hadn't applied the ointment, he'd still be alive.

If he were still alive . . . well, according to Dr. Sanguine, that mental pathway led only to dead ends, since *nothing* would be the same if he was still alive. Not her, not her relationships with her friends. Cleo's dad wouldn't be demanding to control the school board. Cleo and Deuce wouldn't have broken up. And whatever was up with Monster High—the thing that was making it attack the student body instead of protecting them—she couldn't help but think that problem wouldn't exist either.

Or, if it did, that her dad would know how to fix it.

But he wasn't here, and in the past two days she'd faced down scargoyles and blood. She could handle a little sun too.

Draculaura took a deep breath and ran across the road and through the cemetery gates.

It wasn't her name, but the letter was deathinitely for her. Its white envelope was resting against Poe's mom's headstone with five letters printed across the front in blocky script—like the writer was taking pains to be neat.

Laura

She picked it up and opened the flap, blinking at the nearly illegible words scrawled across the piece of notebook paper inside, then scanned down to the signature.

Poe

Draculaura carried the note over to a bench that was shaded by a willow tree and began again at the top.

Laura,

Thank you for the flowers. They were from you, weren't they? They were the exact same color as the stripes in your hair, so I'm assuming. But if I'm wrong—if you never came back and never see this note, I guess I don't really have anything to lose, right?

Man, I hope you can even read this. My hand-writing is the worst and I'm already late for soccer practice. The rest of the team is out on the field and I'm still sitting in the locker room wondering where you are on a Thursday afternoon.

Remember when I said I wondered if anyone would ever treat me normally again? I've found the place: sports competitions. We had our first game yesterday, and apparently not playing at the top of my ability is still "unacceptable"—no matter the excuse. At least according to my dad—who told my coach to "stop taking it easy on me."

I should get out there. But I wanted to say thank you—and that I'm thinking of you. I hope things are going better with your friends. And even if you never see this or I never see you again, I'm still glad we met.

—Poe

It was just a piece of paper torn from a notebook. Probably sandwiched between class notes and math homework. Just a piece of paper, but it felt precious. An acknowledgment that she existed, she mattered, that the time they'd spent together that Monday in the graveyard had impacted *him* as much as it had her.

Wouldn't it have been the worst if she couldn't stop thinking about Poe and he'd already forgotten she existed? If she'd been carrying around a phone number she couldn't call, and he didn't even remember her fake name?

But he hadn't forgotten, and her hand dipped into her pocket, like it had so many times over the past five days, stroking the well-worn slip of paper she'd been transferring from outfit to outfit like a talisman. She pulled it out now.

The original ink had all but faded off the gas station receipt. She could no longer read the date or the price per gallon, but the ink Poe had written his phone number in was still entirely visible. And even if it hadn't been, she'd long since memorized the ten digits. Not that she could call him. But why didn't she have a pen? She couldn't even write back to his letter.

But wait . . . when Lagoona asked Ghoulia how the normies' video had jumped from the human's internet onto MonsterWeb, hadn't the zombie said something about a site on the "dark web" where it was possible to send hexts across the digital divide between the worlds? Could she find that?

Draculaura turned on her iCoffin and began to search.

Ten minutes later, she had entered her number, Poe's number, and a short message into a shady looking cobwebpage. She hoped she wasn't making a dire mistake, signing them both up for months of spam and hoax hexts, exposing them to identity theft, or exposing monster world secrets. Was this even legal? It was quite possible the Monster Bureau of Investigation would be knocking on her door later with some questions about her online activities.

If so, she hoped they were fans of her father and gave her a free pass—because she'd held her breath and clicked on the button marked *Send*, so there was no undoing this now.

Her phone beeped. The screen's message changed to "sent"— but had it? She had no way of knowing. Not unless he wrote back. If he did, the website would supposedly translate between their devices and deliver the message to her inbox.

But would it? How would she know if it didn't? And who else was reading what they wrote?

This was a mistake.

This was a huge mistake. Ramses had just given a whole speech asking them to be "on guard" and warning against humans attempting to infiltrate the monster world, and here she was, practically inviting Poe in.

She should stay far away from him, physically and electronically. She shouldn't have come back to the cemetery again. She should leave. She should focus all her efforts on *not* becoming human. She should attempt to attend a full day's classes.

But before she even made it to the cemetery walls, her iCoffin pinged with an unfamiliar beep, and a new message popped up on her screen.

It's so good to hear from you. I just finished practice and don't want to go home—want company?

Did she? Absolutely. Should she? Absolutely not.

But she was still typing *Yes* into the sketchy cobwebsite. Adding, *Meet where we met?* Because maybe it was marginally safer to arrange a clandestine rendezvous with a normie if you didn't tell whoever might be monitoring a likely illegal cobweb-site where you'd be.

Her phone chimed again with that weird beep.

I can be there in five.

Which meant she had only three hundred seconds to talk herself out of this—or not talk herself out of it. She wasn't even sure which side was right or wrong anymore.

And when a sleek blue car pulled into the parking lot and Poe climbed out, all glistening tan skin and sandy hair curlier than last time, well, she forgot to be conflicted.

He had on a gray T-shirt that did sparkling things to his blue eyes, black sports shorts, and sneakers. She was defrighted to notice that he had some sort of tan line on his calves, just a few inches below his knees. Draculaura was more of a spec-tator than participant when it came to all sports except for fearleading. Which had he said he played? Soccer? It had to be similar to Monster High's scary soccer—and Lagoona, Claw-deen, Frankie, and Toralei were on the scream, but humans—fragile as they were—had to wear so much more protective gear than monsters did. Hence the tan lines and probably the messy hair.

"Hey." Poe paused to smile and gaze at her like he was drinking her in. Honestly, she was doing the same. "Sorry I'm all sweaty. I didn't want to make you wait while I went home to shower and change."

"I don't mind," she said honestly, then asked, "The curls? Are they from helmet hair?"

"Helmet?" He laughed and ran his fingers through his damp hair, making it spiral in a million chaotic directions. "I play soccer."

So, from that she was inferring *no* helmets in the normie version of the sport? Probably not a thing she could ask. "Soccer, huh?"

He shrugged sheepishly. "It used to be my *thing*, you know? I was obsessed and spent all my time tracking stats and training."

She smiled. "I have a few friends like that." Besides Lagoona and her lap time spreadsheets, Manny could be way competitive about casketball. And Operetta had gotten a little too intense about training during the one season Draculaura had tried Skultimate Roller Maze.

Poe nodded. "And now it's finally my senior year, and I'm supposed to be returning all these calls from college recruiters and making highlight reels and networking and *caring*, and I just . . . don't."

She sat on a low stone wall conveniently located in the shade and patted the spot next to her. "You don't like the sport anymore?"

"Maybe? No, I do still like it. I just don't want it to be my entire life." He kicked at a pebble on the path before joining her on the wall. "I don't know. Maybe I'll get back there again, but right now . . ." He looked up from the ground and met her eyes, searching for something there. "My dad's just . . . I'm not saying our grief has to be exactly the same, I know everyone handles things differently—but, like, he's somehow become *more* obsessed with my soccer, while I feel like I'm just going through the motions." He flicked some hair off his forehead and then turned so his intense focus was on her. "Enough about soccer. What about *you*? Are you still into your clubs or sports or things?"

She sucked on the tips of her fangs as she considered this. "No. I don't think so. I don't know though. I haven't had to actually face any of it. My school canceled all sports and clubs for the week."

"Why?"

"Oh, um . . ." Draculaura scratched the toe of her black Mary Jane in the dirt as she came up with a lie. "Gas leak in the gym. No practice until they fix it."

"That stinks. Or maybe it doesn't, if you wanted a break."

Draculaura considered that for a moment. Maybe she *had* wanted a break. A minute to figure out who this new orphaned version of herself was and how she fit into her old hobbies and habits. She gave a startled laugh.

"What?" he asked.

"It's just—" She swiped some book dust off the pleats of her dress. Or maybe it was cemetery dirt; it didn't really matter. "I used to be almost annoyingly optimistic, and then my dad died. And my scare-apist, *therapist*, has been trying to get me to reframe things to find the positives for months now. And you achieved that in just a few minutes. You surprise me."

He grinned. "It's my name, isn't it? *Poe*. People hear it and assume I'm some sort of emo poet. They expect slick dark hair and guyliner. It's always kinda awesome to surprise them with this mop." He pointed at his riot of curls.

"Wait, do you—" she giggled. "Are you saying that's a *perm*?"

His laugh seemed to come from his toes and cover them both like a warm sunset. It echoed off the closest gravestone, contagious and magnetic, so that they were leaning toward each other for support. Though the moment their shoulders touched, the energy changed, the laughter fading into electricity that crackled between them.

"No, I promise," he said, wiping tears of laughter from his eyes. "The hair is all-natural chaos. My dad hates it. Wishes I'd buzz it off."

"Don't you dare." She'd said the words without thinking but didn't regret them. Not when they made him smile like that.

"I mean, I've always gone rather aggressively *against* the sad poet stereotype. But this year, I don't want to worry about student council or homecoming court—you know?" He made a thoughtful noise. "Or maybe that *is* who I am now. I'm already leaving handwritten letters on gravestones to mysterious beauties—that seems pretty emo. Give me another week and maybe I'll move on to poetry. But I'm warning you, it will be *terrible*."

Draculaura could feel her lips fighting to arch upward, instead, she lifted an eyebrow. "Beauties? Exactly how many cemetery correspondences do you have?"

"Just you," he said with a laugh. "But I swear, it's like you're haunting me. I can't think of anything else."

There was something endearing about his honesty. The way he said things directly but dropped his eyes as he did, peeking at her sheepishly through those eyelashes. This was the sort of thing she usually told Frankie, the two of them curled up in a hammock in Clawdeen's backyard or sitting squished together on a brainbag chair in Ghoulia's basement. She'd be giggling and gesturing, and Frankie would get so enthusiastic she'd manage to fling a body part somewhere, and they'd all laugh as they hunted for it. They'd tease her—of corpse—but Cleo would also strategize the best way to win Poe over and probably threaten to curse him with an ancient relic if he didn't return her feelings. And Clawdeen would have fierce fashion insight into what was "cemetery chic."

She could tell them about his broad shoulders, the tan lines, the freckles on his face and neck that she wanted to trace with her fingers. "I've been thinking about you too," she admitted.

"Good. I'm glad it's not just me, because it's been . . ." He shrugged and chuckled. "Embarrassing amounts. I told my best friend, John, and I'm pretty sure he thinks I'm either making you up, or bewitched, or annoying since I won't shut up about you. Not soccer, not my dad hassling me about college apps, not even this whole monster hoax thing that my entire school won't stop talking about. Just you."

If there was any bewitching being done, *he* was doing it right now. But whatever spell his words had been weaving was shattered by the phrase *monster hoax*.

She repeated the words back to him, turning them into a question.

He just shook his head and laughed. "I still can't believe anyone thinks that video—or *monsters* for that matter—are real."

She gave a choked laugh.

Fiction. Poe thought she was fiction. The knowledge that humans used to have about monsters had all faded to myths, stories, and scare tactics. And if those who boolieved were more likely to run screaming than meet the knowledge with any sort of open mind, then maybe all the protections around the monster world and rules against intermingling with normies were necessary.

Dracula had always thought that monster leadership didn't give humans enough credit—that maybe they could coexist peacefully instead of existing separately. After all, hadn't Draculaura's own mother been perfect proof that not all humans hated their kind? And Draculaura herself—she'd been human for sixteen years, and she'd loved her dad long before she had fangs.

Maybe her mom was the reason Dracula had had such a soft spot for human culture and an affinity for bending the rules about crossing into normie portions of the world. An affinity he'd passed down to her, apparently.

But then again, since she'd been born a human, wasn't her curiosity about them understandable . . . even if entirely off-limits?

"That video is . . ." She shook her head and shrugged. "It's *something*."

Poe was grinning at her. "Right? It's all ridiculous. I know the kids on the cross-country team who filmed it. They're the same guys who cling-wrapped the toilets and greased the door handles last April Fool's Day. This has got to be another prank, but how can they even admit that now, when way too many people are insisting it's real and getting all invested? Has your school gone as bonkers as mine?"

She nodded wordlessly. It wasn't a lie; Monster High was fully cursed-chaos right now.

"When you said your school canceled sports practice, I thought it was because of that. They're talking about canceling games at New Salem High. They've already got security patrolling the fields and all over campus. And have you heard they're talking about a citywide curfew?"

"No." But she bet that if news got out that the humans had instituted one, then Ramses might insist on similar precautions for Monster High.

"We had a whole monster-on-campus drill today. Which . . . wasn't different than any other intruder-on-campus drill, except five kids in my Spanish class started crying. And my dad . . . he's all-in. He's bought this 'monster spray' from some online ad and is up all night reading message boards by 'experts.'" Poe picked at the moss growing between two stones. "What about your school?"

She thought back to lunch, when Lagoona had mentioned transferring and Frankie had started whispering, "Don't cry, you'll short-circuit. Don't cry, you'll short-circuit." A mantra that Draculaura hadn't heard since the time Abbey accidentally froze Frankie's science project right before she was about to present it at the Monster National Science Fair.

Cleo had sniffed. "Well, Deuce will probably leave too. Not that *I* care. But that mother of his—ugh! She gets under my bandages. She's wrapped up so tight that it's a shock she ever lets him *breathe* without her permission. And when Medusa goes all overbearing and says he can't come to Monster High anymore, I'm sure he'll just smile and agree. Like *I* would ever let anything happen to him?" She had faltered, glancing across the room to where her ex sat with a table full of mansters. "I mean, like I *would've* let anything happen to him." She'd glanced down at her nails. "Now, who cares, right? Not my problem. He can take care of himself."

As Draculaura answered Poe, she wondered if her voice was as fake-cheerful as Cleo's had been. "Oh, you know. It's . . . a lot."

How many friends *would* she lose? To accidents at the school, to parents who panicked, to students who'd had enough of the danger and discord that seemed to be infecting the halls. And since she didn't have parents, who would tell her when things had gone too far? Where would she even go? Belfry Prep was the vampire-only school, but she'd always gotten the worst vibes from the place, and none of her ghoul friends would be allowed to enroll.

Also, if it was a vampire-only school, she wouldn't qualify for much longer.

The thought sent a shiver through her, and Poe seemed to track the motion. "You're probably sick of hearing about this. I know I am. It's all anyone is talking about. Have you heard about this Van Hellscream Society? Literal monster hunters?

They hung posters in my school overnight—trying to recruit students to hunt fictional beasts. It's like everyone has lost their minds. I just hope it dies out before someone gets hurt, because the monsters aren't real, but the weapons they're talking about using are."

She gasped. The Van Hellscream Society. Every monster knew the violent history of the monster-hunting group, the families it had destroyed and displaced. She used to have nightmares about them when she was newly turned. She'd scream in her sleep, and Dracula would rush into her room and scoop her out of her coffin. She'd wake up in his hug, his steady voice telling her, *It was just a dream, I'm here, the Van Hellscream Society is long gone—*

But now it wasn't a dream, Dracula wasn't here, and the society was back—and recruiting.

She shivered again, more violently this time. Poe turned toward her, his knee brushing hers as he asked, "Cold? And I'm sorry. I said we weren't going to talk about it, and then I did anyway."

She shook her head. She wasn't cold. Which was weird. Vampires were almost always cold, and she was sitting in the shade. Normally this would be teeth-chattering territory, but not anymore. She subtly ran her tongue over her fangs again. She'd noticed she'd started doing this more and more often. A nervous tic to see if they were still there.

As of right now, still there. Still pointy.

"So, tell me," he said. "Have your friends gotten any better about treating you like you're breakable?"

"Actually," she tilted her head as she thought about it. Granted, it was probably because they were all going through new crises—breakups, school attacks, transferring decisions— but still. "Yeah, they have. A little bit."

"Good." He tapped his knee against hers, and she wanted to shiver for a totally different reason. Humanity wasn't so bad— was it? It certainly didn't look bad on Poe.

He glanced down at her and grinned like he could read her thoughts. Draculaura felt her cheeks heating—another new thing: Vampires didn't blush.

"What?" he asked. "Do I have something on my face or something?"

She shook her head. "I just like looking at you."

His grin grew wider. "I like looking at you too."

The one square inch where their knees were touching was absorbing all of her attention. She was in over her head and fall- ing fast. She bounced to her feet. "Let's go for a walk."

Draculaura didn't wait for him to follow, but she knew he would. His longer legs eating up her head start so he could walk beside her down the gravel paths that meandered toward the older parts of the cemetery. This was where she felt more at home, back where there were bowers and crypts, gravestones with elaborate statues and flourishes. Everything modern was minimalist, square—those graves were still tended by people who grieved and remembered. The older plots didn't feel nearly as sad—those who'd missed them had also moved on.

This was a preference she'd developed long ago, one that had made Dracula smile indulgently when she'd shared it. But now, as she explained it to Poe, already bracing herself for him to think it was freaky that she had cemetery preferences—he just nodded thoughtfully.

"That makes a lot of sense," he said. "And I like that you want to make sure people are remembered. It feels like we live in a world that's so quick to forget—and move on to gawk at the next, new tragedy."

He's a human, she told herself. She repeated in her head, over and over, like a meditation mantra. And since he was a human, it wasn't possible that he'd put her under some sort of spell. It wasn't possible that he had magical powers pulling her toward him like a magnet.

This attraction? This head-spinning swoon? It was all natural—or all *unnatural*, depending on who you asked.

But she wasn't going to think about that. Not while his smile drew her closer. Not while he was stepping closer to her too. They were under the shade of a massive witch hazel tree, whose branches were an explosion of yellow firework-shaped blooms, and standing beside a picturesque crumbling crypt covered in trailing vines.

Draculaura couldn't claim the kiss had caught her by surprise. He'd leaned in so slowly, paused to ask, "Is this okay?" Then waited for her response. She'd leaned in even more as she nodded; the movement of her head causing her lips to graze against his.

And while she was igniting, melting from that brief contact, he was pulling back—just for a moment, just long enough to grip her waist and lift her up to sit on the crumbling wall. The inches it added to her height meant she didn't have to crane her neck—meant he was *right there*. And when their eyes locked, his full of smiles and hers full of who-knew-what—she was the first one to lean in again, to grab the back of his neck, to pull his mouth to hers.

There were sparks—not literally—though, even if there had been literal sparks, Draculaura wasn't sure she would've noticed. Her eyes were squeezed tight, and she was blinded by the sensation of his mouth on her own. She gasped when he pulled away, his lips painting a trail of sensation across her cheekbone to her neck. Her neck, where the friction and suction of his mouth made her pulse flutter, had her wondering for the first time how it would feel to have someone you cared about bite you, drink from you.

Before her thoughts could carry her too far down that dangerous path, his mouth was back on hers, his lips opening against hers, urging her lips to do the same. To let him in.

Poe's groan vibrated on her lips as she parted them, and his tongue advanced to twist with her own. He tasted like mint and lemon sports drink; a combination that shouldn't have worked but did. It made her smile, thinking he'd taken the time to eat a mint before driving over. Like he'd hoped for this. He deepened the kiss.

And then—

And then—Poe was stumbling backward. His hands withdrawn from their positions at her neck and waist so quickly that she almost fell off the wall.

"Poe?" she asked.

He was stepping backward, and backward again. Putting a bench between them and holding up a hand. "Stay where you are."

Her eyebrows shot up. "What's going on?"

But even as she asked, she knew. Spreading across her tongue was an unfamiliar taste—salty, coppery, like pennies and sweat.

"You—you—" Poe's face had gone white. He was slightly hunched forward, like he couldn't catch his breath. "You have fangs!"

"Yes, but . . ." But, what? Draculaura had been so careful, always making sure she smiled with her mouth closed, talked with her teeth tucked behind her lips. And she'd somehow forgotten about them in a kiss *like that*? How could she have lost her head so completely?

"You bit me." He reached up to touch his mouth and held up a drop of red as proof.

The sight of it, the knowledge that it was the taste of his . . . his *blood* that traced across her tongue, made her vision go blurry. She slid off the wall, a drop of sweat trickling down her back.

"Don't come any closer!" Poe shouted, holding up his hands to tell her to stay back. The tip of his finger was still red.

"The only thing getting closer is the ground," she mumbled, vision blurry. "I—"

And then she passed out.

CHAPTER 11

Draculaura thought she'd heard Poe call her name as she fainted, but she was alone when she came to. She was still lying in the crushed gravel of the cemetery's path, the sharp points of the small stones pressing into her skin like thousands of acupuncture needles. The sky didn't look darker—it was still that transitional hour between dusk and twilight, where she didn't need sunscream or to use her weakening vampire abilities to see in the dark.

But she was alone. And maybe she deserved it for lying to Poe, for scaring him. He hadn't thought monsters were real, he'd said as much—and here she was, biting him.

Though, not really. She hadn't closed her jaw, hadn't engaged her teeth at all. If you wanted to get technical about it, *he* had caused the bite. His tongue had snagged on her fang. Not that she hadn't liked his tongue-action—the thought of it made her lightheaded in a different, swoony sort of way. But still, if you were assigning blame, it really should've been fifty-fifty.

But Draculaura didn't think this was a technicality that Poe would care about while bleeding and having to reconcile his whole world view with the fact that the things that went bump in the night, the spookiest of Halloween costumes, and the main characters in horror movies were all real.

Though, to be fair, Hollywood got quite a lot wrong.

Not that he'd stuck around to let her explain. Or to make sure she was okay. And the weight of that pressed against her chest and made it harder to breathe, made her want to just continue to lie on the ground as the world darkened around her.

She thought he liked her. *Her*, as she was. She'd known he was a normie this whole time and it hadn't stopped her from caring about him. That didn't stop her from worrying if he was hurt, and if he was scared.

But to be fair, she'd always known normies were real. She'd *been* one, once upon a time. He'd just discovered monsters were real in one of the weirdest possible ways.

Maybe she would've stayed there—lying on the ground, melting into the shadows and her disappointment, if only the stones weren't quite so pointy.

Pointier than her fangs, really.

She groaned and tried to sit up. This moment—after fainting—was always awful. Her stomach twisted, her head swam, her skin felt sticky, and her vision tunneled out.

But worse was the fact that the last time she'd fainted, her dad had died.

The memory was so close, so vivid. She'd passed out and woken up alone. Again.

The thought made her hiccup.

Then, like she'd conjured it, there was a hand at her back, offering support. A warm arm braced around her shoulder. "Wait. Take it slowly."

But it wasn't her father's voice.

When Draculaura turned, Poe's face was right beside hers. As close as it had been when they'd kissed. His breath, still smelling of mint and citrus electrolytes, ghosted across her cheek. Her eyes drifted to his mouth, where a red smear haunted his lower lip.

She dropped her gaze to the gravel and whispered, "I thought you left."

"I ran to my car to get you some water." He held out a sports bottle. "Wait, can you even drink water? And, technically, it's Gatorade. Can you drink that? Probably not. I'm such an idiot."

Her laugh was more of a choke. All the things he must be imagining about her. All the worst-case scenarios. And yet, *he came back*. She answered Poe by taking the bottle from his hand and swallowing a few mouthfuls. The sports drink did *not* taste as good from the New Salem High School water bottle as it had from his lips. And the way he was watching her so warily . . . it made her shiver.

"Here, I brought you this too." Poe held out a blue and silver New Salem Soccer sweatshirt. And even before she put it on, she was already dreading the moment she'd have to return it. She could smell him in the fabric—the combination of tears, sweat, and Poe that made her senses light up.

But when Draculaura pulled her head through the sweatshirt, she blinked to find him a few feet away. He was no longer crouched on the gravel but sitting farther down the low wall that she'd sat on while they kissed. He had his hands clasped together, elbows resting on his knees, fingers pressed to his mouth as he studied her. His hair was even more chaotic than usual, like the worries escaping from his head were ensnared and taking up physical space.

The cemetery birds had taken their silence as permission to sing. If it weren't for the wariness in the angles of his eyebrows, it might be rather romantic to be sharing this moment with a guy you'd just kissed.

Er . . . bitten?

She cleared her throat, and the sound made him jump, so she kept her voice quiet when she said, "You must have some questions for me."

"So . . . you can drink Gatorade. And you have fangs. What are you?" He shook his head and stood, pacing back and forth on the other side of the low stone wall. "I mean, I think I know, but—I need you to say it out loud, because I feel ridiculous even thinking it. It can't be real, right? I mean, you can't be—"

"A vampire." Draculaura interrupted his spiral, saying the words he couldn't.

"A vampire. Right." He nodded and started pacing faster. "Because apparently those are real. And that means other monsters are too? Is that video—is everything everyone is saying—Van Hellscream, a monster uprising—is it all real?"

"Can I?" She pointed to the bench and then sat down slowly so he wouldn't be spooked. Well, not more spooked. She took a deep breath, feeling the press of consequences on her shoulders. What she was about to do was forbitten. It was breaking the greatest ta-boo of the monster world: telling humans they existed.

The buckles on the side of her heeled Mary Janes clinked against the metal leg of the bench as she crossed her legs. The tiny noise made Poe flinch and take another breathless step away.

Her voice and lip trembled as she said, "I'm not going to hurt you. Monsters—we're nothing like you see in human stories."

"Are you going to turn me now?" Poe touched his mouth. "Did you already start the process?"

"What? No! That's not even how that works!" Her hair whipped her face as she shook her head emphatically. "You have to drain a person entirely, then have them drink your bl—" She couldn't say it. The fact that she'd had a few drops of it on her tongue was still making her stomach churn. She'd count herself lucky if she made it out of the cemetery without throwing up.

Though, judging by the way he'd grown impossibly paler, that answer had only made things worse.

"I don't even drink"—she forced the word out around a gag—"*blood*. Or even eat meat. Please don't be scared of me."

"I'm trying, but I'm really freaked out, Laura." He raked his hands through his hair again, gripping the back of his neck. "None of this feels true. None of it makes sense."

Well, if she was going to be honest, she might as well be honest about *all of it*. "Um, my name—well, you see, it's actually . . . It's Draculaura."

"Draculaura." The letters sounded like they were made of glass, like he was saying them carefully so they wouldn't shatter. "Right. Draculaura, because your dad's . . ."

She nodded. "Dracula."

"Uh-huh. Okay. Okay. *Dracula*. Who is apparently not actually fictional."

Was it possible for a teenage boy to have a heart attack? Because Poe was still pacing, but his lips had gone as colorless as his cheeks, and his eyes were startlingly wide. She was starting to worry. Maybe the reason monsters weren't supposed to talk about their world with humans was because normies couldn't physically handle the knowledge?

He nodded slowly, not looking at her. "Was anything you told me true? Or was this all some big elaborate way to con me? I really believed you, about the dead dad and all of it."

"Wh-what?" Her eyes wanted to well and spill, but she forced back the tears. "It was nothing like that. I really came here because I missed my dad and needed space to cry. I didn't know I was going to see anyone. I didn't expect to meet someone who understood me. I didn't expect *you*. Everything I told you was true—except for this one part."

"Except for *what you are*." His eyes slid toward her briefly, then away. Then she felt them back again, like he couldn't help himself.

And she was trying so, so hard not to cry, to keep her voice even and make him understand. "It was the first day of school and everything was different. Everything was changing. Everything still *is* changing. I was just trying to feel connected with my dad, and now he's farther away than ever. I'm not even going to be a vampire anymore and I don't know what he'd think—"

"Wait, what?" Poe asked. Now his gaze was glued to her. "What will you be?"

"Human," she said. "My dad's death means I lose my vampire identity. So, the one thing that's left to connect me to him—the thing that makes me *me*, is going to be taken away."

An unfamiliar melody burst into the air between them. Without moving his eyes from her, Poe pulled his phone from his shorts pocket and pressed the button to ignore the call. "Did you just say you're turning human?"

She could tell he was trying to keep his voice neutral, but there was a hope in his expression that twisted her stomach. "Unless I can figure out how to stop it," she said.

He looked staggered by her words, and it was only when he took a step backward that she realized he'd started to drift closer to the bench where she sat, to be less guarded about the space between them.

"You *want* to—"

His confused question was interrupted by a second call. Again he rejected it but not before she saw the name on his screen: *Dad*.

"Do you need to get that?" It wasn't that she wanted to end their conversation, it was just painful to watch someone ignore their father when she'd give anything to talk to hers.

Poe shook his head and rejected a third call. "He wants to know where I am and make sure it's *not* here. He thinks I visit my mom's grave too much."

"Oh." She wasn't sure how to respond to that. Had Dracula ever tried to limit how she'd grieved her mom? She didn't think so, but it had been so long ago.

"Laur—Draculaura." He shook his head. "That's going to take some getting used to."

Which implied he planned to continue to use it, right? Draculaura squeezed her hands in her lap, like she was physically squashing the hope his words inspired. "Ask me anything," she said. "And if I know the answer, I'll tell you. I'll make you see monsters aren't bad guys."

He chuckled grimly. "I don't even know where to start."

The fourth time his phone rang, Poe cursed and turned it off. "He's not going to stop calling and he's going to get madder if I don't answer soon." He looked away from her to the parking lot, to the time on his watch. "I've got to go, but I can't just leave you like this."

She blinked. "What do you mean?"

"You just told me monsters are real. What am I supposed to do with that information? Where do I find out more?"

She felt her eyes widen. This was on her. She'd broken the rules, inviting him into her world, so now this was her responsibility. If she didn't teach him, he'd still look for answers. But where? The Van Hellscream Society? Somewhere dangerous on the dark web?

Draculaura reached into her pocket for the well-worn piece of paper she'd held on to like a good luck charm all week: the receipt that contained his phone number. She held it out to him. "Give me your address."

He hesitated with his hand half-extended. "You're not going to materialize in my room in the middle of the night, are you? Send the Monster Squad after me because I know too much?"

She shook her head. "Yeah, that's not a thing. I was thinking more like I'd mail you an iCoffin—a phone that can connect to mine. Don't hext—*text* me again with your normie phone. I had to go to a creepy cobwebsite to make our phones communicate and I don't think we should take that risk again."

He turned a little green as he pulled a pen from his pocket and scribbled down his address. "How does an i—did you say *coffin*? How does it work?"

She held up her own phone and gave him a quick overview of the functions he'd need to know: calling/ hexting/ video chat. "It isn't all that different. Well, except for that it functions on an entirely separate, secure, monster-only network."

He nodded. "Got it. So don't contact you until you send me one of those?"

Draculaura sucked on a fang because the sending wouldn't exactly be easy or legal. But he didn't need to know that. Not while he was still so pale and anxious. "And you should probably delete the messages we already sent."

"Right. Sure." His hand shook when he powered up his phone again. It rang immediately.

"You should go," she told him.

"I don't want to," he said. "I mean, I do—I want to hide under my bed until I can make all this make sense—but I'm scared that if I leave, I'll get scared of *you*. When I look at you, I just see the girl I met—the one who turned one of my worst days into one of my best—but that's not all you are . . ." He squeezed his eyes shut and shook his head. "I don't want to forget that version."

"I don't want you to either." Holding her hand out toward him felt like one of the bravest things she'd ever done.

She wondered if he felt the same way when he clasped it. If he still felt the tingles when they touched, because they hadn't changed for her. If anything, they'd intensified. Did that scare him?

They held on for several precious seconds until the now too-familiar ringtone tore through their moment.

"I'll be in touch as soon as I can," she told him, reluctantly pulling her hand away. "Wait to hear from me. Don't go looking for answers."

He nodded somberly. "Bye, Draculaura." His eyes were as sad looking at her as they'd been at his mother's grave, and she wondered if, like her, he was thinking that he'd lost yet another precious thing in his life.

She swallowed around a lump in her throat. "Bye, Poe."

It was supposed to be vampires who had the ability to melt into shadows (not that Draculaura had ever mastered this)—but clearly human teen soccer players had skills too. In the time it had taken her to reluctantly peel Poe's sweatshirt over her head so she could return it, he'd gone.

She heard a car door close, an engine start.

Then it was just her.

And the gravestones.

A receipt scrawled with a forbitten address.

The delicious-smelling school sweatshirt of a normie boy.

And the knowledge that she'd broken her world's biggest ta-boo.

CHAPTER 12

Draculaura woke up the next morning with a sense of new purpose. And, no, it wasn't just from responding to all of Frankie's panicked hext messages:

Are you sure you're up for ghouls' night?

(Yes.)

It's not disrespectful?

(No.)

Would you tell me if it was?

(Yes.)

And are you still handling those kelp cupcakes for Lagoona?

(Ms. Heaves is making them right now.)

Thanks! You're the beast!

But even with Frankie keeping her busy, part of her was on edge, wondering when her package would be delivered. And every time her iCoffin buzzed with a message from one of the ghouls, part of her was disappointed that it wasn't the hext she was waiting for.

Draculaura had made two stops on the way home the night before. The first—buying a new iCoffin and programming her number into it—had been the easy part. It was getting the phone to Poe that had been stressful. Still, she'd kept her shoulders back and marched into that FedHex store with all the confidence she could fake.

She'd selected a mailer envelope and slid the new phone and a note to Poe with directions on how to operate it inside, sealing it up with a healthy sprinkling of her hopes and fears. She'd filled out the label with the address Poe had given her.

That's when she'd hesitated, telling the impatient clerk, "I just need a minute," when he'd asked, "Are you ready to mail that?"

She was pretty sure she was a breaking a half dozen monster laws. It was probably *illegal* to mail things to the human world. But there also had to be exceptions. Dracula had told her that there were a select few normies "in the know"— leaders of states and countries, certain scientists. So, there had to be legitimate reasons that monsters could send things to normies, right?

She'd taken a deep breath and tried to look and sound authoritative as she'd slid the package across the counter: "I'd like this delivered as soon as possible, please."

The clerk had frowned at the address, his teal-colored tusks quivering in disapproval and alarm. She'd seen the questions he'd been preparing to ask and acted to preempt them by placing her ID and credit card on the counter with sharp clicks.

She'd watched the clerk's eyes shift to them—saw them widen as he took in her name and made the connection to her father, his back straightening, his attitude changing.

"I was so sorry to hear about your dad," he'd said. "I was a huge fan."

She'd never felt guilty name-dropping her dad to cut a line or get a table at a crowded restaurant when her dad was undead. But now that he was gone . . . it had felt icky to benefit off their connection. Like the worst type of entitled necro-baby.

But since the alternative had been the clerk refusing to deliver the package to a human address or possibly alerting authorities, she'd swallowed down that feeling and asked, "Can you make sure this gets delivered tomorrow?"

"I'll deliver it myself," the clerk had said. "Anything for Dracula's daughter."

And now it was tomorrow, and the package could be delivered at any time, so she was never far from her phone as she flitted around, making sure Ms. Heaves was following Frankie's explicit instructions on the cupcakes (*Can they have teal and blue frosting? Maybe sprinkles that look like scales?*), catching up with homework, and watching the news—where information about the Van Hellscream Society's reemergence dominated every broadcast, alongside warnings to stay inside the gated monster communities, report anything that looked suspicious, and not do anything to attract human attention.

Somehow Ramses had finagled guest spots on three different shows, using the time to talk about his own importance and how "vital" it was for him to "helm the school board and save our school."

Medusa appeared on one show, her hands and snake-hair all a-flutter as she gasped, "All this news about the normies, about what's going on at Monster High—it's just terrible. How's a mother supposed to keep her baby safe?"

Draculaura was pretty sure that Medusa's "baby"—aka Deuce—was going to be horrified by this interview. She was equally sure than Manny, Clawd, Heath, and the other mansters were going to be dielighted and tease him mercilessly.

At least it was keeping her distracted between taking out her phone, unlocking it, checking for messages.

Then finally, one came.

Hi. Did I do this right?

She typed a quick hext, then paused and deleted it. How did she know the iCoffin had been delivered correctly? What she was doing was super forbitten, so how could she confirm it was Poe on the other end?

She ran her tongue over her fangs as she thought, then typed: **What's your superhero alias?**

His response was quick: **Oh man, did we ever come up with something cooler than Captain Cemetery?**

Draculaura was still laughing when she switched over to a video call. When he answered, he was laughing too.

She'd already spent some time brainstorming where to take the call. The setting especially mattered since it was *all* he'd see—her floating outfit and the room behind her. So . . . not her bedroom. Poe was hanging on by a thread; she doubted he was ready to see the pink satin–lined coffin where she slept. The kitchen might remind him about food—and she wasn't sure he was convinced about her bloodless diet. The bathroom was just weird; Dracula's home office was too formal and emotional. So, she'd settled on the second-floor wraparound porch. It was covered, of corpse, and cozy. The shady outdoor space was where she and her dad would sit after dinner, sipping their preferred beverages (Dracula's always, *always* in an opaque cup). The porch was filled with clusters of potted plants and groupings of comfy couches. There were space heaters and baskets of blankets. Bat boxes lined the rafters.

It was her favorite part of the house, and it was super gratifying that after Poe said, "Hey—oh, do you not, um, appear on video?" his eyes had widened even more and he'd added, "Whoa. Is that your house? The view is amazing."

"Nope, and um, yes, and thanks." She hadn't explored the grounds lately. Hadn't taken any walks in the night-blooming garden or tried out Mr. Taur's latest hedge maze creation. She hadn't gone for any midnight swims in the bioluminescent pool or laid on the lawn and read by the light of the constellations.

Truthfully, she didn't *need* the light of the stars—vampires saw really well in the dark—but they added a great ambience. She wished she could invite Poe over to experience *any* of these things, but after the latest news report she'd seen—where monsters were organizing patrols to keep an eye on normie patrols—meeting over video was much, much safer than smuggling him into her gated, protected neighborhood.

"How are you?" she asked. "Was your dad really upset when you got home?"

He shrugged and looked away, setting the phone down for a moment when he crossed the room to shut the door. It gave her a chance to take in his surroundings. Is that what a normie teen boy's room looked like? Blue comforter hastily pulled up on his bed, pillows crookedly tossed against a dark wooden headboard, a sweatshirt very similar to the one she'd accidentally stolen last night draped over the back of a desk chair. Which, did that mean she didn't have to give it back? She could see a corner of a bulletin board. A series of triangular pennants for soccer teams tacked to the wall. And then he looked back at the camera and wholly consumed her attention again.

"My dad wasn't super happy with me," Poe said. "But that's nothing new. He's never happy unless he has something to criticize. At least these days he's too busy obsessing over . . ." He trailed off, his cheeks flushing.

Draculaura didn't need him to finish that sentence to know the thing Poe's dad was obsessing over was the same thing that had kept her up last night.

"I tried to talk to him about it," he said softly, and when she gasped in alarm, he quickly added, "Not you! I didn't say anything about you or anything like that. I just, uh, tried to float the idea that maybe monsters—if they did exist—maybe they weren't so bad."

"How did that go?" she asked, then based on his grim expression, said, "Oh. Well, um, thanks for trying?" She tried to keep her voice and expression sunny. Er, not that he could *see* her expression. "So, anyway, maybe I can at least convince *you* we're not so bad? I think you have some questions for me?"

He chuckled and held up a notebook, flipping through pages covered in his messy scrawl. "Just a few—want to go grab a snack? This might take a while."

"Oh, I came prepared." Draculaura heard his quick intake of breath, watched his nostrils flare before she flipped the camera to show a tray covered in chopped veggies and hummus. She'd purposely left off beets, turnips, tomatoes—anything with a hue that even vaguely resembled blood.

"You really don't—um, eat a traditional vampire diet?" Poe asked, and she wondered if he knew that the fingers he'd crossed in his lap were visible.

"Really, truly. Honestly, just thinking about it makes me a little woozy." She crinkled her nose. "Is that your first question?"

He set the notebook down and leaned in. "No, that wasn't on my list, but before we start—can you tell me the whole part about turning human again? If you already don't drink blood—how are you different from us now?"

"Besides the part where I live forever, don't have a reflection or a shadow, but do have fangs and other vampire powers?"

"Yeah." He sucked in a breath. "I guess that's pretty different. So, then, *why* are you turning human? What happens?"

He listened as she walked him through it—her dad's death, the transformation, Ghoulia looking for a way to prevent it. Unlike yesterday, when he'd gone glassy-eyed and distant, distracted by his shock and his dad's repeated calls, she could tell he was hearing her today. He was nodding, making little listening noises, jotting down notes. Asking her to repeat or clarify things. Asking more and more questions, expanding them beyond just her to the whole monster world.

Dracula had had hundreds of biographies written about him over the centuries, but only one had been authorized. For that, he'd sat down with the author for days and days of interviews. He'd told her afterward that it was one of the most exhausting types of work he'd ever done. It hadn't made sense to her then, but it did now. She was mining her memories for specific examples, things that would make Poe see and understand. Anecdotes that would invite him into her world, instead of scaring him off. The time she'd tried changing into a bat and only managed extra pointy ears and oversized furry eyebrows—both of which didn't go away for a week and *would've* been documented in the yearbook if she'd shown up in photographs. The time she and Clawdeen had a campout creepover and forgot to check the moon-phase. That had resulted in one seriously shredded tent and a seriously annoyed Dracula when she'd woken him up to help her track down her much, much furrier friend. The time Nefera had tricked Cleo into wearing a cursed scarab necklace to school and the day had been awful, arrival to dismissal— pop quizzes, mystery mush at lunch, timed sprints in Phys Dead, homework that mysteriously vanished from their bags.

"I don't think we stuck the landing on a single stunt that day at fearleading practice." She laughed. "Cleo was so mad. Nefera is the worst."

"And Cleo is . . . a mummy? Is that right?"

"Yup," Draculaura managed around a mouthful of scarrot and hummus. Poe wasn't kidding when he said she'd need snacks. Pretty soon she'd need to get a charge cord for her phone too. It'd be worth it. Every five percent her iCoffin's battery dropped matched a five percent relaxation in Poe's body language. While she doubted he'd be volunteering to stick his tongue in her mouth anytime soon, she hoped he wouldn't feel the need to keep ten feet and a bench between them if they met again. She'd call that progress.

"I've still got tons of questions about your world—" He tapped his pen on his notebook. "But—do you have any about mine? I've been thinking about this part a lot. I know you're scared about turning human. I know you're looking for a way to stop the change from happening, but . . ." He swallowed and it looked like he was bracing himself. "If you have questions or if it would make you feel better to have a plan B, I can tell you what I love about being human. I can show you my favorite parts. And—and then, maybe, if you can't prevent it, at least it won't be so scary."

He'd said the second part in a rush, the words blurring together so that it took Draculaura a moment to decipher them, and then another second to process what they meant.

He looked down, the tips of his ears red as he mumbled, "Never mind. That was stupid. Sorry, I—"

"That would be fang—fantastic," she said breathlessly. "I am so scared, all the time, of everything. School is scary, my friendships are all different, and I literally don't even know *who* I will be when I wake up each day." Her eyes were welling up and she didn't even know if her tears would be clear or red if she cried. "If you're willing to be my tutor in the strange new world of the normies, I will gladly sign up for every lesson you think I need."

"Careful—" His mouth tipped up in one corner, and this new type of smile had her stomach fluttering even before he added, "I might start making things up just to have excuses to spend time with you."

Draculaura knew that playing it cool meant not blurting out, "So you're not scared of me anymore?" But then again, when had she ever worried about being cool? Her heart was in her throat as she asked the question; it stayed there as he paused to think about his response.

"I'm scared of how much I want to *not* be scared of you. Logically, I know I should be, but I'm . . . I'm not."

Draculaura wondered if she should be going through a similar mental debate. She'd spent the morning eagerly telling a human all about her life—she hadn't even hesitated. But how could she be worried when he was smiling at her every time he looked up from his notepad?

"What should I know to keep you safe when I play tour guide to humanity? And when are you free?"

"I've got a ghouls' night tonight—and Frankie will kill me if I miss it, but I could do something this afternoon. Just nothing too sunny." She rubbed at her arms. Nightmares about sunburns still woke her up most nights.

"Minimal sun. Got it." He jotted that down. "I've got some ideas already, but also a few more questions so I don't mess this up."

So he didn't *mess this up*. Not because she scared him, or because she was some weird thing he wanted to analyze like a bug beneath a microscope. His list of questions was because he *cared*.

Draculaura thought she might cry again, but there wasn't time. He had his pen poised, ready to record her answers. "What *do* you eat, besides carrots? What's your favorite food? Anything I should avoid?"

"Avoid garlic," she said. "It won't kill me, but it's not pleasant."

Poe laughed and shook his curls out of his face. "Please, give me some credit. No garlic is just good date etiquette."

She could've stayed on the phone with him all day, talking and laughing right up to the moment she had to hang up to rush through getting ready for their—he'd called it a *date*. Should she? And she also had ghouls' night. After sitting home alone all summer, the idea of back-to-back plans was frankly exhausting, but it helped that she was genuinely looking forward to both. It helped that Poe's blue eyes smiled at her as he sat backward on his desk chair, his chin resting on the top of it, biting his lip in concentration. His new iCoffin was propped against something so his hands were free to record all her words—not like some class notes he might get tested on later, but like they mattered, because *she* mattered to him.

"Where's your dad today?" she asked. "Do you have anything else planned?"

His face lost all its softness as he sat up straight. "He went fishing with my uncle. My friends are playing a pickup soccer tournament in the park. I told my dad I was doing the soccer tournament and told my friends I was going fishing with my dad." His face went red. "I'm not normally a big liar, but I wanted today to—to process everything. And I was really hoping you'd figure out a way to get in touch."

A hext flashed across her screen: I'm about to call you. It's important. You MUST pick up.

She hadn't even finished reading it before her phone began to beep with an incoming call from Cleo.

Draculaura sighed. "I need to take this. But . . ."

"I'll see you later, right? I can come pick you up if you tell me where."

She thought of the news broadcasts about monster patrols in the neighborhoods. Hers was gated, high security, even before all of this. Warded to be invisible and keep humans out. It was the only way Dracula had felt comfortable leaving her alone with Ms. Heaves when his travels took him away for extended periods. She hadn't realized then that it would be practice for when he was gone for good.

But, inviting Poe into her house—wasn't safe. For either of them. "How about we meet somewhere?"

You sent ME to voicemail?! Pick up! This is an eekmergency!

"Sorry, I've really got to—" Cleo was calling again, and Draculaura was trying not to panic about the urgency in her hexts. Had something happened? At the school? To one of the ghouls? Where wasn't dangerous right now?

"Go," Poe said. She was clicking over to Cleo's call while halfway through her goodbye, and maybe Cleo caught the last syllable and interpreted it as a hi, because she didn't pause for a greeting but jumped right in.

"Took you long enough to answer!" she sniffed. "You should know, I'm not going to ghouls' night. I won't go anywhere near Clawdeen. You'll never boolieve what she said to me."

Draculaura collapsed back against the cushions of her seat. Clearly Cleo's definition of "eekmergency" wasn't one you'd find in any dictionary. "I'm sorry to hear that," she said. "We'll miss you."

"Don't you even want to know what happened?" Cleo demanded.

"Um, sure?" She wasn't actually sure she did and was already not looking forward to hearing Clawdeen's version later tonight. When those two had a common goal, they were unstoppable, but when they disagreed—well, the rest of them had learned to stay out of it. Lagoona had once mused that maybe Headmistress Bloodgood had lost her head because she hadn't kept it down during a friend fight. If her friends were anything like Cleo and Clawdeen, Draculaura thought it was entirely possible.

She tuned out as Cleo started listing all the ways she'd been wronged, from Clawdeen wearing golden claw polish (*"And she knows that's my signature color"*) to being excluded from snack selection for the night, to comments made about her dad.

Draculaura let the ghoul rant while she made her way to her bedroom and scanned her closet—she'd need an outfit that could transition from a date to ghouls' night.

Her attention snapped back to the conversation when she heard Cleo say, "So, you're coming to my house instead, right?"

"Wait, what?"

"Oh my Ra, were you even listening? I just said that since I'm blowing off ghouls' night, I've decided to throw a little soiree among the who's-who of the Monster High community to raise support for my dad. The more people badgering Headmistress Bloodgood to instate him, the better. She's really being insufferably slow about the whole thing—something about wanting to research 'the process and precedent.' Blah, blah, blah. Anyboo, I can count on you to be there tonight, can't I?"

"Oh. Um. While that sounds fangtastic and I bet you'll have a blast"—she needed to figure out the right way to word this—"you see, Frankie is counting on me to bring kelp cupcakes for Lagoona."

"Blech, those things are vile," said Cleo. "We'll have much better canapes. And a whole dessert banquet."

Draculaura wracked her head for another excuse, but it turned out she didn't need one, since Cleo wasn't done talking. "Well, I'll put your name on the guest list in case you can stop by. I'll include Frankie and Lagoona too. And since I'm feeling generous, I'll even include Clawdeen and Toralei—though they better not even scream of coming if they're not ready to apologize for being so rude."

"Oh, um, I think they have a double feature planned for ghouls' night? *To All the Boys I've Bled Be Gore* and *P.S. I Still Blood You.*" Despite the titles, they were surprisingly bloodless vampire rom-coms. And the fact that they were two of *her* favorites made Draculaura pretty sure this ghouls' night wasn't only about convincing Lagoona to stay at Monster High.

"You won't let them play Gargoyles to Gargoyles without me, will you?" Cleo demanded.

"Um, no?" Cleo was the only one of them who actually liked the game, so Draculaura could guarantee they wouldn't play it if she wasn't there.

"Good. I've got to run. Nefera is trying to take *all* the credit for my soiree. The nerve!"

Draculaura set down her phone with an exhausted chuckle. Cleo was always going to be Cleo—and Clawdeen, she was more stubborn than dog fur on black pants. If she thought she was in the right—and especially if she was being encouraged by Toralei—this was going to be an epic battle of the wills.

But that was a problem for later. Right now she needed a day-to-night outfit that would wow Poe without raising too much suspicion with the ghouls.

CHAPTER 13

It was time. Draculaura double- and triple-checked, comparing her watch to her iCoffin to the immense grandfather clock that stood in the entrance hall. She had Poe's directions in a hext, their meeting spot entered in her phone's GPS, and her mother's words in her head.

Maybe choosing her mom's diary as pre-date reading hadn't been her wisest choice, but it was the closest she could get to parental advice. And somehow, across the span of centuries, her mom had given her so much to think about.

20 Aprilis 413

I find my soul unsettled tonight—for it is my soul that was up for debate. While I know Dracula to be the best of men: wise, compassionate, generous, and loyal—I also must never forget that he is not a man. Not human. But how can a monster of such kindness have no soul? This is what is reported about his kind—but I wonder if it can be so.

I have no doubt of the veracity of the feelings he professes to have for me. I find myself reciprocating them, but it can never be. At least this is what

I have told him. I tell it to myself too, but in the darkest hours of the night, it is hard to convince myself it is true.

But of my soul, I am certain. I must not, cannot succumb to Dracula's offers to make me other than I am. I am not meant to be immortal. I desire to experience life in all phases—if the fates are willing—and to watch my dear daughter grow and change as well. Change is life's truest gift—the ability to wake each day and experience things that are new and fleeting.

I cannot sacrifice my humanity.

Had Draculaura truly never read this entry before? Or, in the past had she only focused on her mom and Dracula as star-crossed lovers? That had always seemed so romantic. But now, her focus switched.

Her mother hadn't wanted to be anything but human. Her mom had wanted her to be human.

But Dracula had saved her life. If he hadn't changed her into a vampire, she would've died from the same plague that had killed her mother. Draculaura had never regretted his decision, had never questioned it.

But now she had a choice—just like her mother had. And unlike her mother, she *wasn't* certain. Her mother had written: *I am not meant to be immortal.*

Was she?

Draculaura tucked the memory of the journal in the back corner of her mind. It was time to go begin her own star-crossed romance with Poe and hope their ending was happier than Camilla and Dracula's.

"Ms. Heaves?" Draculaura leaned through the kitchen doorway and smiled when the older vampire fumbled with her e-reader, almost dropping it onto the tray of freshly frosted cupcakes. "I'm heading out. Are you still okay to drop those off at Frankie's house? They look fangtastic."

"Of corpse, my dear." Ms. Heaves peered over the top of her light purple glasses, taking in the outfit Draculaura had spent way too much time choosing.

Did Poe realize what a wrench he'd thrown in her plans when he hexted: Wear comfortable shoes? Because she was pretty sure it was the sneakers—granted they were pink, sparkly sneakers, a gift from Frankie who had a matching pair in green (they matched her green, sparkly phone case)—that had Ms. Heaves doing a double take.

"I'm happy to deliver the cupcakes, but why can't you bring them yourself, dear, since you're headed there anyway?"

"I have to run an errand first," Draculaura said.

"Can I do it for you? I'm just so glad you're getting out of the house and that you and the ghouls are fanging out again. I don't want you to miss any of it, and I have no other plans tonight except for finishing this cozy mystery."

Draculaura shook her head. "Thanks, but I've got it. And I'll call if I end up deciding to stay over at Frankie's."

Yet even after Ms. Heaves sent her off with a "Sounds

good, dear. Say hello to the ghouls for me," Draculaura hesitated at the front door.

This was the first time her dad wasn't here to insist her date come inside to pick her up so that he could meet/intimidate them. Dracula hadn't even had to do an overly tight handshake; all he needed to do was arch one of his eyebrows and any manster who'd been brave enough to ask her out would be quaking in his boots.

Poe would not have been able to handle that . . . but then again, she wasn't sure she could handle this—a date without her dad's approval. A date her dad would certainly *disapprove of*.

These thoughts chased her out the door until she was practically running toward the GPS coordinates Poe had sent her. So maybe it *was* a good thing he'd recommended comfy shoes. But that didn't mean she had to show up gross and sweaty. She slowed to a walk.

Draculaura's hesitation melted like a popsicle in Heath Burns's hands when she reached their meeting spot—a tucked-away road at the edge of a half-finished construction project. Poe was waiting against his car, looking like something from her daydreams: one foot propped against a tire, a lazy curl unspooling on his forehead, a delicious grin on his face as his eyes tracked her approach.

He stood and walked toward her. "Hello, beautiful," he said, then blushed. She loved watching him blush, the intimacy of seeing his emotions on his skin. "That sounded less cheesy in my head. But, hi."

"Hi," she said back, letting him swing the car's passenger door open for her and help her inside. "Where are we going?"

"You'll see," he said with a smile, and a few minutes later, she did.

"A hike?" It wasn't what she would've chosen for a first date—or any date, actually. Frankly, it sounded ghastly, but she was going to give him the boonefit of the doubt as he parked his car alongside a dirt road and gestured for her to lead the way toward a trail.

Branches arched overhead, creating a shady green canopy that cast dappled shadows on the packed dirt, roots, and rocks that made up the path. Each time she scuffed a toe or stumbled, she kicked up a cloud of dust. Her sparkly shoes were significantly less sparkly.

Poe whistled cheerfully as the incline increased.

Draculaura gave him a skeptical glance over her shoulder as she huffed ahead of him, determined not to slow him down. But not everyone had a soccer star's endurance. "Is this truly the best part of being human? Getting sweaty and walking through spiderwebs?" She tried to shake the offending strands off her hand and managed to get them in her hair instead.

"I like hiking," he said, offering her a fallen branch as a walking stick. "And let me go first—I'll take the brunt of the spiderwebs." He held out a water bottle, and she took a grateful sip. "But if you can trust me for another five minutes, I think you'll find this worth it."

"Five minutes?" That didn't sound too bad.

"Yup. You ready for a little more?" he asked.

She nodded—not sure if it was the walking stick, the hydration, or his smile—but she felt revitalized for the last part of the hike. And as the trees cleared to reveal a bluff that overlooked the ocean, Draculaura had to agree. She grasped his arm and gasped, "Whoa, look at that view."

Poe grinned at her excitement. "Isn't it gorgeous? The water is way too cold to swim in, but I could watch the waves hit the rocks forever." He shrugged off the backpack and pulled out a blanket, spreading it on a mossy outcropping of rock and gesturing for her to sit. "My mom and I used to hike here when I was little and being cranky. She used to tell me that there was something so validating about feeling like you'd earned the view through hard work." He handed her a water bottle. "My mom had this whole thing about saltwater being the universal cure—tears, sweat, or the sea. Not going to lie—sometimes this hike was a combination of all three."

Draculaura pretended not to see that he was wiping at his eyes. It was only fair, since he was giving her the same courtesy. She was trying to imagine what her dad would've said if she'd ever come home and told him, "I just went for a hike!"

Probably, *Why?*

But then, if she'd explained it like Poe had—about accomplishment and the hard work being the point—he would've hugged her and said, "I'm proud of you, darling girl."

She nestled down onto the blanket, pulling her eyes from the horizon to glance at him. "Your mom sounds like she was wonderful."

Poe's eyes got a little far away, focusing on something in the distance that she couldn't see. "She really was. She would've loved you."

Draculaura snorted and fidgeted with a fold of the blanket. "I'm not exactly the ghoulfriend that most normie mothers dream of for their children."

He sat down beside her, folding his hand over her own. "Maybe not, but you make me happy. That would've made her happy."

Draculaura stared at their hands, fingers intertwined, then she looked away to watch a wave slam down on a large rocky outcropping, spraying foam and droplets into the air like sparkling jewels. The water retreated, pulled back by the ocean, and regrouped to do it again and again. The rock didn't change. The rock didn't appreciate the beauty or how hard the water was working—it just existed.

Immortal monsters, she realized, could be a lot like that rock. "Thank you for bringing me here—and making me see."

Poe nodded, his eyes focused on her lips for a long moment before he pulled away and unlaced their fingers. "I should unpack the picnic." He fumbled with the zipper of his backpack, pulling out some apples and foil-wrapped sandwiches. "You don't have to eat them if you"—he looked at her mouth for a moment, as if trying to see her fangs through her lips—"if you don't want. It's nothing fancy, just some peanut butter and jelly."

Instead of answering, she plucked a quarter of a sandwich out of one of the foil wrappers and popped it in her mouth. But, *bats*, that was a lot more food than she'd imagined. It coated the inside of her mouth in a way that wasn't graceful or alluring—Cleo would've had an absolute fit if she'd seen it, but Clawdeen, Frankie, and Lagoona would've laughed. And, as she struggled to chew and swallow while maintaining a smile, Poe did too.

"I *may* have gotten a little heavy-handed with the peanut butter," he admitted.

And the only thing that could've made the scene worse was if she snorted sandwich out her nose, so Draculaura had to bite back her own laughter until she managed to swallow it down and chase it with some glugs of water.

It was too easy to sit on a blanket with Poe—to stare at the waves, or into his eyes—and talk about anything or nothing. It felt too nice to press her arm against his, to lean her head on his shoulder. To exist in this moment without missing the past or dreading the future.

"Oh, it's about to start," he said, leaning back on his elbows.

"What is?" Draculaura looked around, but all she saw was the sun starting to dip lower in the sky. They'd have to leave soon in order to get back in time for ghouls' night.

"The second part of my plan to show you humanity's best hits. Lesson one was: Hiking—it's worth putting in the time to get somewhere. Not just poofing in or whatever you all can do—because the journey can be the best part."

Draculaura nibbled a sandwich crust and thought about that. She couldn't "poof"—that was more of Spectra and the other ghosts' thing. But she also didn't have an easy, loping run like Clawdeen or the other weres. Abbey could create ice patches to glide along. Her dad and other vampires could change into bats and fly. She'd always resented that she didn't have a short-cut, that she had to work when others could get places faster with a fraction of the effort. But this was a new way of thinking about that—what if the work was the *point*? What if it was as important as the destination?

She was going to think more about that on the walk down—which, yay hard work and all—but she still hoped it would be easier than the walk up.

"I'm still not seeing lesson two?" She looked around again. Just the sky and the ocean and the rocks. Pretty and all, but nothing they hadn't been staring at for the past few hours.

"The sunset." Poe pointed to where the bottom edge of the sun was almost kissing the horizon.

Draculaura wasn't sure what to tell him. She did some quick math in her head to see if it would help make her point. "I've seen more than a half-million sunsets. What makes this one so special?"

"Me?" Poe chuckled as he picked up her hand and laced their fingers together. "It's special for humans *because* we don't get a half-million. We get each day as it comes, and there's no promise of a sunset. Knowing that you only get so many makes the experience different." He raised their joined hands to press his lips to the back of hers. "So, you've seen a half-million of these, but have you ever stopped to really enjoy one? And you'll never have *this* sunset again. In this spot, on this day, with this company." He squeezed her fingers. "Hopefully that makes this one more memorable."

She squeezed back. "Of corpse it does."

Poe's smile was more beautiful than the sunset, but she didn't tell him that. The light painted the horizon with the same palette that had been used to create him. Golden curls, bronze skin, pink cheeks that flushed so easily. The blue of the sea that sparkled like his eyes. If the sunset had looked to him for inspiration, it almost measured up.

"I could be wrong," he said, "but it seems like immortals treat days like they're disposable. Humans can't . . . or at least we shouldn't. If we waste one, we never get it back. So when you get one—and when you get one with great company"—he squeezed her hand—"it's a crime not to stop and appreciate it. To acknowledge it."

She wondered if she should be offended that he was talking about monsters like that—criticizing them. But . . . he wasn't wrong. And with his human pulse beating against her own wrist, she could feel how precious a gift this was—he had finite days, finite sunsets, and he was sharing this one with her. She rested her head against his shoulder, murmured the words, "Thank you," into his shirt as she watched the sun paint a one-of-a-kind masterpiece across the surface of the water.

"C'mon," Poe said twenty minutes later, tugging on her hand. "It's time to go."

"But the sunset's not over," she protested. Now that she understood, she didn't want to waste a moment.

"We have to go before it gets too dark to see the trail. Not all of us can see in the dark, you know."

Her smile felt strained—as strained as her weakening night vision. But the hike back to the car was easier—she wasn't sure if she should attribute that to the help of gravity, all the things he'd given her to contemplate, or his hand in hers.

As he held the car door for her, Draculaura had a pang of regret. The date had been too perfect. Even though the ghouls were waiting for her, part of her wanted to skip their plans and stay with Poe forever.

And part of her realized that if she made certain choices—she could.

CHAPTER 14

Draculaura asked Poe to drop her off as close to her neighborhood as she dared. Even that was a risk, but Frankie's wrath at her being later than she already was seemed riskier.

As his car idled alongside the thick trees that edged her monster community, Poe looked at her uncertainly. "Are you sure it's safe for me to leave you here?"

"I mean, I don't see any other normies, do you?"

He palmed the back of his neck and snorted. "It's still unreal to me that literal monsters exist—and that the things they're scared of are *humans.*"

She shrugged and quoted facts she knew from Lagoona. "Can you name one environment humans haven't polluted or one food web where they're not the apex predator?"

"Sharks?" he guessed.

She knew this too! Lagoona would be so proud—not that she could tell her. "Nope, humans kill far more sharks each year than the other way around."

"Okay, point taken. If you tell me you're safe, I trust you."

But did he? Enough for a kiss? That was the way good dates traditionally ended—but was it appropriate here? Poe leaned in and brushed his hand, then lips across her cheek. She wondered if she should be disappointed? But it was hard to feel anything but sparks and anticipation when he touched her.

"Thank you for sharing your world with me," she whispered against his cheek.

She could feel him shiver and shift in his chair before he hurried out of the car and opened her door. "Thank you for trusting me with the secrets of *your* world," he said.

"We'll talk soon," she said—but based on the frequency with which her iCoffin was buzzing, if she didn't show up ASAP, Frankie was going to start a search party. And the last thing she needed was Clawdeen sniffing out her location while she was standing far too close to a normie.

Draculaura waved, Poe returned it, and she disappeared into the trees, his headlights fading off into the night. Then she was grateful her night vision was still somewhat intact, because navigating this dark forest without it would've been impossible. On the other side of the trees was a row of backyards. She'd come out about a house and half away from Frankie's—though she could already hear the ghouls' voices and laughter.

"Draculaura, is that you?" Clawdeen's voice echoed across the lawn, chasing her into the woods, where she had paused to put on her game face.

"Who else could it be?" asked Abbey. "She is small, but clumsy—like a baby yak."

Draculaura stepped out of the woods and waved as she crossed the open grass toward the Stein's backyard patio. "Yes, it's me. Hi. Did the cupcakes make it? Is there any pizza left?"

A moan drifted out of the hammock. She hadn't even real-ized someone was in it. Frankie was sitting in a hanging chair. Clawdeen was sitting by the firepit with Toralei right beside her. They were both tossing in bits of twigs and bark—presumably seeing which of them could create the larger sparks. Lagoona was in the hot tub, and Abbey was perched atop the cooler— about as far from the fire and hot water as she could get. They were all wearing gloppy green face masks. Probably something of Lagoona and Frankie's joint nature-science invention; her pores were practically begging for her to slather some on. But since Cleo had said she wouldn't be coming and that Ghoulia would be at her house too—who was in the hammock?

A second moan drifted out of the hammock, and everyone else groaned too. Clawdeen lifted her eyes to the sky in her patented *give me patience* look—the one she used with Cleo or when dealing with her younger siblings.

"Don't say that word," came a muffled voice from inside the hammock.

"Which word? Me? Cupcakes? Left? I'm confused." Dracu-laura looked to the others for clarity, but they were busy rolling their eyes.

"Pizza." A pair of black-and-white checkered sneakers appeared over the edge of the hammock as the monster sat up.

"Deuce?" asked Draculaura. "What are you doing here?"

"Moping," said Abbey. "He mopes like a yeti whose favor-ite icicle has melted."

"*Pizza*," groaned Deuce. Even his green face mask looked

droopy. "It reminds me of Cleo. We had pizza on our eighth date."

"And yet," purred Toralei, "this didn't stop you from devouring eleven slices."

Draculaura noticed the evidence of quite a few murktails around the hammock as well. In fact, looking around the patio, all the ghouls seemed to be hyped up on sugar, giddy with good company.

"No offense, mate," said Lagoona, slurping the last inch of a blue beverage in her glass. "But everything tonight has reminded you of Cleo. Pizza, napkins, the rude delivery driver."

Deuce's face went soft. "She sounded like Cleo. She's agoreable when she's all snippy and—"

Clawdeen cleared her throat. "Nope. Stopping you right there. Like we always tell Cleo—we do not want to know what you two get up to when you're alone in her tomb."

Deuce continued as if she hadn't interrupted. "And if I sound like everything reminds me of her, that's because everything *does* remind me of her. She was my favorite snake charmer. My bandaged babe. My venomous vixen. My everything." He dropped his face in his hands, forgetting all about the face mask, which squelched between his fingers. The snakes on his head all reared back to avoid being touched, and it was only then that Draculaura noticed they were wearing face masks too. The green of it perfectly matched their scales.

"You are all so lucky," groaned Deuce, his face still buried in his now-gloppy hands. "You've never had your heart broken."

Lagoona raised an eyebrow, and Draculaura wondered if she was finally going to dive into some details about what had gone down with Gil. Lagoona had dated him for *years*; it was hard to boolieve she was truly as indifferent as she seemed, but what she said was, "Personally, I say good riddance. No offense to Cleo, of corpse, but we're young! Single is the way to be."

Or . . . Draculaura shrugged, pouring herself a generous murktail from the pitcher and settling onto the hanging chair beside Frankie, who beamed and snuggled into her—maybe Lagoona really was just fine with the breakup.

"Another option"—Clawdeen cut in—"is just be more patient. You don't have to go out with the first monster to wink at you. I mean, just look at me and Toralei. I never would've seen that coming."

The werecat purred and curled her tail around Clawdeen's waist, nuzzling her neck.

Draculaura smiled. "I don't think any of us could've seen that coming—but you seem really happy together." And if they *really* wanted their minds blown, she was pretty sure she could accomplish that by telling them all about the date she'd just gone on. Would they even boolieve her if she said she'd been hiking with a human?

Each half of that sentence sounded improbable on its own; together, it was beyond impossible. She still wasn't sure *she* boolieved it. Or boolieved how much she'd enjoyed it. And part of her wanted to steal this moment for herself, spill everything into their willing ears. But before she could, Clawdeen gushed on.

"We're *so* happy." Her grin was practically face-splitting. "Who knew all those times we were bickering, it was just—"

Frankie reached in her drink and threw an ice cube at the were-pair. "Stop right there. Do we need to implement a Cleo-overshare rule for you two too?" She turned to the manster slumping half in the hammock. "No offense, Deuce, but we have heard *way* too much from Cleo about"—she waved her hand wildly, then had to grab for it with her other hand when the stitches at her wrist started to fray—"*everything*."

Deuce shrugged. A glop of facemask dripped off his chin and plopped onto a half-eaten slice of pizza on the plate in his lap. "It's all good. None taken."

Toralei waggled her eyebrows. "You wish we would overshare."

Abbey stood up off the cooler. "*I* wish to be rid of gunk on my face. I feel like Uncle Ivan after he fell into a mud puddle during spring thaw."

Frankie immediately transformed back into hostess mode, offering everyone washcloths and bowls of clean water. "Lagoona," she said tentatively, "my dad says you can't rinse off in the hot tub this time, because last time it clogged the filter."

Based on the apologetic look on her face, Draculaura knew Frankie was still stressed about the whole school transfer thing—worried that *any* inconvenience might be the thing to tip Lagoona into leaving, but she just shrugged and boosted herself out of the hot tub.

"No problem, love. It was time to get out anyway—all that hot water, I was starting to feel like a poached fish. Too much longer and I'll have global warming nightmares tonight." Lagoona gave her face a quick wipe, then plucked another kelp cupcake off the half-empty tray beside the hot tub.

"Speaking of nightmares—well, *not* nightmares—but sleeping, does anyone want to stay over?" Frankie looked so hopefully at Draculaura that she felt herself nodding. "Not you, Deuce," the ghoul added quickly. "My dad would blow a fuse."

The manster promptly broke into sobs so loud that even his snakes looked embarrassed. "Do you think—do you think she even *misses me*?" he managed to choke out.

Lagoona passed him a napkin as the ghouls exchanged looks.

"Cleo's head—I'm not sure there's room for anything in there but Cleo," said Abbey, who was transforming Deuce's messy tears into snowflakes and blowing them away before they could land on the snack food.

Frankie jolted upright. "That's not true!" She ignored Toralei's scoff and added, "She can be incredibly loyal and helpful. And no one plans a party like Cleo."

Toralei opened her mouth but rethought whatever she was about to say after Clawdeen whispered something that sounded suspiciously like "*Kitten, tone down the cattitude*." Instead, the werecat gave her ghoulfriend a quick smooch and stood up. "I've got plans in the morning with Purrsephone and Meowlody, so I can't stay. I'll makes sure the big guy gets home in one piece." She pawsed to consider, then added, "Is it catty if I say, well, *one piece* if you don't count his broken heart?"

They all nodded, but it was Abbey who spoke first, "As rude as the frost that comes after spring planting."

"Hmm. Then pretend I didn't say it." Toralei held out her paws toward the manster and hauled him out of the hammock. "C'mon, Romeo. Fur what it's worth, I bet your Ghoulliet realizes her hisstake."

"You really think so?" Deuce leaned against her with a sniffle. Toralei rolled her eyes but didn't pull away—not even when he blew his nose with a resounding honk that appeared to disgust his snake hair. "Thanks for having me, Frankie. I'm glad you all are still my friends, even though Cleo doesn't w-wa-want me anymore."

"There, there, big guy," said Toralei as she led Deuce around the side of the house. She pawsed at the corner to glance back over her shoulder with a look that screamed *You owe me one.*

Clawdeen blew her a kiss, calling out, "You're the best, kitten."

Draculaura grabbed a plate and scanned the spread of snacks, looking for some that weren't contaminated by Deuce's tears. So, this was a different sort of ghouls' night than usual . . . but as Lagoona mixed up another pitcher of blue murktails, Abbey and Clawdeen demonstrated the latest EekTok dance craze, and Frankie tugged Draculaura back down on the swing chair beside her so she could steal pretzels off her plate, then braid her hair—some things felt exactly the same.

And maybe she *should* tell them what was going on—with her blood, with her crush, with all the things that were changing—but for just one night, maybe she could pretend they were like they'd been before.

"After you're done braiding my hair, want me to do your nails?" she asked Frankie.

The other ghoul beamed. "Don't I always?"

Always. Draculaura held on to that word as she caught the pillow Clawdeen tossed her way, then threw it back with a laugh.

She hoped they *always* had nights like this.

CHAPTER 15

Draculaura spent Sunday waiting for her iCoffin to ring and dodging calls when it did.

When it was Poe's name on the screen, she accepted—gleefully, giggly, chattering, flirting, planning. But when *Cleo*, *Clawdeen*, then *Frankie* called in quick succession, she didn't answer any. That pattern could only mean a battle; that Clawdeen and Cleo had figured out yet another thing to fight about and wanted her to choose sides. Frankie would be panicking about being caught in the middle and want to brainstorm ways to make everyone get along.

At least, those were Draculaura's predictions as she hit the ignore button three times in a row—and they were confirmed by the string of hexts that followed.

Can you boolieve Clawdeen?

You'll never guess what Cleo did.

I'm about to blow a circuit!

"At least they're not treating me like I'm breakable," she told Poe. Truthfully, any distance she felt from the ghouls right now was probably of her own making. It was because of the secrets she was keeping.

"I wish I'd kissed you last night," said Poe—and just like that, all her attention was back on the conversation she was having instead of those she was avoiding. Just like that, all her secrets felt worth it. "I mean," added Poe, "*if* you wanted to kiss me."

"Of corpse!" she said—then felt her cheeks heat. Is that what it felt like to blush? How very human. "I just—I don't want you to worry. I won't—"

"I know," he said quickly. "And now that I know about, you know, your . . ."

"My fangs," she said, prompting him, because they weren't something she was ashamed of—and if they couldn't both say the word, then they had no business swapping saliva.

"Yeah." He was blushing now too—enough to be visible over the iCoffin screen. "Now that I know about your fangs, I'll be more careful."

"I wish you were here—or that I was there." Basically, she wished for the impossible.

"And I wish I'd had my epiphany twelve hours sooner," Poe said with a chuckle. "Maybe I'll write some angsty poems after all, because my dad will be home soon and this whole upcoming week is packed with soccer. When am I going to see you?"

"We'll figure something out." Draculaura was very aware that with fearleading practice canceled, her schedule was a great big blank, so she could be flexible. And after all, nothing had stopped them so far—even though many things probably should've. Of all her problems, Poe seemed the most manageable. The ghouls' fights, Ghoulia's research dead ends, missing her dad, the school board takeover, and Monster High being in attack mode—while also needing to be in defense mode because of the normies searching for it—*those* were reasons for her sleepless nights and nightmares.

Poe was the inspiration behind her sweetest daydreams.

The other problems? They were the reason she should get off the phone *and* the reasons she didn't want to. But Ghoulia had asked her to search through the books in Dracula's home office, Frankie was calling again, and Ms. Heaves was knocking on her door and asking about dinner. However perfect this stolen time with Poe was, it was over.

"Talk soon," she said, and when he echoed the words back to her, she knew she could trust them.

Monday started with a security scan at the front doors of Monster High. Draculaura wasn't sure what the purpose was—to find mysterious normies trying to sneak into the school? And she wondered how enrolled normies, like Jackson Jekyll, felt about the process, which was made all the more chaotic by Nefera and Cleo competing to see who could move more students through their scanners.

"Come to my line, it's shorter," called Cleo.

"Yeah, because everyone can see that *my* line is more efficient," countered Nefera. "Everyone who chooses your line must really like waiting around."

Cleo stomped and fumed. Nefera preened and hurled insults at students who weren't keeping up with the line or emptying their bags quickly enough. Obviously, all the zombies chose Cleo's line, which wasn't helping her temper.

Anytime Draculaura regretted being an only child, she only had to think about Cleo and Nefera and she got over it. Those two were rivals at the best of times. But now, with their father pulling on their insecurities like a puppet master, they were terrifying. An enemy who also knew all your childhood secrets and embarrassing moments? Yeah, Draculaura gave that a hard pass.

"Who authorized this?" asked Lagoona as she queued up behind Slo Mo. "And isn't it weird we didn't get an eek-mail from the school telling us to expect it?"

"And who made the mistake of putting these two in charge?" added Clawdeen.

Draculaura was pretty sure those were rhetorical questions with the same answer: Ramses.

But in this one instance, she was grateful for the de Nile daughters' dramatics. Not because she was going to choose a side (if forced to pick, she'd say they were both wrong! #TeamNeither!), but because when they repeated the process after school (what, were they worried a normie *in* the school would now sneak out?) they created so much chaos that it was the perfect distraction to slip away from the crowd and sneak off campus to meet Poe.

Or at least it *would've* been, if the secret passage was where it always was. She pulled on the middle head of the hydra statue, glanced back over her shoulder to make sure no one was watching, and . . . walked into a solid wall. She slammed into it, really, bouncing off and falling on her butt in a way that was neither graceful nor dignified—and also hurt!

All those students who hadn't been watching before? Yeah, she'd grabbed their attention now. Draculaura gave an awkward laugh. "No worries. I'm fine. Just a stumble."

Slo Mo offered her a hand up, but after he'd shambled off, she kicked at the wall where the passage should be and muttered, "Stupid school. What is wrong with you?"

It shouldn't have been possible, but if anything, it felt like the wall in front of her grew *harder*. She should probably be grateful it hadn't done worse. Monster High had been in rare, rotten form today. First, the school's PA system had broadcast the same Catty Noir song for two hours. Draculaura loved Catty's music but not when played backward at disorienting double-speed for one hundred and twenty minutes while Mr. Rotter tried to yell-teach over it. She was pretty sure most of the student body still had pounding headaches. Nefera and Cleo's escalating voices at the scanner exit lines were deathinitely not helping.

She headed away from their commotion to her second-favorite escape route, a tunnel behind a cyclopes tapestry by the catacombs. This exit was a bit like an awful version of hiking, actually—all the cobwebs, but none of the fangtastic views or the company. She swiped another web from her cheek and picked up the pace. If she didn't hurry, she was going to be late.

Poe's school had finally done what they'd been threatening: canceled all after-school activities. He'd called with the news as he was walking to his car. "Someone in the marching band claimed they saw a zombie running across the football field. Or to be more precise: They said they saw 'the reflection of a zombie on a tuba, but when he looked, they'd already vanished.'"

"There's too many impossible things about that statement to count." Draculaura had laughed. "Zombies do *not* move quickly. They cannot run or vanish. Boolieve me, if they saw a zombie on the field, there'd *still* be a zombie on the field. But I'm sorry about your practice."

"I'm not," Poe said. "Well, at least I won't be if there's any chance you can meet up."

It was a risk, but she was taking it, stepping from the shadows at the tunnel's exit and crossing the empty sports scaredium's parking lot where she'd told him to meet her.

Seriously, Poe should do car ads. They could just be this moment: him leaning back against a vehicle with a pair of sunglasses on his face that he removed and tucked in the front of his shirt as she approached. All the better to see how his eyes lit up and his face split into the most welcoming grin. Whatever car they put behind him would sell out immediately. Or, maybe not immediately, because it might take a couple replays before viewers could move their eyes from Poe to notice the vehicle behind him.

Or, at least, it had taken *her* that long to notice.

"That's a different car," she said, pointing to the convertible.

"My dad's. Mine's in the shop getting an oil change—he didn't trust me to drive my mom's, so I got his. Which is perfect for my plans."

"Which are?"

"Driving with the top down on a warm day at the end of September when you know fall is coming is one of life's greatest pleasures." He glanced up at the overcast sky. "Is it cloudy enough today?"

She'd fully admit that she swooned a little at his thoughtfulness, and that *she* was the one who made the first move, looping her arms around his neck, pressing up on her toes, and carefully grazing her lips across his.

"It's perfect," she said when she pulled back. "You're perfect."

He laughed and brushed his lips across her forehead. "Not according to my dad or my history grade." Poe leaned back slightly to look at her, his brow creasing as he caressed her cheek. "I want to ask *the* question, but I know you hate it. So, what if I put it this way: Will you tell me if you're not okay?"

It would be a lie to say yes. Draculaura wasn't sure if she was—and was equally unsure what to say about it—but she knew why he was asking without asking. She had dark shadows under her eyes—not that she'd been able to see them firsthand, but the ghouls had commented on them. She was not cool with turning human if it meant she was turning hideous.

Also, she wasn't cool with turning human at all. And so far neither she nor Ghoulia had turned up anything about how to slow down, stop, or reverse the process. Those undereye bags? Probably courtesy of the hours she and Ghoulia had spent in her dad's home office the night before. Hours of searching instead of sleeping and still finding . . . *nothing*.

"I'm just . . . tired of things being so complicated," she said. "Remember when the hardest decisions you had to make were lipstick color or what sort of highlights to get?"

He laughed and held open the car door for her. "While I can't say I relate to those specific examples, I know what you mean. When I left this morning, my dad was installing cameras on our garage that are supposed to record 'monster energy.'"

She snorted. "If they locate any, could you send it my way? Not even an ogre-sized coffinchino has enough caffeine these days."

He chuckled as he started the car and smoothly reversed out of the lot. "Since I'm the one who mows, I'm secretly hoping it catches whichever neighbor's dog keeps pooping on our lawn."

Her laughter was carried away in the breeze.

It was hard to remember her problems with the almost-autumn wind in her hair, or with Poe's fingers woven through the tangled strands when he pulled over and kissed her senseless. But it was equally hard to forget them when his human phone beeped with emergency broadcast messages of imaginary monster sightings.

She knew they were imaginary because the news alerts on her own phone only warned of potential curfews and human patrols.

And when the sun broke through the clouds and Poe tipped his head up to bask in the light while she dove for her high potency sunscream, it highlighted the differences between them.

This time Poe wasn't pulling the car over for kisses but to raise the convertible's roof.

This was a human experience they couldn't share—at least not while she was a vampire. But it made her think of her mom—of a memory so old and faded she had to hold her breath to recall it. Wind in her face, a field blurring past. Leaning into her mother's shoulder as they bounced around in the back of an open, horse-drawn cart. The large wooden wheels bumping down a dirt road near Dracula's Dacia estate. They were laughing, heads thrown back, sunlight on their skin. She couldn't have been more than twelve—she didn't recall where they'd been, just that they were coming home. Just the music of her mother's laugh, the sun-drenched happiness of it. And while she couldn't have her mother back, and modern transportation was much smoother, she could have sunshine. She could have moments like that.

If she became human . . .

Both of their phones beeped simultaneously, shaking Draculaura out of her inner debate. The messages on the screens emphasized just how impossible their situation was: *New Sighting of Monster School* versus *Humans on Campus: Monster High's Protections Fail for a Second Time.*

Nowhere was safe anymore.

CHAPTER 16

Draculaura's days slipped into a pattern. School, with Monster High's new, innovative, sometimes-scary forms of torture. Thankfully, there'd been no more bleeding walls, but students had bled from accidents ranging from lockers closing on fingers to test tubes spontaneously shattering to self-inflicted scratches when an entire Hisstory class had hallucinated that spiders were crawling all over their faces.

Fewer students showed up to pass through the de Nile sisters' scanners each day. Ramses's face seemed to glare imperiously off every flat surface—posters demanding he be appointed school board president and listing his anti-normie strategies had been posted everywhere—and she did mean *everywhere*. She'd been startled by one on the underside of a toilet lid, and somehow they magically reappeared inside her locker each day. Clearly Nefera and Cleo were in some sort of competition to see who could hang the most. It all felt vaguely threatening, or at least abrasively aggressive. He was still hassling her to publicly endorse him as a replacement for her father. Draculaura was still managing, barely, to be noncommittal, but if he truly cornered her, he wasn't going to be pleased when she turned him down.

Deuce and Lagoona were still enrolled at Monster High—so far—but she held her breath each morning until she saw them, because it felt clear that some morning soon, she wouldn't. Even more so after that second breach of the school's invisibility protections—the alert that had lit up her phone and Poe's had been for a normie mommy-blogger who'd been in the forest photographing the early fall foliage. When she went to post her pictures, she realized Monster High was right there in the background of the images. She'd already had a huge following on the human-web, so the photos had gone *beyond* viral.

Poe said his dad had printed out copies of the images and hung them and maps all over their wall, like some twisted scene from a crime movie. "We used to go camping and do geo-caching—now he does this."

Draculaura spent her Study Howls in the library searching for answers and avoiding the ghouls' fights. After school, Poe showed her more and more of his world. Some of it she loved (catching fireflies had been magical), some she didn't (mosquito bites, ugh! They were terrible!), and some human things didn't seem all that different from her own (apparently, coffee was coffee—whether bought at the Coffin Bean or in a to-go cup from Poe's favorite café).

And then, after spending time with Poe, Draculaura would attempt to cram her homework into a few hours before she fell into her coffin and slept like the dead until it was time to wake up and do it all over again.

Zombies hated being rushed, but as the week dragged on, Draculaura began to despair about her or Ghoulia ever finding a solution. "Do you think we should tell Headmistress Bloodgood or ask any of the teachers for help?"

Ghoulia only looked up from whatever book she was studying long enough to shake her head, before she resumed reading.

Draculaura slumped against the library shelves. "Right, with all the anti-normie sentiment, it's probably not the best time to announce that I'm becoming one."

Jackson Jekyll had stopped attending school, and she didn't blame him. She missed him—and hexted him to let him know he was missed—but she'd seen the looks he got from other students when he'd set off the human-detection scanners. No, she didn't blame him at all. And . . . *since* mosquitos were biting her—did that mean she had human blood to drink? If so, how long until the change was irreversible? How long until *she* set off the scanners? How long until she no longer fit in at Monster High?

Maybe that was why she'd taken a creeptacular risk and said yes when Poe asked if she wanted to come to his house after school on Friday while his father was away on a business trip.

"I guess we better hope that those 'monster energy' cameras really are bogus," she said with an uncertain laugh as he parked in his driveway and led her past the three lenses mounted on the garage and up the path to his front door.

"I promise they're total crap," Poe answered, fitting his key in the lock. "They're supposed to turn red when they detect monsters. Look."

She glanced over her shoulder and confirmed they were still glowing green.

He let himself in, then turned to grin at her. "You coming? Or do you want to run back and forth in front of them to see if

189

you can get them to trip? You can try, but so far the only thing that's set them off is the garbage truck."

"Oh." She felt her cheeks flush. "I can't—I can't come in without an invitation."

His grin faltered. "Right. Come in, please. I forgot—vampire."

Then again, maybe she *could've* gone in without an invitation? With each passing day she felt less like a vampire, more like a . . . human? She couldn't remember what that felt like. But *if* she decided to continue down this path, she'd find out soon enough.

Not that she'd have much choice.

She wasn't sure she wanted to. Wasn't sure she didn't. She'd been rereading the last entry in her mother's diary, the Latin words burning into her brain as she memorized her mother's final wishes.

13 Februarius 412

> *I can make no foothold in my battle against this ill-ness. It grips me, stealing my vitality and breath. I fear that this may be my final entry, as my fingers are flagging, lacking the strength to grip this quill. But before I pass into the unknown eternity, there are some things I must commit to paper.*
>
> *It pains me to know that Dracula may not return from his trip abroad before I pass. That I may never get to tell him of my great esteem for him. It is akin to love—an emotion I had thought never*

to experience again after the passing of my husband. While my heart aches to be reunited with Gaius and to tell him the news of our remarkable daughter, I do not desire for him to meet her so soon.

I suffer to see her suffer so. I have many hopes for her life, much I want for her—and though I will not be here to witness it, I want her to have the chance. I have made peace with my own mortality, my own death.

For Draculaura, I desire more.

Dracula—I pray when you arrive home, it is not yet too late for our beloved daughter—for though you are not her father by birth, you have raised her as your own, with a love that is a marvel to observe. If thou canst preserve her life, I beseech you to do so. Teach her your ways. Let her live.

And tell her that I have loved her.

The words were spattered, smeared, blotched. Her mother's final signature nearly indecipherable as her strength faded. But the meaning in this entry was absolutely clear—her mom had given Dracula her consent to change her daughter into a vampire.

Camilla had made her own choice; she'd made a choice for her daughter. It was time for Draculaura to decide for herself. But she wanted it to be a *choice*. Not a decision that was made for her because of a lack of answers.

"What are you thinking?" she asked Poe, when she realized he'd been silent just as long as she had. Both of them standing awkwardly in his front hall, surrounded by framed family photos from a time when Poe's family had been a trio. One wall was suspiciously blank—but peppered with hundreds of tiny tack-holes. This, she realized, was where his father had hung up the photos of Monster High. His "conspiracy wall," as Poe called it. He must have taken it down for her.

"Do you really want to know?" Poe asked.

"Of corpse."

She'd seen the inside of his house before, but only on the screen of her iCoffin from when he walked around during video calls—where she frequently asked him to aim the phone's camera at things so she could see them closer. Fake plants! These still fascinated her. Why? But there they were, in all their plasticky glory. She gave one a subtle poke as she waited for Poe to formulate his answer.

Draculaura desperately wanted Poe to reach over and hold her hand, but he curled further into himself, shoving his fingers in his pockets. "I'm thinking that I have no right to think this—but I love seeing you in my house. And the idea of you being in my world is potentially the best news I've had in a really long time."

"Oh." Draculaura swallowed around a lump in her throat, trying to decide if she felt flattered, or fear-pressured. Poe-pressured? Her cheeks flushed hot as she fought against a smile. "Thank you."

"I know—it's not fair of me to say that, but . . . am I allowed to hope? If I do it silently? Based on what you've told me about your friends, I doubt they're keeping their opinions to themselves."

She laughed. Oh, he was absolutely right they wouldn't. Except . . . "I haven't told them yet."

His brow scrunched, and his confused expression was scary agoreable. When would just looking at him not make her stomach twist in the best possible way? When would a simple thing, like him touching her arm as he led her into a bright, sunny kitchen, stop making her breath catch?

"Why not?" he asked.

"The ghouls are already so stressed about *everything*. And they're just starting to treat me like I'm me. I think if Frankie had one more problem she felt like she had to solve, *she* might break. And not in a way that would be easy to reassemble."

"Got it. My friend John keeps teasing me about my 'girl from the graveyard'—I'm pretty sure he still thinks you're imaginary, since he hasn't met you yet—but it's more, like . . . if it's not safe to tell him *everything* about you, I don't know how to skip some of the most important parts? So, I'm just saying nothing and accepting the teasing. Does that make sense?"

She nodded. It did, but also, she was fascinated by his kitchen. She wanted to open all the cabinets and drawers, poke around in the contents, then explore the rest of the house—attic to basement. It looked so . . . so . . . *normie*. The cabinets were white with a pale gray subway tile backsplash. It was clear someone had once taken a lot of pride in the room. There was an empty fruit bowl with a floral print that matched the faded towels hanging crookedly on the oven handle. The fridge was covered in photo magnets—but even the most recent were at least a year old. The room was pretty—but a little dusty, a little neglected. Draculaura chided herself for the thought—not everyone had a Ms. Heaves.

"Hungry? I'm starving." Poe pointed her toward a chair and opened the fridge, scowling at the bare shelves. "Dad said he was going to go grocery shopping before he left for his trip. I guess he forgot."

She pointed to a note and some cash clipped to a magnet on the freezer. Poe scanned the message and snorted. "Right. He 'ran out of time.' Probably too busy on his monster message boards." He sighed. "I wish I could take you to the grocery store so we could get ingredients for my mom's famous pancakes. Or omelets. Those are the only two things she taught me how to cook. Mom was really into breakfast."

"We can make them next time," said Draculaura. "And thanks for sharing your world with me, even if we can't do everything. I feel like I understand it better now. I wish I could do the same for you in my world, but—"

"That's okay." Poe shook his head quickly. "I know enough to know I'm glad it exists—I'm glad *you* exist—but your world, it's not for me."

The conviction in his words, the absolute certainty in her mother's diary—it baffled Draculaura. "How can you be so sure? I'm not judging, I just want to understand—because I'm—I'm *not*."

Poe pulled out the chair beside hers and sank onto it like his legs had gone heavy. He looked down at the hands he'd clasped so tightly in his lap. "My mom. I don't know if *I* believe in any sort of an afterlife—but she did. And if one exists, I want to see her again someday."

He glanced up at Draculaura, his eyes deep with sadness. "The last thing she said to me was to live my life to the fullest and always be me—never change for anyone."

Draculaura's thoughts felt like a flock of bats leaving their cave for a night of flying—they scattered and spiraled in a dozen different directions: What had been the last thing her dad said to her? Did Dracula not get an afterlife? Would she? And would turning human make it more likely that she'd have a someday-reunion with her mom? What was the last thing Camilla had said to her? That time was such a fever dream of hallucinations and pain, but maybe her mom had advised her on which choice to make—in case of this highly improbable scenario sixteen hundred years later . . .

Poe reached over and took her hand. "I think my mom was really talking more about her and my dad than *me*, but I promised her. And since then, I've been second guessing everything, trying to figure out who *I am*, so I can always be myself. Like, with soccer and everything—it took me a minute to double-check if I really loved it. And I do. Maybe not as much as my dad does, but I do love it. I want to keep playing in college.

And did I love hiking? Or just love the memory of doing it with her? Nope, I love that too. And Mom hated when I stayed up all night, but I still love it—so that's a true thing. Something I shouldn't change. Though, lately it's been less night owl and more insomnia, so that's not the best."

He squeezed her hand. "But what I'm *not* is a monster, and I can't change myself into one. Not for you. Not for anyone. I can't ask you to be a human either. I don't want to do that. It has to be your choice."

Her thoughts—still bats. A group of them was called a *colony*—and it could range in size from ten to a hundred times bigger. Right now these decisions felt a hundred times bigger than her capacity to make them. Her feelings were swarming from all directions—tenderness, defensiveness, frustration, exhaustion. And even a prickle of resentment, because wouldn't it just be easier if someone else made this decision *for* her? But even as she thought it, she knew that wasn't fair, wasn't actually what she wanted.

"Now it's my turn to ask," he said, lifting her hand to his lips and pressing a kiss to her palm. "What are *you* thinking?"

She leaned into his touch, resting her head on his shoulder as she tried to focus on a single thought—a single thing that made sense right now. "Do humans get—we call it *fangry*—when you're cranky because you're hungry?"

"Hangry," he said with a chuckle. "Why don't I order pizza? And while we're waiting for it to get delivered, you can snoop around my house. I can tell you're dying to."

"Really?" she probably looked like a toddler, clapping her hands in excitement, but she didn't care. "Where can I look?"

"Have at it," he said. "Nothing's off-limits except my dad's room and office."

Draculaura snooped until the pizza arrived, defrighted to find a drawer full of old school pictures and report cards where Poe's elementary school teachers had called him wiggly and *more focused on socializing than math facts.*

"Honestly, that hasn't changed," he said with a grin, handing her a photo of him around that age with missing front teeth and eyes that looked comically large and full of mischief.

"Who could possibly get mad at that face?" she cooed, before moving on to the next room. She paused to eat pizza, then went back to exploring, pouting briefly when Poe refused to model anything from the plastic bin marked *Halloween costumes* that she found in the back of the coat closet.

"I haven't trick-or-treated in years," he told her, taking her hand and towing her toward the family room couch. "I promise you, nothing in there is going to fit me."

"You say that like it doesn't make it better," she giggled. "I think I deserve to see Poe the pirate with a crop top and a major pirate-pants wedgie."

"Next time," he chuckled, flopping down on the couch and pulling her beside him. He snapped a quick selfie of them—her head on his chest, his arm around her shoulders, lips pressed to the top of her head—before tossing his phone on the coffee table. Draculaura didn't have the heart to remind him that she wouldn't appear in the photo. Especially when he sighed contentedly against her hair and said, "I really needed this."

"But . . . we're not doing anything?" she noted with a giggle, wriggling out of his embrace to lean back so she could read his expression.

"I know." He made the "c'mere" gesture with his fingers, and when she relented, tiptoeing her fingers up his chest as she snuggled back in, his exhale felt like it contained all the stress inside his body. "Isn't it the best?"

Draculaura tilted her head. "I get lazy sometimes too. And Lagoona once wore the same lucky shirt for a week. What makes this version of doing nothing particularly *human*?"

"Because we're choosing this." He leaned up on one elbow to see her better, drawing soft lines across her back as he spoke. Her Poe, he was a toucher—it was one of her favorite things about him. And he was *hers*, she was sure of that. He was hers for as long as this lasted—but whether that was this week, or a whole human lifetime—that was the question. His fingers trailed up her neck, across her shoulders, down her arms to clasp her hands. If she'd been made of butter, she would've melted all over him. Instead, she just gave a happy hum.

"Humans know they only have so many days," said Poe. "And we're choosing—not to be lazy but to relax into these minutes and just enjoy them without pressure to *do* anything but savor this time and each other."

She considered this, weighing her words before she spoke. "I'll accept this premise, but so far, humanity seems to be a whole lot of thinking about time."

He tilted his head, looming closer—she could see the thought of their next kiss on his lips. "At the risk of sounding like an emo-poet, isn't immortality the struggle to make time have meaning? When you have endless amounts of it, it's not precious anymore."

"So what you're saying is"—Draculaura wanted to kiss him, would kiss him soon, but this temptation was too delicious. She whipped a throw pillow from behind her back and smacked it into his stomach—"I should *savor* this pillow fight, and the victory will be so much sweeter, since you poor mortal can only experience a finite number of pillow defeats?"

He oofed, then laughed. Then he grabbed a pillow from the couch beside him to launch his counterattack. "You're asking for it."

"Oh yeah?" she teased, maneuvering to straddle him, a pillow held above his head. "What *exactly* am I asking for?"

He grasped the pillow, tugging it from her hands and tossing it aside. "Whatever it is," he said, as she lowered her mouth to his. "It's yours."

I'm yours, she thought—thought it so hard, it felt like it was being broadcast through every kiss, caress, and breath. *I'm yours. I'm yours. I'm yours.*

Later, they'd put the pillows back on the couch to cuddle up and watch some movie about a normie high school. Draculaura doubted the plot was actually hard to follow, but then again, she was watching him more than the screen.

His freckles were constellations across his face—no, that comparison was too cliché, but it also kind of fit. They were landmarks she could use for navigating this strange new human world. When the one above his left eye disappeared with his raised eyebrow, she knew he was struggling to wrap his mind around one of her Monster High stories. The ones about Cleo especially seemed to baffle him, which, *fair*. When the trio of freckles on his nose converged as he scrunched up the skin there, it meant he was trying not to laugh. And when he gnawed on his bottom lip, making the freckle that was normally hidden below it suddenly front and center—then he was concerned, or hesitating to ask her something.

This expression always made her want to kiss it right off his face. Often she did. At first she'd been worried about kissing him again, about accidentally biting him again, but with each passing day, her fangs grew noticeably duller. Also, they'd had plenty of practice.

She was changing in other ways too. Her skin had darkened, it tolerated the sun better. Maybe, eventually, she'd have freckles too.

Maybe soon that idea wouldn't feel like a tragic failure of research and instead like a choice.

CHAPTER 17

found the answer.

The hext from Ghoulia arrived sometime after one a.m. on Wednesday, but Draculaura didn't see it until she woke up to pee around four.

Her replies of all exclamation points, then all question marks, then You have my undead gratitude, but I'm dying of impatience over here! all went unanswered.

Understandably, Ghoulia was sleeping. She should be too. Instead, she climbed out of her coffin; straightened the pink satin sheets, because there was no way she was falling back asleep; and began to pace her room.

She'd wanted a choice—and now, presumably, she was getting one. So why, instead of relief, did she feel dread?

She'd started to come to terms with this being an unsolvable mystery, started rehearsing what she'd tell her friends: *I tried looking everywhere for answers—Ghoulia did too—but we ran out of time. I had to turn human.*

But that wasn't true anymore.

Alongside the privilege of choosing her own fate came the ability to choose *wrong*. That was a lot of responsibility. A lot of pressure.

And she still didn't know what the choice entailed.

She sent one last hext, crossing her fingers that Ghoulia had her iCoffin set to *do not diesturb*.

Meet at Coffin Bean before school?

Then she set down her phone and picked up her mother's diary.

Her mom and Poe would clearly both be Team Human, and maybe it wasn't fair not to tell the ghouls and let them make their best counterargument. Except, she'd had sixteen hundred years of experience as a vampire, versus sixteen as a human. If her math was correct, that was only one percent of her life spent human. So surely it made sense for her to consult some outside experts to balance the scales. But this wasn't Poe's decision, it wasn't her mother's, it wasn't her friends'. It was hers and hers alone. And alone was what she didn't want to be anymore.

By the time Ghoulia shambled into the Coffin Bean, Draculaura was on her third coffinchino. She'd never managed more than the slightest hover off the ground, and these days even her mediocre vampire skills were waning—but between the caffeine and the anticipation, she was practically levitating as she rushed toward her friend, herded her toward a seat, then scurried to place and collect the other ghoul's usual order of an eekspresso.

She set the mug down in front of the zombie and scooted her chair closer.

Ghoulia took a long, slow sip, and Draculaura had to sit on her hands to keep herself from snatching away the drink she'd just delivered. Zombies didn't respond well to being rushed. And why should they? While Ghoulia's movements may be slow, her brain worked at speeds Draculaura couldn't dream of comprehending.

She channeled her anxiety into slurping down the dregs of her own drink and debating whether a fourth one would be a mistake. Seeing as her legs were jittering at frequencies that could set off a seismograph, the answer to that was . . . probably.

Finally, Ghoulia set down her cup and pulled a dusty book from her bag. She hesitated before sliding it across the table, and Draculaura had to work hard to tear her eyes from the brightly colored *Dead Fast* comic book her friend had used as a bookmark and listen to the speech in Zombie that Ghoulia had clearly rehearsed.

"The reason these answers were so hard to find makes much more sense after you know the solution. The fact is, this problem wouldn't be a problem for most vampires. They wouldn't even know it *could* happen, because they'd have prevented the transition to human before it even started."

"Um . . ." Had Ghoulia meant for that to sound like a riddle? Because she hadn't followed that explanation at all. But either the somber look on her friend's face or all that coffee on an empty stomach had left Draculaura suddenly feeling nauseated.

She reached across the table and pulled the book close, flipping to the marked page.

She skimmed the words, then read them slowly, then scanned the page a third time. If she'd been hoping their meaning would change, she was dead wrong.

Ghoulia was correct. Most vampires would never realize the risk of turning human *because* they'd preemptively evaded it.

The solution was simple and obvious and impossible.

Blood.

Blood drunk directly from a human source, if she wanted to be precise.

The caffeine jitters drained from her body, replaced by a sucking lethargy and head-spinning wooziness. "That's what the school meant," she whispered. "The message on the wall—*sanguis requiritur*. 'Blood is required.' The message was for me—the school was basically doing my homework for me, telling me what I needed to stay vampire."

Ghoulia shrugged and said in Zombie, "That seems likely."

And apparently there was risk—the longer a vampire delayed their "affirmation of their vampyre identity," the greater the chance they wouldn't survive the *re*-transformation process.

Delays longer than one lunar cycle often fail to achieve vitality.

"Vitality?" she asked Ghoulia. "Does that mean they die?"

The ghoul nodded grimly.

This shouldn't be a surprise. The creation of *new* vampires was incredibly rare—but Draculaura knew that not every human who'd been bitten, drained, then fed vampire blood reawakened as a member of the undead. Some never woke again. It made sense that this re-transformation process had risks too—*more* risks, it sounded like.

She had waited more than *three* lunar cycles—aka months—did that mean she had three times the chance of dying? One-third the chance of surviving?

So, even if she *could* drink human blood—and she couldn't—it was unlikely she'd survive?

And just in case she'd thought there was a loophole, the text made it clear that de-vampired humans could not be reawoken through the original process. There'd be no going up to Elissabat or Gory Fangtell and asking if they'd "drain and drink" her to vamp back up.

There was *one* procedure. One impossible, risky procedure. Draculaura shut the book and blinked back tears. She'd wanted a choice—but this felt more like a dead end.

Ghoulia offered her a napkin and a nonjudgmental expression. She asked in quiet Zombie, "What will you do?"

She *did* have a choice. Draculaura knew she need to acknowledge that—but it wasn't a choice she could make. Blood and a potentially painful death versus a future as a human? One that her mom would want for her, a future full of all the possibilities and small joys Poe had shown her.

She drummed her fingers on the book's cover. "Do you think they'll let me attend Monster High after I'm human? How will I even know when I'm fully changed? What are the ghouls going to say?"

Ghoulia stood and circled the table to hug her. "I don't

know—but I know you're stuck with me as long as you want me."

"Forever, then." Draculaura returned the hug with the word burning like a lie on her tongue. Humans didn't get forever. A clock was now ticking down her mortal life. She needed to start making the seconds count.

"You need to tell the ghouls," Ghoulia said in Zombie. "I can do it with you, if you want—except not until later. I've got to head to a meeting with Headmistress Bloodgood and Mr. Rotter. We're researching potential causes for the school's . . . um, crankiness."

Draculaura gave her friend a watery smile. "Thank you— for everything. And good luck with the research."

Ghoulia gave her an encouraging nod before shuffling off. She called back over her shoulder in Zombie. "Could be worse. Could be more star charts for Cleo."

But neither ghoul laughed.

"It could be worse," Draculaura whispered to her collection of empty mugs. After all, it wasn't as if Poe and humanity were rotten consolation prizes. This just wasn't the way she'd wanted to make this choice.

It could be worse.

Draculaura held her breath as she stepped through the scanners to enter Monster High. They were no longer free-standing devices—they'd been mounted above all the entrances to the school instead. Which meant there was no longer a need for the de Nile daughters to run the lines. Draculaura was surprised to realize this disappointed her—it would've been nice to have Cleo's friendly face waiting for her, because she now knew that one of these days, this device *would* sound the alarm for her. In fact, in all likelihood, the alarm would be how she learned that her transition to human was complete.

She exhaled as she made it to the other side without any lights or bells going off—today was *not* that day.

But it might be tomorrow; it might be the day after. She was vamping on borrowed time, and she needed to get ahead of this. She needed to schedule a meeting with Headmistress Bloodgood to discuss her ability to have a human future at Monster High. She needed to tell her friends.

She needed to tell Poe.

"Did you hear?" Clawdeen ran down the hallway to meet her. "What am I thinking, of corpse you did. Were you in the super-secret meeting where it was decided? How mad was he?"

Draculaura blinked in confusion. She *had* been in a super-secret meeting where a big decision was made, but she doubted it was the same one Clawdeen meant. Or, at least, if it *was*, she was slightly hurt that Clawdeen was *this* excited about her impending humanity.

And who would be the "he" who was mad?

Before she could clarify any of this, Cleo rushed over and grasped her arm. "Draculaura, be honest," she said earnestly. "Who do you think would make a better campaign manager: me or Nefera?"

"Campaign manager?" Draculaura asked.

"Yes. Oh my Ra, please keep up. For the *election* they're going to hold for the school board vacancy." Cleo fluttered a handful of posters at her. Draculaura made out the words *Rameses for School Board—Dynastic Deaducation*. "My dad will win, of corpse, but he's graciously decided that this is the best way to ensure he gets the *most* attention and shuts up any naysayers."

This last part was very clearly aimed at Clawdeen, but the werewolf just shrugged and smiled. "Ghoul, I've got to tell you—I've been furrious about this whole school board takeover—but this way feels fair. I'm down with an election. Letting monsters vote and giving others the opportunity to campaign—I'm satisfied. And I'm sorry I gave you such a hard time before."

"Thank you." Cleo pressed a hand to her heart. "I'm going to be gracious and accept that apology—along with your promise that your whole pack will be voting for my father."

Clawdeen's face turned sour. "I don't even know who the other candidates will—"

Cleo's eyebrows were climbing higher than the pyramids, and Clawdeen's temper was likely doing the same. Before either of them could tip back toward hostility, Draculaura tugged one of the posters from Cleo's hand.

She held it out like she was admiring it, but really, her head was swimming with information overload. All she registered was *gold.*

"I love a good election," she said with false enthusiasm. She gave the poster a quick thumbs-up, then handed it back to Cleo.

"Speaking of the school, Ghoulia said there's a whole committee researching why Monster High is behaving so strangely—so hopefully we'll get those answers soon too."

"If Ghoulia is part of the team, of *corpse* we will." Cleo sniffed, sounding insulted that Draculaura had presented her beastie's skills as anything but absolute.

Draculaura bit back a laugh and managed a contrite nod. More than anyone else in these hallways, *she* had reason to extol Ghoulia's talents as a researcher.

Though this was clearly *not* the time to share all of that. She shut her locker and left them to their squabbling. At least now Clawdeen and Cleo were bickering for fun, instead of contentiously. They were focused on fashion and weekend plans, not moral matters of the school board—though, no doubt there'd be more of that before elections.

As Draculaura walked toward class, she realized there *was* someone who already knew everything. Everything, that is, *except* her decision.

And her decision would thrill him.

She could use some joy—and maybe his would kickstart her own. She felt relief at having made a choice but not peace. Not . . . glad.

She pulled out her iCoffin and tapped out a message: How do humans celebrate big decisions? Asking for reasons.

Then, in case that was too vague and because it felt scary unfair to tease him about this, she added: I've made my choice. A really great tour guide convinced me to give humanity a try.

That was an oversimplification. It wasn't *because of* or *for*

Poe. She'd make that clear later. Her decision was her own, not his responsibility or victory. And while he was persuasive, it was her mother's journals that had haunted more of her thoughts. It was that the monster world didn't feel hers anymore, and the price she'd have to pay to remain in it was too high. But that felt like too much to put into an early morning hext.

New Salem High School started before Monster High. And it wasn't like Poe could use his iCoffin in public, so she expected to have to wait hours for a response.

It came in less than thirty seconds.

And not words, but a photo of Poe's face, beaming from ear-to-ear. His smile felt like moonshine, felt like home, felt infectious. Her own mouth curved in response to his.

And for the first time since she read that book in the coffee-shop, Draculaura felt like she could take a full breath.

She was standing in the chaos of a hallway that was depressingly empty, surrounded by only a few dozen other students dealing with their own victories and defeats. She could acknowledge the monsters who *were* here while missing the increasing number of those staying home. And she didn't know where she would end up. She was half in this world and halfway out of it.

Her mother had written in her last journal entry, *For Draculaura, I want more.* Draculaura had embraced more. She had chosen a life that was shorter but *new*—opening herself up to a human lifetime's worth of fresh experiences.

She wished she could send a picture back to Poe—show him how happy his reaction had made her. Tell him how much she'd needed someone to celebrate with.

Draculaura pushed open the door to her Clawculus class—where Frankie was waving her sparkly green iCoffin case to get her attention. Pointing to the seat she'd saved beside her, the one Draculaura sat in every day. The seat she hoped to continue to sit in, even after she'd gone normie. If the school would let her.

"Hey, ghoul," she called out.

"Hey! Was it just me, or was last night's homework shockingly killer?" Frankie asked, her bolts sparking. "Can you show me how you did number thirteen?"

But as Draculaura pulled out her decomposition book to help her beastie, a thought occurred to her. It was only vampires who didn't appear in photographs.

So, soon enough, she could.

She could send selfies to Poe. She could capture these moments with her ghouls—Clawdeen crowding in to offer her own advice, Lagoona accidentally dripping pool water on her homework. She could record these memories—document how time now mattered so much more.

CHAPTER 18

Draculaura tried to celebrate with Poe, she really did.

They'd met at one of his favorite parks at sunset. He led the way past a castle-shaped playground to a shadowed grove of picnic tables. "Technically the park closes at dusk, but my friends and I used to come use the swings after dark all through middle school, and no one ever stopped us."

Draculaura brought murktails, Poe brought veggie burgers and a variety of strangely sour candies in weird shapes. They smiled a lot during the meal, but neither said much. It all felt . . . serious, scareful.

And when she tried the sour candy, Poe kissed her puckered mouth. He shrugged and laughed when she asked why they were shaped like small humans with big heads, or bears, or worms.

"And you say *monsters* are confusing," she said—but it had been hard to feel present, to match his smile and his enthusiasm.

"Are you sure about this?" he asked, rubbing his hands up and down her arms, which were dotted with sudden goose bumps. "I won't be mad if you change your mind. I don't want you to have regrets. I tried really hard not to pressure you—but are you sure I didn't?"

"You've been fangtastic. This *is* my choice." She couldn't promise she'd never regret the choice, but she knew she wouldn't resent his role in it. "But thanks for checking."

And truly, it wasn't second-guessing her decision that held her back from celebrating, it was the fact that keeping this a secret from the ghouls any longer felt like betrayal.

When she told Poe that, he kissed her fiercely. But the hand she thought was aiming for a butt-squeeze was actually him fishing her iCoffin out of her pocket. He pulled back and pressed it into her palm. "Tell them. You're not going to feel better until you do."

"But—we had plans?" There'd been talk of a moonlit walk, of looking for more straggler fireflies. Of swings and kissing.

"We have *lots of* plans," he said, stroking her cheek. "But now we also have lots of time. I'm not going anywhere."

Impulsively, she aimed the iCoffin's camera at them both and clicked the button. The picture should've shown Poe embracing an empty pink ruffled sweater. There should've been floating skullete earrings, a hovering black velvet headband.

But—that was *her* beside him in the photo. She looked overexposed, like the lighting on her was brighter than on him, making her faded or washed out. But she was *there*. In the picture.

It was so strange to see herself on-screen. But even stranger to see how right she looked beside him.

"We have time," she said back to him. "I like the sound of that."

"Come on." He clasped her hand in his and picked up the bag of their trash. "Let me drive you home—or, as close to your home as you'll let me."

She squeezed his hand. Poe's acceptance in the monster world—or her own future in that world—those were problems for another day. She had enough to worry about right now.

And plans—different plans—to make with the ghouls.

Except, it turned out the ghouls already had plans. Clawdeen was babysitting her youngest siblings, Cleo was in a strategy session with her father's campaign staff, Lagoona was swimming, and Frankie must've been in her lab, because that was the only time the ghoul's sparkly green iCoffin went unanswered.

Resigned, Draculaura changed into pajamas and sat down on the edge of her coffin. Humans must need more sleep than vampires, because lately she'd been exhausted.

Or that could be grief.

She'd scheduled a call with her scare-apist, who kept saying grief wasn't linear, it couldn't be predicted. That *mourning* had a *u* in it because it was personal. Unlike morning, it didn't show up every twelve hours, and it didn't go away on a schedule. Dr. Sanguine had affirmed that it made sense Draculaura missed her mom more *now* than she had in hundreds of years. It made sense if she was tired or irritable or a million other emotions and understandable that she was having a hard time being vulnerable or sharing secrets with those who knew her best—because then she'd have to face those emotions. Then they could hold her accountable.

But her scare-apist, like Poe, had urged her to be brave. To trust and try . . . even if Dr. Sanguine didn't know the extent of the trust or secrets she'd be sharing.

Draculaura squeezed her phone. It wasn't fair to be annoyed that no one was available right now when she hadn't been around for them for months. If anything, she'd been actively avoiding them. That ended now.

She typed up a quick group hext and pressed send: I have something I need to tell you all. Meet me in Study Howl before first period.

Now all she had to do was wait for morning, wait for them to show . . . and not lose her courage.

Draculaura had gotten to the classroom where Study Howl was held extra early. She'd spent the time rehearsing what she was going to say and staring at the photo of her and Poe. It felt like proof she could do this. Proof he was real and this change, this choice, had already been made.

Lagoona arrived first. Her hair hung damp against her shirt, and her blue scales were tinged a stinging pink. She was walking scarefully, holding her arms away from her body and wincing as her flip-flopped feet hit the floor.

"You okay?" Draculaura asked.

"Oh, mate." Lagoona sighed. "Apparently the school's not done messing with students. I was just at the pool, and in the middle of my eight-hundred-meter beaststroke, the water started to *boil*."

"Boil?" Draculaura looked closer at Lagoona's pink scales. Those were burns. Like her dad had suffered. Her throat felt tight. "Are you okay?"

"Well, if I ever wondered what global warming on fast-forward would feel like, now I know. It's going to be bloody gruesome." She pressed a finger against her shoulder and winced. "I don't understand why the school is doing this. And I'm sorry—because I know Frankie's going to be so upset, but I can't—"

"Upset by what?" asked Frankie as she entered the room leading a visibly trembling Cleo.

"Osiris-ly! By being locked in the dark! Haven't you been listening?" asked Cleo through a sob.

"I was actually asking—" Frankie pointed at Lagoona, but the sea monster cut her off.

"You were trapped in the dark? What happened, Cleo?"

All the ghouls knew of Cleo's exscream nyctophobia. It was understandable she'd fear the dark after having been trapped in a pyramid for millennia, but anytime it was triggered, the mummy's emotions were as wild as the Nile during flood season. Draculaura knew she wasn't the only one taking a deep breath and preparing to be swept up in it.

"Well," Cleo sniffled and straightened, glancing to make sure she had everyone's attention before she continued. "So, I thought I'd hang up a few of my father's new campaign posters on the way here. Nefera says the ones *she* designed are more persuasive, but she's clearly dead wrong. Anyway, I went to stick one to this door, but it swung open when I pressed the tape to it. And something tripped me and then the door slammed shut and locked, and I couldn't open it. I was banging on it, and I knocked over all these shelves of cleaning stuff, and no one could hear me, and my iCoffin wouldn't work."

"Cleaning stuff?" Now that Draculaura stopped to sniff, Cleo did have a distinctly ammonia aroma. "Was it the custodian's closet? That doesn't even have a lock." She knew that from her school board meeting adventures. Except for the catacombs, there were very few parts of this school she hadn't explored.

If the ghouls expected Cleo to be indignant about having been trapped with cleaning supplies—something the princess had certainly never touched before—she wasn't. She sniffed and burrowed into Frankie's shoulder. "I can't boolieve how *dark* it was. It felt like being entombed all over again."

Frankie patted her back. "You're safe now."

"Yeah, but . . . for how long?" asked Lagoona. She'd sat on one of the tables and pulled her feet up, gingerly hugging them to her chest.

"How did you get out? Did Frankie find you?" Draculaura asked.

"No—it was the eeriest thing. Just when I felt like I might *scream*, the door unlocked and opened. My iCoffin worked again."

"At least there's that?" Draculaura exchanged baffled expressions with Frankie.

Cleo wearily lowered herself onto a chair. Draculaura assumed she must be feeling at least a little better, because as Clawdeen arrived—panting and with sweat dripping down her reddened face—Cleo gasped and declared, "Oh my Ra! Talk about a *purrspiration* problem! You *must* let me recommend my scarab-scented deodorant. It's dynastic and clearly you can use the help. I've never seen sweat that bad."

Clawdeen stepped in front of the other ghoul and bared her teeth. "That's funny, because all I see is a cheating traitor."

Cleo gasped, but Clawdeen ignored her and turned to Draculaura. "Sorry I'm late. Abbey and I got trapped in the furnace room. And I don't know if it malfunctioned or what the school was doing, but it got so hot in there that Abbey's ice powers were evaporating and she was overheating. She passed out, and I had to carry her to the nurse."

"Is Abbey okay?" Lagoona squeaked.

"I think so," said Clawdeen. "Or, at least, she will be once she cools down a bit. Nurse has her soaking in an ice bath."

"Crickey, ice water sounds pretty fintastic right about now," Lagoona said. "My scales are still smoking."

"Um, ghouls, not to downplay any of your mornings, and I'm scary glad you're all okay, but I think Draculaura wanted to tell us something," said Frankie.

"Before she does," Clawdeen interrupted, "I think *Cleo* needs to tell us something about buying votes."

"What are you even talking about?" Cleo asked, picking a

piece of lint off her jacket and scrunching her nose. "Is this mop fuzz? Is there mop fuzz on me?"

"Don't even try and deny it," Clawdeen practically growled. "Nefera already admitted everything. She wasn't even ashamed."

"Nefera admitted *what*, exactly?" Cleo dropped the lint. Her jaw and voice had hardened. "Because I have no idea what you're blabbing about."

"Your dad gave her permission to offer to *pay* monsters for their votes. Bribe them. And he promised her a position on the school board after he's elected in exchange for her help."

Had there been any zombies around, Cleo's jaw could've caught a whole lot of flies in the two seconds before she snapped it shut and growled between gritted teeth. "She's getting *what*? Why wasn't *I* offered a similar deal? That's so unfair! I'd be so much better at—"

"To clarify," said Frankie, "I'm hoping you mean 'it's unfair' to buy votes and that you'd be 'much better' at being on the school board—not that you're bragging about being better at bribery?"

"Of corpse," said Cleo. "Obviously. But also, how dare she? How dare Daddy! I'm going to give him a piece of my mind if he sphinx he can get away with—" She dashed off, grumbling something that sounded like *Why am I never the favorite?*

The ghouls watched her leave—Clawdeen still looked furrious, but Draculaura was fairly certain that Lagoona and Frankie felt as conflicted as she did. It could not be easy being Ramses's child. Especially not when he was playing his daughters off each other for his own gain.

Frankie cleared her throat. "So, um, you wanted to tell us something?"

"Right." Draculaura took a deep breath. After everything they'd been through today—boiling and entrapments and furnace malfunctions—did she really need to put them through this too? But Clawdeen caught her eye and nodded encouragement, and Poe's and Dr. Sanguine's voices echoed in her mind, so Draculaura smoothed down her skirt and spilled it all—about her symptoms and the book in her locker, the research with Ghoulia, the solution . . . and the decision she'd made.

Okay, fine, she didn't tell them *everything*. She'd left out all parts Poe. Not because she was ashamed of him, but because everything about him was so expansive and important. This decision wasn't about *him*; it was about *her*. She wanted the focus on that. She wanted Poe to have his own moment. She wanted them to meet him when she knew they'd be accepting and open-minded. But the rest—she was honest, she was vulnerable. She quoted her mother's journals: *"Change is life's truest gift—the ability to wake each day and experience things that are new and fleeting."*

"It was a fangtastically hard choice. But I've been a vampire for sixteen hundred years—I think it's time I try human. I want to know how my mother felt—to understand her life, her experiences—why she felt like her own humanity was so precious."

They let her talk and talk and talk. It was like she'd released a pressure valve on the secrets she'd been keeping, and none of them was brave enough to interrupt for fear she'd shut down again or explode.

But as soon as she'd stopped, taken a breath, and looked to them for reactions, Lagoona stood up. Her laid-back posture and chill attitude were replaced by crossed arms and an expression like she'd eaten an oyster full of sand and sea scum. "Humans are polluters. They're poisoning the planet and hunting your own kind. Not to mention they're destroying our school. I can't boolieve you'd want anything to do with them."

"But not all of them—"

"There's a right and wrong side here, Draculaura," Lagoona said as she flipped her beachy waves over her shoulder and spun toward the door. "You're on the wrong side."

Draculaura's eyes stung. "Frankie, Clawdeen, you don't agree with her, do you?"

"I think you should do whatever you want," said Clawdeen.

Relief coursed through Draculaura. "Thanks. I know it's—"

"I mean, why should you care what we think now?" Clawdeen continued, curling her claws into fists. "You clearly haven't before. So it's not like anything *I* have to say is going to matter to you."

"What? That's not true." Draculaura put a hand on the ghoul's arm. "Clawdeen—"

The werewolf shook her off. "I need time to process this, and I have somewhere else I have to be. Toralei, Deuce, and I are going to tell monsters about Ramses's bribes. He must be stopped."

"Wait! I could help," she called after Clawdeen.

"No thanks." The other ghoul shook her head and kept walking.

Draculaura barely dared to peek at the one ghoul who remained. "Frankie?" She hardly recognized her voice; it sounded so small.

The other ghoul engulfed her in a hug. This time, Draculaura didn't find it suffocating. Sparky, yes, but suffocating, no. She squeezed back just as tightly.

"Are you mad too?" she whispered.

"No. Of corpse not. I'm surprised, but—also, I feel like you've closed a circuit. Things I've been trying to figure out about you make sense now. I knew you were dealing with *something*; I just didn't know what."

"I didn't know how to tell anyone. I didn't want the choice to be more complicated."

"And *I* didn't know how to help." Frankie pulled back and was hugging herself now. "All quarter, I've felt so, so—like our polarities were crossed—you know?"

"Kinda?" Draculaura's knowledge of volts and circuits only went so far, but she got the gist. "My scare-apist has been on me to *tell* you all what I need. Whether that was space, or quiet, or company. But half the time, I had no clue what I needed—so how could I tell you?"

"I could've asked, though," said Frankie. "Instead of assuming or just *doing* things so that I felt helpful. I mean, you clearly didn't want or need someone carrying your books—but I just felt like I had to do *something*."

Draculaura gave the ghoul another hug. "I love you, you know that, right? I love all of you—and this school, and the monster world. I'm not making this choice because I don't."

Frankie squeezed her until her stitches strained. "You are the most voltageous monster I know—even once you're not a monster anymore, you're still stuck with me." She pulled back and added, "The other ghouls will come around. They're just—this year has been *a lot*. And they all had gruesome days—and classes haven't even started yet."

Draculaura scrunched her forehead and looked around at all the empty tables and chairs surrounding them. "Frankie, did the school do anything to you?"

Frankie froze, her heterochromatic eyes growing wary as she also eyed the room, assessing potential threats. "Not yet?"

"Me either. Does that mean we're next?" The door was still open, and the room's temperature was still stable, but either of those things could change in an instant. Or maybe the school was working on a new, creative form of torture for them. Maybe the walls were about to bleed a new message, or the rugs were going to turn to quicksand. The tables and chairs could form a cage with their metal legs. The lights, the outlets—who knew how those could clash with Frankie's voltage. She shivered.

"Before the school gets all, um . . . *punitive*, let's see if we can talk to the ghouls." Frankie checked her iCoffin and held up the screen to show that there were no new messages. "I'll take Clawdeen and Lagoona. You go find Cleo—she didn't even get to hear your news, and you know how she'll be if she feels like she's last to know or hears it from someone else."

"Be scareful." Draculaura didn't love the idea of splitting up—if ever there was a time for using the bloody system, this was it—but the plan made sense. Cleo needed to hear this from her, plus she was too hurt to face Lagoona yet. Also, she'd be forever grateful if Frankie managed to talk Clawdeen down.

"You too!" said Frankie. The ghoul visibly gulped before squaring her shoulders and turning down the hallway to the right.

Draculaura turned left, the ghouls' angry words echoing in her head as she gave feeble waves in response to greetings called her way. Not that there were many; the hallways were half-empty, with fewer monsters coming to school each day. And before she'd been interrupted, Draculaura was pretty sure Lagoona was about to announce that she wouldn't be back.

After being boiled during swim practice? Draculaura didn't blame her.

But were Lagoona and Clawdeen right that she was wrong? What would her father have said about this choice? There were so many things she wanted to ask him. To tell him. Hex, she'd even patiently sit and listen to one of his long-winded lectures on the evolution of coffin design.

Instead, she'd head to his office—which was no longer his but covered in Egyptian artifacts and more gold than any one room should reasonably contain. Because that's where Cleo would be: confronting her cheating father—hopefully about his cheating and not about leaving her out of the cheating schemes. Though with Cleo, it was quite possibly both.

Before she could reach the office door, a ghoul flew through the wall and blocked her path. Well, not literally. Draculaura could've walked right through Spectra, but passing through a ghost without permission was incredibly rude.

She skidded to a stop. "Oh, hi."

Spectra smiled at her. "Draculaura! I keep meaning to find you, but this school year has been—" She flung her arms out, as if the gesture could encompass all the chaos of attacks and humans and the Van Hellscream Society. "I've practically unlived at the *Gory Gazette* office trying to keep up with the news. And now an *election*? Can you boolieve it?"

Draculaura felt a pit growing in her stomach. "I don't have anything to say. I don't want to be quoted."

Spectra tutted. "Shame. But that's not what I meant or why I stopped you. I wanted to make sure you got the book I put in your locker."

"*You* put it there?" Did that mean Spectra knew she was turning human? If so, why hadn't the ghoul done a big article about it before? She lived—er, unlived—to be the first in the know. "Why? Where did you get it from?"

"Did you *not* want it?" Spectra's eyes narrowed, and Draculaura recognized the look. It was the ghoul's *I-smell-a-story* face. "I saw it fall from one of the boxes the de Niles's servants were carrying out of your dad's office. I thought you might want to have it, but then I wasn't sure if it should go to *you* or with the other boxes."

Draculaura paused and gave her full attention to the ghost. "What do you mean? The boxes came to my house."

"Not all of them." Spectra shook her head. Draculaura had always been jealous of how the ghoul's sleek lilac and lavender hair floated so gracefully—it was almost mesmerizing . . . but now was not the time to be distracted! "The other boxes went to the old library. The one down in the catacombs."

Draculaura shook her own head to clear her thoughts. "But—I went through the boxes myself?" At least twice when she was looking for more information about turning human. "That wasn't all of them?"

"Nope." Spectra pulled out her iCoffin. "Now, would you like to go on record about Ramses stealing your father's books? Because you've got an eyewitness: I saw the jackal-headed servants carry the boxes down there."

"Actually, I would." Draculaura ground her fangs together. Ramses had so much to answer for—and she wanted him held accountable. "But I can't right now. Find Clawdeen. She'll have plenty to tell you about the election. And I *will* go on record saying I have never—*will* never—endorse Ramses to replace my father as head of the school board."

"A tip! I love it."

"But first—can you do me a favor?" Draculaura didn't wait for a nod. "Find Ghoulia. Tell her about the books. Tell her the answer to what's going on with the school might be there."

"Oooh, I can help," said Spectra, her transparent thumbs a blur in her iCoffin's notes app. "A good journalist is a great researcher, you know."

"That would be fangtastic! If you do . . . I'll—I'll sit down with you for a full interview later." Draculaura didn't add *if things go well*.

But Spectra didn't wait around to hear it anyway. She floated away, shouting, "I'm holding you to that. I love the smell of a scoop in the morning."

CHAPTER 19

When the sirens first started blaring, Draculaura was only a few steps from the school board office. At first she didn't know what they were. Her eyes flew to the fire alarm, but it was silent, unblinking. Other monsters were pulling out their iCoffins, checking to see if it was some weird alert of an approaching tornado or exscream weather. It was only when Toralei yowled and pointed to the doors that the pieces clicked into place.

The sensors above the main entrance were flashing. The screeners she'd resented until this moment were shrieking.

"Humans!" yelled Deuce. "That means there are normies on campus."

And, as if his words had drawn them from the shadows, they began to appear.

The humans were dressed all in gray. Balaclavas, shirts, pants, socks, shoes, gloves. Even their faces were covered in grimacing gray masks with screens in the eye holes, so that the only thing visible was their teeth, which flashed in sneers as they shouted back and forth into the walkie-talkies they pulled off the gray belts cinched around their waists.

They'd blended with walls, appeared out of shadows—

looking for just a moment like stone gargoyles, before it was clear they were much more menacing.

Students began to run. It reminded Draculaura of a terrified game of hide-and-shriek because monsters scattered without intention. They headed in every direction, knocking into each other in their panic to get *away*. To get anywhere but where the humans were.

But it seemed as if the humans were everywhere.

The normies didn't seem organized so much as angry. Scared. But they had the element of surprise—nothing like this had ever happened in the school before. Unlike the drills Poe mentioned in New Salem High School, Monster High didn't practice being invaded. They didn't run scenarios for if intruders got on campus.

They never had. They never *should*. Yet here they were.

The humans ran at students, then jumped back when they got close. Draculaura cowered behind a stone pillar and watched as a normie screamed threats at a fleeing group of zombies. The human could easily have overtaken them, but he was keeping a consistent distance between himself and their group, and he screamed in fear when Slo Mo glanced over his shoulder to check how close they were to the human's pursuit.

"Don't eat me," the normie shrieked, before switching back to "You freak! You abomination. You don't belong!" once there was a bigger distance between them.

Draculaura added confusion to fear, and anger, and betrayal, and exhaustion, and all the other emotions floating in the adrenaline soup of her blood. How could the humans act as if *they* were being threatened when they were the threat?

This was a school, a building full of students—teens, children—the only freaks, abominations, or things that didn't belong were the invading normies.

She thought she'd seen chaos before. She'd been run out of towns, pursued by mobs with torches and pitchforks, been forced to flee from her homelands. But she'd never seen mass panic like this. A scenario where the attack was so one-sided—so nonsensical, so incomprehensible. The humans had chosen this, they'd made the plan, they'd been the ones who invaded—yet she was pretty sure that at least one of them had wet their pants. They were choosing to interpret the students' retreat like it was an assault. How could the humans be this scared when they were the aggressors?

But maybe that's how it always worked—maybe it was fear that made people fight. Fear of the unknown, fear of change, fear of some imagined threat to their privilege or status quo. Maybe this entitlement was what made normies so adept at playing both villain and victim. Implementing unprovoked attacks, then claiming ownership of the resulting trauma.

Through the blare of walkie-talkies, Draculaura heard a triumphant "Got one. Mobilize. Out. Out. Out."

And then they were melting out the doors, exiting like the shadows they resembled, the alarms cutting off as they passed back through.

The resulting silence felt heavy—like the intense pressure of breathing against humidity right before a storm explodes.

This explosion was held breaths, it was sobs, repressed screams, shuddering calls home. A collective gasp of *what* and *why*. The blare of the intercom system broadcasting a demand that everyone report to their first period class *now*. *Mandatory. Immediately. Attendance.*

And, as Draculaura rushed toward Clawculus, dodging around backpacks, water bottles, sweatshirts, and other items that had been abandoned in the hall as students had rushed for cover or concealment, a vortex opened in the bottom of her stomach.

The front door to the school still lay open—it was foolish, really, to think that invaders would pause to close it politely as they exited. But as she passed it, Draculaura saw something winking in the sunlight from the edge of the top step.

When she tried to go outside—to examine it closer, convince herself she'd mis-seen and didn't recognize it—an unseen force slammed the doors in her face. They weren't locked, but she couldn't open them. And a hand—Deuce's? Lagoona's?—she wasn't sure, she couldn't see anything but the image of a green phone case sparkling in the sun—dragged her away from the doors, her legs too boneless to protest.

Her heartbeat didn't so much skip as it felt like it stopped altogether—then beat frantically, like it was trying to escape through her ribcage. Either to go searching, or to avoid hearing her suspicions confirmed.

Before she even reached her seat. Before she zeroed in on which chair stayed empty. Before they had even gone through the attendance roster. Before Mr. Mummy had called a name once, twice, three times—his voice becoming increasingly loud, like volume alone could summon a response from a student who clearly wasn't there.

Before Clawdeen gripped her hand, squeezing it frantically, forgetting she'd yelled at her less than an hour ago. Before Mr. Mummy picked up the class phone and called the office.

Draculaura already knew.

Frankie was missing.

Frankie had been taken.

CHAPTER 20

Draculaura was pretty sure that every screen in the school was playing the same video. She didn't know who'd hacked the humans' internet and cloned it to the MonsterWeb already, but there it was on every single monster news channel. All over social medea. Frankie's scream echoed on a loop—even when Draculaura couldn't determine whose device the noise came from or if it was just in her head. She wrapped her legs around her chair to stay upright. The sound and emotional barrage was so disorienting—and yet she couldn't look away from the news playing on the screen mounted at the front of her Clawculus classroom.

The screaming cut off abruptly when a man off-screen held out an oily rag, his silky voice asking, "Do I need to gag you, or can you shut up?"

On camera, Frankie shook her head vigorously as the man said, "At least you monster scum have some sense of self-preservation."

Then the man stepped into view.

Objectively, Draculaura knew the human was probably considered goregeous. Not that it mattered when his actions were so ugly. He had Frankie! He'd threatened Frankie.

Draculaura catalogued him, studied him—so she could figure out how to beat him. His hair was arranged in dark, glossy curls, his eyes the thick green of goblin ooze. His features were straight, symmetrical in that boring way normies preferred—except for when he turned toward the left. Across his cheek and neck were four massive scratch marks—not fresh, but old and faded, yet immediately calling to mind the size of the claws and the strength of whomever was behind them.

The man's voice was deceptively calm as he stepped closer to the camera. "For those of you who don't know me, you can call me Van. Van Hellscream." He pointed to his scars. "I've spent my life pursuing the creature that gave me these. I've been telling anyone who'd listen that monsters were real, monsters were dangerous—" He chuckled in a way that felt practiced. "You can imagine how well that was received. I've been laughed at and called a fool, or insane, or worse."

Van stepped to the side so that Frankie was back in the shot. "Monsters are as real as you and me. As your grandparents or children. And those grandparents and children will never be safe, so long as they exist."

Draculaura had to remind herself that she wasn't his audience. No one in this classroom would be taken in by his slick, smarmy charm. But scared humans? They might boolieve him. Poe's dad had. So had all the invaders. Humans might see sweet, sparky Frankie as a threat. They didn't know the ghoul would rather fall to pieces than hurt anyone.

If *he* hurt her . . . Draculaura ground the nubs of her fangs and watched as Van stepped toward Frankie and kicked the leg of her chair. "Today I have proof. Look at this creature. Its scars are worse than mine. And it's just the tip of the iceberg. There's a whole school full of this sort of abomination. Some even worse. I implore you to join me. None of us are safe until that school—and all the monsters in it—are destroyed."

As he went to kick Frankie's chair again, she shot a jolt of electricity through the metal frame. His expression hardened as the shock passed through his body, his stylized curls frizzed out, and his shoe smoked. "You see the danger? All of them must die."

The next things to appear on the screen were GPS coordinates and a call to action. Draculaura didn't bother to enter the numbers into her iCoffin—so many of her classmates already had. They confirmed what she suspected: Van Hellscream had broadcast the exact location of their school.

"We've got to get out of here," called a voice from the back of the room. Students began to flood from the rear of the classroom toward the door. "They're coming back!"

Apparently Clawculus wasn't the only class that'd come to this conclusion—rooms up and down the corridor were opening, the students inside spilling into the hall, that terrible video still looping on a dozen unsynchronized phones.

"We've got to save her!" yelled Heath.

Draculaura agreed, but she couldn't find her voice, she couldn't catch her breath. Clawdeen had practically dragged her out of their classroom. Lagoona was all but propping her up right now. Apparently their disagreements were insignificant and forgotten in the face of this danger, but Draculaura was reeling. Humans were doing this. *Humans*. And she was . . .

"Me-*how*?" asked Toralei. "What's your big rescue plan?"

"I'll show those normies!" Manny had literal steam coming out of his nostrils as he stomped a hoof on the ground. He looked like he was gearing up to charge—but who?

He clearly wasn't going to stop for answers or plans—he ran straight at the front door.

But instead of crashing through it—he collided and ricocheted.

Manny stood and tried again, lowering his head this time and aiming his razor-sharp horns at the wood. Again, he smashed into the surface and rebounded. There was not even a scratch on the door.

While he lay dazed on the floor, Slo Mo grasped the handle and pulled.

Nothing.

"Need help, buddy? I got you." Heath took the other door, but even when he walked his feet up the wall and heaved with all his might, it wouldn't budge—not even when Clawd Wolf stood beside him, muscles straining as he added his strength to their failed efforts.

"Are they locked?" asked Mr. Rotter.

"No," panted Heath. "They just won't open."

"Oh my Ra, there's normies out there," called Cleo. She was standing by a window, peering around the frame. "Big groups of them. But I don't sphinx they can *see* the school? They're all facing different directions."

"Good. Those protections are holding." Mr. Hackington swiped a hand across his sweaty head.

"Be scareful, ba—*Cleo*," called Deuce.

She rolled her eyes at him, but then shrieked and backpedaled when there was a crash outside.

"Seems like they have found the school," said Abbey. She was pale and still had ice packs strapped across her torso like bandoliers, but she was upright.

There was another crash as something slammed against the outside of the building. Then another.

"We've gotta get out before they get *in*," said Operetta.

"The windows won't open either," said Lagoona. "The latch is unlocked and there's nothing in the way; it just won't slide up."

But as she stood there in front of it, the glass over her head shattered. Shards rained down on her and the other ghouls as a rock landed in the middle of the hallway. The jagged opening above them let in the triumphant shouts of the mob outside and let out the terrified cries of the students around them.

It took Draculaura a moment to realize she'd been cut. At first she was too distracted by Lagoona's fear and by the red scratch above Meowlody's eye. Purrsephone was shaking glass fragments off her jacket, and Toralei was yelling at the werecat twins to step away from the window.

It was only after looking around and realizing that no one else was seriously injured—yet—that she began to register that her own arm stung. That the sheer pink sleeve of her blouse had been slashed midway between her elbow and shoulder—and the fabric around that tear had darkened to red.

Now that she was paying attention, she could feel the wetness running down her arm, dripping off her wrist.

But the floor around her was clean.

As she watched woozily, another scarlet drop fell. But when it hit the stone floor, it was immediately absorbed. She blinked. This was stress, this was the disorientation that preceded fainting. There was no way what she'd just seen was real. Stones didn't drink. And based on the number of times things had been spilled, exploded, iced, or oozed in this hallway, she knew the marble floor wasn't even porous.

Clearly it was time to sit before syncope set in. She lowered her head between her knees, grateful when Lagoona ran over with some seaweed wraps and bandaged her arm. "You're okay, love. It doesn't look deep, and it's stopped bleeding already."

"Thanks." Draculaura lifted her head and met the other ghoul's eyes. She was sure they'd exchange actual apologies later—*if* they made it to later—but right now, they were good.

"Hey!" Heath, never one to use common sense as a compass, had crept back to the window and was peeking out. "Hey, something freaky is happening. The humans—they're complaining. And look—" He pointed out the window, but Draculaura and most of the other students were in no rush to get that close to the glass. She stayed put and let Johnny Spirit drift over and float his ghostly top half through the wall to catch a glimpse of what was happening.

Except . . . "If he can go through the wall—" she started.

"The doors are open," called Deuce. He shut the front entrance quickly, then opened it again—stepped outside, then danced back in. "We can leave."

Johnny pulled his head back into the building. "Everything the normies are throwing is ricocheting off an invisible barrier and bouncing back at them. And everyone who'd been climbing the gate has fallen off. Based on the way they're walking aimlessly and what they're shouting—I don't think they can see the school anymore."

"The protections are back!" said Clawdeen.

"Yeah, but for how long?" asked Lagoona. She was still scarefully shaking bits of glass out of her hair. "I don't trust it."

"We can go after Frankie," Draculaura said softy. The scratch on her arm throbbed, and her head swam. She didn't have time for either of these. They needed to find Frankie, save Frankie—and if the doors were open, that meant they had the chance to leave . . . but go *where*? Do *what*?

"Cleo, it's time to go!" Ramses stormed down the hall, as imperious as ever. Which was impressive, since clearly he'd been hiding in her father's office this whole time. Nefera was right behind him, and two pairs of ushabtis were behind her. They all had their arms full of the golden treasure that had, until recently, lined the shelves of Dracula's office.

"What do you mean? I can't go anywhere," said Cleo. "We've got to rescue Frankie!"

"That's not your responsibility," said Ramses. "Leave that to others. Your job is to—"

"Flee when things get scary?" challenged Clawdeen.

"What? No! It's just—" It was the first time Draculaura had ever seen Ramses flustered. In another situation, it might have been funny. "Let's go, Cleo. We're leaving."

Cleo crossed her arms and took a step backward. "I'm not going anywhere."

Ramses sighed in annoyance and snapped his fingers. Two of the ushabtis immediately dropped the treasures they were carrying and advanced on the ghoul. They each grasped Cleo under an arm and picked her up, then began to march forward, falling in line behind Ramses and Nefera as they continued toward the main entrance doors.

"Put me down! No. Help!" Cleo thrashed her legs and tried to yank her arms free, but the ushabtis didn't slow or even flinch from her kicks.

"Deuce!" she wailed.

The manster's head snapped up from across the hallway and he assessed the situation in a glance. "On it, babe," he called, sprinting to be in front of the servants. "I *see* what's going on— it's *stone-cold* wrong."

It was a code—and not even a hard one, but everything was happening so fast that Draculaura barely had time to shut her own eyes when Deuce called, "Hey, jackal-dudes, look over here" and whipped off his sunglasses.

Ramses and Nefera were ahead of him, too focused on their own escape to notice what was happening behind them. Cleo, the ghouls, and most of the students were savvy enough to have looked away.

But no one warned the ushabtis carrying Cleo. Apparently no one had warned Invisi Billy either—because those three had looked directly into the face of the gorgon when his eyes were unshielded. They were now a trio of stone statues.

"I got you," said Deuce as he helped Cleo down from the servants' stone grasp, adding, "Sorry, Billy," as he passed his statue-classmate.

"Yeah, maybe hold on to that apology, mate. For about twenty-four more hours until he's unstoned and can hear you say it," teased Lagoona.

"At least he went rock-steady while he was visible," said Deuce. "An invisible statue in the middle of the front hall would be concussion city." He seemed reluctant to let go of his ex but did as soon as she reached toward Lagoona.

Cleo stumbled into Lagoona's arms, the other ghoul rubbing her back as she cried.

It took another five steps before Ramses even noticed. He called, "Cleo, keep up," before turning to check. His eyes narrowed on the stone servant statues before he turned his glare to Deuce, nostrils flaring. "I thought we'd eliminated your meddling."

Deuce placed a hand on Cleo's shoulder. "Turns out I'm pretty hard to get rid of."

Cleo covered his hand with her own. "I'm staying. Frankie needs my help."

Nefera stamped a Nile blue wedge sandal. "Daddy, what's *wrong* with Cleo?" She tugged on Ramses's arm. "She's always so—so stubbornly . . . *loyal* to her friends!"

Ramses shook his head, his gaze lingering on his youngest daughter for one more second before he turned back to Nefera and the exit ahead of them. "Not to worry, daughter, she'll grow out of it . . . eventually."

"Well, *her* problem shouldn't be *my* problem." Nefera's lip was quivering. "I can't get locked in again, Daddy. It's too much—too much like the pyramid."

"Quite right," Ramses said firmly. He snapped his fingers at the remaining ushabtis and pointed to the door before addressing Cleo. "Daughter, you *will* outgrow this childish impulse, and when you see the folly of your ways, we can only hope the exits will still be unbarred and you'll be able to rejoin us at the estate."

One more snap of his fingers and he was moving forward without a single glance back at the daughter he was leaving behind.

Cleo kept her chin up, her shoulders back. By silent agreement, no one acknowledged the trembling fingers causing her bandages to flutter. She squeezed Deuce's hand, then stepped away from him, closer to Lagoona.

"Thank you," she told him. "I owe you an apology and I'd like to talk—but I must rescue the school first. Talk after?"

Deuce gave her a half-smile and one of those cool nods that Draculaura was pretty sure had half the remaining monsters swooning just a little. "I'd like that. I'm going to go help Slo Mo, Clawd, and Manny blockade the front door. Stay safe, babe, okay?"

"Of corpse," Cleo said, her smile caught on his.

"Is that a hairball in my throat, or are the two of them just making me gag?" Toralei asked in a faux whisper as Deuce and Cleo watched each other walk away.

It felt wrong to laugh but also impossible not to. And then impossible to stop.

"Ghouls! Now is not the time for hissterics," snapped Headmistress Bloodgood. She had a line of students behind her and was directing them to various exits. "Mr. Hackington, evacuate this group of students through the western catacomb's passage. Mr. Rotter, take the group over there through the tunnels behind the painting in my office."

She pointed to a student with an iCoffin pressed to her ear. "Twyla, if you are talking to your father, ask the Boogey Man *not* to come to the school. That goes for everyone here. We need *fewer* monsters on campus, not more. Hext all your parents or goredians, tell them we're evacuating. Tell them you'll meet them at home." She dropped her voice and muttered to Nightmare, "The last thing we need are clashes between normies and monster parents happening outside the gate."

Draculaura and her friends hadn't been assigned to any evacuation groups, and as the others sped off, the headmistress turned her head toward them. Lagoona still had her arm around Cleo. Clawdeen and Toralei had their hands clasped and faces defiant. Draculaura had her feet planted wide—but that was more to counterbalance the dizziness of her headache and inner turmoil.

"I presume you aren't going anywhere?" asked Headmistress Bloodgood.

"Not until Frankie is back," said Clawdeen, widening her stance like she dared anyone to try and move her.

Headmistress Bloodgood nodded, and if Draculaura wasn't mistaken, there was a gleam of approval in her eye, but she forced a frown and made her voice firm when she said, "I'm meeting with Frankie's parents and a Creature Intelligence Agency team in my office—you may stay, as long as you stay out of the way and out of trouble."

They all gave their agreement in quick, overlapping answers. Draculaura knew that none of them had any intention of staying put or staying out of it, but if a fib was what it took, they'd all nod and lie like their afterlives depended on it.

Because it was possible that Frankie's did.

Giving them one last wary glance, Headmistress Bloodgood turned Nightmare back toward her office and clomped off.

Right before she disappeared from view, a window shattered across the hall. The screams from the evacuees echoed from all directions. Nightmare reared and whinnied. "Ghouls, be scareful," ordered the headmistress before reigning in her horse and galloping away.

"Yeah, so those protections on the school? Sounds like they're gone again," said Toralei.

"They're going to get in. What if they take us too?" Lagoona's eyes were wide with panic as she eyed the windows.

"If you want to leave, it's not too late," said Cleo. And even though she'd just rejected that possibility for herself, there wasn't judgment in her voice as she offered it to Lagoona.

The ghoul chewed her lip, glancing between the broken windows and the hall leading to the closest evacuation route. The hallway chandelier was still swinging from the impact of the last direct hit, the floor was glittering with broken glass.

"No," said Lagoona. "I want to help. Let's rescue Frankie."

"Okay, what's the plan?" asked Clawdeen. Her eyes gleamed with determination. "Maybe we let them take us—and then we stage a rescue from the inside?"

"Is that rescue before or after they *kill us*?" asked Cleo. "Because you heard that Hellscream normie—they want us *dead*."

"Sorry, poochie, I agree with Cleo on this one," said Toralei, though she looked like the idea made her want to vomit. "Voluntary kidnapping is *not* happening."

"Hey!" Spectra floated through the wall a few rooms down from their huddle. Though "floated" felt like the wrong word to use for a ghost moving at such breakneck speed. Gusted? Galed? She was breathless—Draculaura hadn't known ghosts could get breathless—and everything about Spectra's arrival raised goose bumps on her arms.

Another window shattered down the hall, followed by a boom that shook the walls and rained dust down on all their heads. Well, not Spectra's; the dust passed right through the ghost.

"Ghoulia f-found something in the-the Old Library—" Spectra gasped. "In the books that were moved from Dracula's office. She says to follow me. Quickly."

Not for the first time, Draculaura reflected on the impracticality of running in heels. Especially when it was heels on the slick, uneven stones of the catacombs. At least down here they couldn't hear the normies' attacks, but that also meant they wouldn't hear if the normies breached the school.

Draculaura's mouth settled into a firm line. If humans thought they could take on the catacombs, it would be their funeral. Not everything belowground was friendly . . . some of it was fatal.

As they jogged, the ghouls filled Cleo and Toralei in on Draculaura's transformation—taking turns as they ran out of breath. It was clear from Lagoona's sharp tone that she still didn't agree with Draculaura's decision, but then again, Draculaura wasn't sure she did anymore either.

"But you said you might've waited too long, and it might not work, right?" said Clawdeen.

"Maybe there's an amulet in our mansion that could help," said Cleo.

"Purrsonally, I'd rather be dead than human," said Toralei. When Clawdeen shook her head, she added, "Not that you asked *my* opinion."

"No," agreed Draculaura. "I didn't." And if the ghouls were surprised by her stern words, they kept it to themselves. She didn't need more criticism, more opinions. She already had enough pressure, enough voices in her head.

Ghoulia was waiting at the entrance to the Old Library. Draculaura had been in this room only a few times before, but she didn't have a chance to take in the towering shelves stacked haphazardly with rare and ancient tomes before Ghoulia shoved a book in her hands.

It was in Latin, of corpse, but two words immediately jumped off the page. The same two words that had seeped through the library walls: *Sanguis Requiritur*—"blood is required." Draculaura scanned the rest of the passage, then read it again more slowly before setting down the book.

"Well," demanded Cleo. "Are you going to tell us, or are you going to make us wait here until the school walls are breached and our outfits are out of style?"

"It's my—my *blood*." Draculaura met Ghoulia's eyes. "The message on the wall, it wasn't about me turning human. Or, at least, not directly."

Ghoulia nodded, her mouth pressed in a grim line.

Turning toward the other ghouls, Draculaura gestured helplessly at the book before she could find the words. "The protections on the building are based on blood from Dracula's line. The school needs my blood—literally—to protect itself."

"So, the reason the doors unlocked to let monsters out and that the humans temporarily stopped being able to see or attack the school—" Clawdeen's eyes were huge as she pointed to the kelp bandages on Draculaura's arm.

"And the reason it only lasted for a little while is because you're almost not a vampire anymore," said Lagoona, gnawing on her lip. "Which means Dracula's line is ending."

"This was what my dad was trying to tell me the night he died." Draculaura's legs felt weak, and she sat on the floor amid the piles of books that Ghoulia had removed from their boxes during her search. "He wanted to warn me what was going to happen—not just to me, but to the school. I didn't listen—and this is all my fault. If I'd heard him . . . I'm such a deadweight."

"That's not helpful right now," said Cleo, placing a hand on her shoulder. "Plus, I won't let you talk about my friend like that. She's bloody fangtastic, and I won't let anyone say otherwise."

It felt wrong to smile—Frankie was in danger, they were *all* in danger. But Cleo sounded so indignant—both scolding and protective—that Draculaura couldn't help but grin. In doing so, she realized just how blunt her fangs had become.

"Not to add too much pressure, love," said Lagoona. "But what are you going to do?"

The smile slipped from her face, replaced by a sinking, drowning sensation. It was as if the stones of the school were sitting on her chest. They might as well be—because this choice, to save or doom the school, was all on her shoulders.

This decision was supposed to be made. She was supposed to have moved past the part where she was creating mental pros and cons lists all day long and living in limbo between two impossible possibilities. But maybe the reason she hadn't felt at peace with her choice was that she'd chosen *wrong*.

How could she want to be human when humans did this? How could she blame all humans when Poe was so good? How could she turn her back on monsters and her school?

Once, when she'd been dithering about something stupid, something trivial, like whether to go to a party or say yes to a date with a manster whose name she couldn't remember, Abbey had told her, "You do not have all day. It's like cracking ice—you must decide to swim or leave. Wait too long, and the decision is made for you."

It was possible she'd already waited too long. It was possible her indecision had doomed them all.

But it was impossible not to at least try . . .

Before she could open her mouth to say as much, Toralei hissed with impatience. "I'm not sure why we're all acting like there's a choice here. She has to get fanging—she has to save us . . . and the school."

"Um, thanks for stealing my moment," Draculaura said with a forced laugh. "I was already going to say I'd do it. But— what about Frankie? Shouldn't we worry about her *first*?"

"You focus on protecting the school," said Cleo. "We'll save Frankie."

"She's right," said Lagoona, cutting off Draculaura before she could protest. "What's the point of rescuing Frankie if they can just turn around and take her again? Or take one of us? Or destroy all of Monster High? Frankie would want you to protect the school—she's spent the whole school year trying to convince everyone to stay."

"Okay." Draculaura nodded and stood. "I just need to go . . . drink some blood." Her stomach rebelled at even saying the words, but she could do this. She *had* to do this. "I'll just close my eyes, pinch my nose, and gulp down a few sips of bloody beet smoothie from the creepateria. Then, easy-queasy, school saved."

Ghoulia shook her head and spoke in Zombie. "It must be directly from a human source. The book was specific about this. No blood banks, no infused baked goods, or spiked smoothies."

"Oh. Right." She'd read that, she knew she'd read that. Apparently she'd just blocked those facts.

"So fresh from a vein. Or is it arteries? I always mix those up," said Cleo.

"Not helpful, love," whispered Lagoona.

"New plan," said Clawdeen, as Draculaura braced herself against a bookshelf and tried to stop the room from spinning. "You sneak off campus and literally just grab the first unarmed human you can find. Give them a quick bite and get back as fast as you can. She doesn't have to drain them, right?" The werewolf turned to Ghoulia, who nodded to confirm this.

"Sure. Right. Quick bite. Back." Draculaura took a wobbly step toward the door, trying to hide that even the thought of this plan made her dizzy.

"Do you want company?" asked Clawdeen. "Or need someone to, like, hold a normie down?"

Draculaura shuddered away from the violence of that image. This was going to be scareable—probably the worst thing she'd done or would do in her whole afterlife. She didn't want— couldn't have—one of the ghouls witness it. What if afterward it was all they pictured every time they talked to her: the moment she'd attacked a defenseless normie?

It might save the school, but it simultaneously proved that the humans were right about their worst accusations: that monsters were bloodthirsty, violent creatures who attacked and harmed innocents.

"I have to do this alone," she said softly. "I appreciate the offer, but since I have to do this, I want privacy." The thing she still hadn't told them, the piece that only she and Ghoulia knew, was that she might not survive. But that information would only make them worry—and it was something she *couldn't* let them witness.

"As long as you don't use *privacy* as an excuse to chicken-out," purred Toralei.

"*Kitten*." Clawdeen's voice was as sharp as her claws, and her ghoulfriend blinked a few times before lowering her eyes.

"Honest to claw, I'm sorry," said Toralei. "That wasn't okay. I'm just—tired of feeling helpless. You know?"

Draculaura gave a small nod. She knew that feeling a little too well. "What will you all do while I'm gone?" She asked the question but didn't stick around for the answer. When Ghoulia began assigning the other ghouls jobs—something about hacking the human internet and replacing anti-monster posts with footage from today that showed the humans as aggressors and made it clear the monster students hadn't fought back—Draculaura took the opportunity to slip out.

CHAPTER 21

Draculaura's iCoffin began to vibrate as soon as she stepped out of the passage and into the forest. She assumed it was an update or a scolding from the ghouls—annoyed she'd left before they could make a whole big thing about her leaving. Or maybe an Eekmergency Broadcast about the attacks on the school. She'd tried squeezing a few additional drops of blood out of the cut on her arm as she exited, hoping it would provide even a temporary boost in the school's protection, but the crimson drips had pooled on the floor—not been absorbed by the stone like when she'd first been cut. And there hadn't been even a momentary pause in the bombardment. The walls of the tunnel had vibrated with the impacts of the nonstop rocks and bricks being thrown at the school.

Like she'd needed more proof there was no time to waste.

She pulled up her hexts as she ran through the forest. She needed a human, any human—well, any human she could surprise and overpower, which meant not a member of the angry armed mob outside the school gates.

I have to see you. It's an emergency.

I mean it—not joking. Not an emo-poet emergency. A real one.

You're in danger.

She was already in danger. Everyone at Monster High was. Frankie was. Honestly, she didn't have time for *more* danger or emergencies.

She tapped out a quick message: I'm a little busy—stuff at school.

Poe's reply was immediate. Call me, please. It's important.

She didn't want to. And she knew why she didn't want to. Because the last time he'd seen her was the last time he'd get to see her in this almost-human state. The last time she'd seen him, they'd celebrated the fact that she wasn't going to change back. They'd toasted with sour gummy animals and kisses on swings and made a list of future plans—pancakes and camping trips and prom. The last time she'd seen him, she'd told the truth— but that truth had changed, and she worried he'd feel lied to.

Despite all this, she pulled up his number and dialed. Because if she was honest, she wanted to hear his voice. She was still jogging down the path toward New Salem and she'd hang up as soon as she found a human to bite—but until then, was it wrong to want him to distract her?

The phone didn't even ring once before he gasped, "Where are you?"

"Just outside campus. Why?" She looked around the woods, keeping her head and voice low, because there were humans nearby and she didn't know if they were armed. She'd need the element of surprise on her side and couldn't afford to be caught unaware.

"My dad—" Poe swore under his breath. "Draculaura, it's bad. He wasn't going fishing or on business trips. He's *in* it. He's in the Van Hellscream Society—and I tried to talk him out of it, but he didn't even *hear* me. He just kept saying that they're planning something big."

Something *big*? She hoped he was just behind on news—that the *big* had already happened—because the thought of *more* felt like more than she could handle. And Poe—the heartbreak in his voice broke her own.

"Oh, Poe, that's awful. I'm so sorry—about your dad. I'm—" She didn't have the words to tell him she understood what he was feeling, because *she didn't*. Betrayal like that was unfathomable. She pressed a hand to her chest. "I'm so sorry."

"*I'm* the one who needs to be apologizing. That's not the worst part." He sounded so hollow that she braced herself against a tree as he continued, "I didn't know. I didn't mean—what I'm trying to say is—" She heard the wince in his voice as he swore again. "He found my notebook. He brought it with him to go meet them."

"Your notebook? What—" And then it hit her—a combination of the desperation in his voice and her own worst fears. "The notebook—the one where you wrote down all my answers? The Van Hellscream Society has it?"

If so, they knew everything. They had Frankie and the notebook, and as soon as they connected her to what he'd written there, they'd know way too much. Her goals, her fears, her vampire weaknesses. They'd have all the ammunition they needed to hurt her in the most manipulative ways.

And then they could use that intel to attack the rest of them.

"I never should've written it down. I just—I wanted to know everything about you." Even over the phone, Draculaura could hear the tension in his voice, knew he'd be pacing, vibrating with it. "I wanted to make sure I never accidentally hurt you—and now I've given it to people who *will*."

This was her fault. Her responsibility. Telling normies about monsters was forbitten, but she had answered every one of his questions. And now all that information was in the hands of those who would use it to harm. She'd told them exactly how they could . . .

"I'm going to get it back," Poe said. "My dad asked me to come along to the meeting and I said no, obviously, but I could call him, tell him I changed my mind—ask where to meet them. I'll find it and get it back—"

"Don't go anywhere near them," she said. "I'll figure it out. I'll do that as soon as—as . . ."

Her voice broke and she could hear the alarm in his when he asked, "What's wrong? I mean, what *else* is?"

"Things have changed, and I have to—" No, that wasn't right. She couldn't present this to him in a way that made her the victim. If she was going to do this, she was going to own it. "I've changed my mind. I'm going to transform back."

"What?" She could hear how staggered he was in that single word; she felt it like a blow to her chest.

He deserved a full explanation. He deserved to hear this face-to-face and with time to process and understand. But she couldn't give him that. Instead, she offered the briefest rundown she could manage—the attack, Frankie's abduction, Dracula's bloodline, and her role in the protections.

"You don't owe them this—" Poe said softly. "You don't owe them your life, your future."

"Except, I want to." Saying the words out loud was hard because it meant admitting she'd been lying to herself. "I think—no, I *know*—I was scared before. You made humanity sound like such a prize—and it *is* a prize. But not mine. I was so focused on what I'd gain, I lost sight of what I'd be giving up. And I can't give that up. I can't give up who I am—I don't want to be someone else."

She swatted a low branch out of the way. "I don't *want* to drink from anyone. I really don't want to have to do that—but I *do* want to stay a vampire and stay part of the monster community. I don't like the choice I have to make, but it is my choice—and I desperately want the outcome, to keep my school safe." She'd kept her voice firm, but tears coated her cheeks. She was going to do this—and she was going to have to live with that decision. She wasn't sure she could.

"Then drink from me," he said.

"What?" She dropped the phone and had to fumble in the fallen leaves and underbrush to find it. Even after she did, she couldn't raise it back to her ear right away because there were voices nearby. Too many voices. Too close.

By the time she looked at the screen, the call had disconnected. But there were five new hexts instead:

I meant it.

If you have to—let me help

On my way to our spot.

Let me

Please

She wondered if he was being vague in case his dad got ahold of his iCoffin. She didn't blame him—couldn't think about his notebook just now or all her indiscretions it contained. What were the chances the Van Hellscream Society couldn't read his handwriting? It was scary messy. She'd had a hard time deciphering it on his note to her, and she'd assumed he'd used his neatest writing then, not the speedy scrawl he'd have used to keep up with her prattling.

She clung to this wishful thinking as she crept cautiously through the woods. Avoiding the groups of humans searching for the school but tromping right through a grouping of three shiny leaves. Venus McFlytrap had told her all about that plant— humans got poison ivy, vampires did not. At this point she was somewhere between the two. She deserved an itchy rash. She deserved so much worse for doing what she was about to do.

But she couldn't think about it as she put one foot in front of the other, forcing her mind to focus on anything *but* what was next.

Poe had beat her to the cemetery. His blue car was the only one in the parking lot, and he was pacing the path by his mother's grave, his face paler, his shoulders bowed. Those eyes—red rimmed, but still the clearest blue Draculaura had ever seen. A window right into how much he was feeling. It hurt to meet them.

She wouldn't let herself look away.

"I've said all along that I won't pressure you—and I'm not going to ask you to change your mind now," he said softly. "But I just want to make sure that this is what *you* choose. I don't want you to have any regrets."

"I'm going to have regrets—no matter what I choose." Draculaura reached for his hand. "And that decision has been tearing me apart, Poe. I wish I could be both. I wish I could make a choice that didn't involve . . . *you know*." She ground her dull fangs. "If I thought I could leave Monster High behind and be a human, be happy—without being haunted by everything I'd abandoned . . ." She shook her head. "Part of me wishes that I could live with that choice—but I can't."

She watched his jaw go tight as he swallowed, his answer a stiff nod.

She forced her voice to sound light—aiming for teasing and landing somewhere more desperate: "And I don't suppose you've changed your mind? Want to come join me on the freaky side? Enroll at Monster High? You could escape all your dad's . . . um, pressure. We have soccer too."

Poe slid his hand from hers and raked it through his hair. Today's curly chaos didn't feel as charming; it was a visual demonstration of his torment. "I can't leave him. I hate him *and* I still love him. He's a mess right now—and everything he's caught up in with Van Hellscream—it's vile, unforgivable. But he's going to need me. Someone's got to protect him from himself. Someone's got to convince him he's wrong."

She wanted to tell him that saving his dad wasn't his job—but saving the school wasn't hers either. And of corpse they were both making the choices they were to protect their families. Because the ghouls were all the family she had left. Just like it was only him and his father.

Neither of them lived in a world where they'd give up on those they loved.

"Do you know where they're meeting? Where they'd have Frankie?"

He blinked, then nodded. "I can find out. I'll track his phone and send you the location." He pulled his human phone from one pocket and took a picture of the screen with the iCoffin he pulled from his other. She felt hers buzz in her pocket with his hext. "And, for what it's worth—what the humans have done, with the school, with the videos, with Frankie—I'm sorry. I know that's not enough, and I'm not just saying that to you— I'm going to say it to everyone who will listen. There are already anti–Van Hellscream protests popping up. I'll be at every one. Do anything."

"Poe," she said.

"I don't expect you to ever forgive my dad," he said, eyes bright with apology, "but he wasn't always like this. Before Mom died . . . he wasn't perfect, but he wasn't like *this*." He gnawed on his lip. "More than anything, I hope Frankie's okay."

She wanted to spend hours studying his face. Memorizing the constellations of his freckles, the roadmap of his expressions that would no longer guide any part of her journey. But any lingering, any delay felt indulgent, reckless, selfish. His words were a reminder of the urgency—*was* Frankie still okay? Was the school?

"Ready?" he asked her. "If we're doing this—I need you to do it now, before I chicken out."

She wasn't ready. She'd never be ready. She nodded.

He sat down on a bench, sliding an arm around her shoulder when she curled up beside him. Her knees resting on his thigh when she tucked her feet up beside her on the seat. They'd sat like this before—in very different situations.

She leaned closer. Her nose nuzzling against his neck, her hitched breath ghosting across his throat as she parted her lips.

Poe turned his head, not away from her, baring his neck, but toward her. Leaning down to capture her mouth in a searing kiss. "I needed that," he said against her temple. "I needed one last kiss."

"Last?" she asked, pulling back to see his eyes.

They were so close that she could see herself reflected in his irises. The image began to shimmer, distort, and it took her a moment to realize that the pain in them was brimming, about to overflow.

Her eyes welled to match his—and it made it easier, not being able to see him clearly as she asked, "We're never going camping, are we?"

"No," he whispered.

"Or riding roller coasters."

He shook his head, jarring a single tear free to slide down his cheek.

She pressed her lips together, hoping she could hold in the sobs long enough to reach the conclusion of this conversation, the conclusion of *them*. "You're never going to teach me to surf, or drive. I'm never going to see one of your soccer games or try your mom's pancake recipe." All these plans they had. All these things for once she was human.

"Love, after today—after *this*—we're never going to see each other again."

The sob that burst from her throat felt like it had been ripped from her hollowed heart.

He looked just as shattered as he pressed a kiss to her temple and whispered, "We can't."

"Please," she begged.

"After this—" He shook his head, a second tear, his other cheek. Hers were already coated. "The Van Hellscream Society wants to *kill* all monsters. I won't be the one who leads them to you." He swore and tightened his grip on her. "If anything happens to Frankie because of what I wrote in that notebook, I won't be able to forgive myself." Poe swallowed and leaned his head against her, his voice desperate against her hair. "But if anything happened to *you*? I couldn't live with myself."

"And if monsters found out about your notebook—even though you didn't give it to Van Hellscream on purpose . . ." She shivered. The context mattered, but the monster world wasn't dealing in nuance and details right now.

"I'd endanger you—you'd endanger me. And I love you too much to let that happen." He pressed his mouth against hers again and repeated himself, "I love you."

The words were raw. They scraped all the way down to her broken heart where they stung instead of sang. He pulled back and looked away from her, offering his throat bare and vulnerable in the fading light. It didn't matter if she felt it too. She wasn't sure if it was crueler to tell him or keep it secret.

In the end, she whispered her declaration against his neck—right before she bit.

The salt from her tears—or maybe they were his—mixed with the salt from his blood.

She drank.

CHAPTER 22

The pain began as soon as the blood hit her throat. The first swallow was hard, the second was agony, the third impossible. She was pretty sure she only managed to choke it down because her throat was open in a silent scream.

That would have to be enough.

Poe was there. Then he wasn't. He'd laid her down on the bench, kissed her forehead, whispered something, and left. His too-pale hand pressed to twin wounds on his too-pale neck.

Was that real or something her imagination had conjured?

The same way it'd pulled out images of her mom—coughing, dying, laughing, running through a wildflower meadow in Dacia with a crown of them in her long hair, her arms spread wide as she told her daughter, "This world, it's so beautiful." Dracula—flying, using hypnosis, and attempting to teach her to drive, as well as the vampire lessons she'd repeatedly failed to master. The ghouls.

She was pretty sure she'd called all their names.

Or maybe it had just been screams.

For someone who passed out frequently, fainting sure failed her now. Instead she was forced to stay conscious and experience this.

Pain. Like each vessel in her blood was bursting. And maybe it was. Maybe the transformation was cellular. Maybe she wouldn't survive it.

Maybe that would be a kindness. Pain like this didn't feel survivable.

She was bleeding. She could feel blood seeping from her nose, her ears. Her mouth still tasted full of it, but when she swiped her tongue along her teeth, it was clear her gums were bleeding. Her fangs were still dull, maybe even more so. How had fangs that blunt managed to pierce Poe's skin? She held up a trembling hand and saw the shadow it cast on her stomach.

Those didn't feel like good signs.

She'd waited too long. There hadn't been enough vampire in her blood to resurrect the protections at the school. There hadn't been enough to complete the transformation.

She'd waited too long.

She'd waited too long—and she'd lost it all.

CHAPTER 23

When the pain began to recede, it left behind a dull cold. *I'm going numb*, thought Draculaura. *It didn't work. This is how I die.*

But then the numbness collected in a spot at her abdomen. She closed her eyes, waiting for the end, hoping it would be quick and that she wouldn't have to carry this guilt and regret into whatever came next. *If* anything did.

No.

The word was in her own voice first. Then her dad's. Her mom's. Poe's. Cleo, Clawdeen, Frankie, Lagoona, Ghoulia. Ms. Heaves. Headmistress Bloodgood. Their voices joined hers in a chorus that rejected this fate.

Her hand still trembled, but she ignored that and used it to grasp the back of the bench and pull herself into a semi-upright slump.

She wouldn't go down like this. Monsters needed her. And she needed this sacrifice to have been worth it.

There was a flair of heat in her stomach. It spread quickly—like flames along her veins, arteries. It was a new pain, but she welcomed it. She exhaled through it, let it warm her body, flow through her to her teeth. She felt her fangs elongate—razor sharp against her tongue. Sharper than they'd ever been before.

She sat up, no longer needing the support of the bench. And though she was tentative when she stood, expecting her legs to wobble beneath her, they were steady. Strong.

That was the word.

She felt *strong*. Not just stronger than she'd been while in pain, but stronger than she'd been since . . . since before she could remember.

She flexed her fingers, curled her toes. Focused her thoughts— and flew into the air.

Her transformation into a bat happened somewhere around the tree line. She wasn't sure exactly when because the change—one she'd always failed to accomplish before—was seamless, painless.

Her laughter was bitter as it echoed into the night, unable to keep up with the speed of her wings as she soared back toward campus. *Dad would be so proud.* He'd always loved flying— said it was the truest form of freedom.

She added that thought to the heap of others she couldn't process right now. *Dad.*

Poe. What he'd said. What they'd agreed to. What she'd done. Goodbyes and declarations and blood. She was locking all these topics in a mental coffin. One she wouldn't reopen until she had the time and space to process them.

Draculaura lowered her left wing and glided downward toward the spire of Monster High's bell tower. There were clusters of normies at the gates. They'd encircled the school and some were scaling the wall.

Their hatred, their prejudice—they weren't welcome here. And she was about to let them know just how very uninvited they were.

Draculaura knew the school needed Dracula's blood—her blood—but did it matter where she put it? She'd changed back to her ghoul form and hovered over the building, ignoring the shout of the humans massing outside the gates as they spotted her and voiced their horror at her very existence. Their opinions didn't matter to her. The one human whose voice she wanted to hear had gone silent, had left his iCoffin beside her in the graveyard—making it impossible for her to even call to check if he was okay and to hear his voice.

Message received; he'd meant what he said about final good-byes and permanent distance.

Two hours ago, when she'd cut her arm on the broken window—a cut that was now fully healed with no trace of a scab or a scar—the school had absorbed the blood like dry sand. When she'd tried a second time, the blood had pooled, the stones rejecting it. Maybe it didn't matter *where* she bled. It was the blood itself that was important.

But just in case, she floated slowly down to the front steps, landing beside a group of creatures.

"Draculaura, get inside," ordered Mr. Rotter. "No students should be out here. The normies are almost through the gates. It's not safe."

"It's not safe for you either," she said, before turning to Headmistress Bloodgood and pointing to the weapon she was brandishing from the back of Nightmare. Draculaura wasn't exactly sure what the headmistress planned to do with the sword, but the blade looked lethally sharp.

"I need to borrow that," she said, infusing her words with the convincing charisma that her father had tried (and failed) to teach her on so many occasions. Now the power came effortlessly, and she watched the protest melt off Bloodgood's face as she handed over the weapon.

"Thank you." Normally the heft of a sword that came up to her shoulder would've staggered her, but Draculaura carried it with ease as she glided down the steps, pausing before the gray block of marble in the lower right. It was carved with the year of the school's founding. *A cornerstone*, her father had called it. Telling her it was *the foundation, the first piece of the school, the most important.*

Tonight, it would be the bloodiest.

Just because there wasn't time for hesitation didn't mean Draculaura didn't want to hesitate. Every woozy lightheaded feeling was still there, shimmering under the façade of her determination. *The school.* She was doing this for Monster High. For *Frankie.* For herself.

She'd given up a lot to be here in this moment, and she wasn't going to waste that sacrifice.

So, she raised the blade of the sword to her palm, then looked away. She thought of her dad, her mom, her friends, the creatures, and all the monsters who needed this place to exist. It was so much more than a building or pop quizzes or sports teams—it was a place where *all* monsters belonged, where they were *all* accepted. She wasn't letting anyone take that away.

Draculaura lowered the sword to her skin.

And perhaps the cut went a little deeper than she intended, or perhaps it was only as deep as the school's protections demanded.

At the top of the stairs, Ghoulia pushed through the door, calling her name. But Draculaura barely glanced away from where the blood was flowing from the cut, coating her cupped palm. Ghoulia handed a book to Headmistress Bloodgood, pointing to something on the page. The woman started to read some sort of chant aloud. Mr. Rotter and Mr. Hackington joined in.

Draculaura could feel the throb of pain, the blood dripping off her wrist. Her vision was starting to warp, so she averted her eyes as she took a deep breath and pressed her wet hand to the cornerstone.

It heated beneath her touch, seeming to suck in even the blood that was rolling down her arm—absorbing it like a pumice stone placed in water at the start of a pedicure.

Draculaura dared a glance and saw the rock was doing exactly that. There was no blood visible—as soon as it hit the surface, the stone drew it deep inside. And it was glowing. First pale gray, then white, then gold, then red—so hot to the touch that she could feel her skin cracking. When she finally wrenched her hand away, she expected the palm to be blistered with burns.

Instead it was smooth, unmarked—all traces of the sword slash healed.

"Well done, my dear ghoul," said Headmistress Bloodgood. "Now, we wai—" But before she could finish her statement, that red glow spread outward from the stone—not toward the building, but across the grounds. It moved through the statues, the fountain, which boiled briefly as the glow passed over it, and continued toward the fences.

All those humans who'd been climbing them? The ones clustered in the mob trying to break down the gate? The ones waiting just behind with torches and threats of what they'd do when they got inside?

They were too preoccupied with their fear and hate. They never saw it coming.

The jolt of power propelled them backward—almost as if the fence had been suddenly electrified. They landed on their backs and faces a hundred yards away. The first to clamber back to their feet did so shakily, dizzily. Their disorientation extended beyond the physical effects of the blast. They turned in confused circles, cupped their eyes, and asked, "Where did it go? What *was* that? Did we blow it up?"

Draculaura wasn't sure what they saw—or what they didn't. She didn't much care, so long as the school was invisible to them. So long as the school was safe. She nodded once and cradled her palm against her chest. There might not be a mark, but there was a memory.

Draculaura locked eyes with Ghoulia. "Do you know where the ghouls are? We need to go get Frankie." And they needed to do it before the normies figured out they'd failed here. Before the Van Hellscream Society decided to make an example of her.

Ghoulia pointed behind her to where the ghouls were watching wide-eyed from the school's double-doored main entrance.

"Fangtastic." She hovered up the stairs and hugged Ghoulia. "Do you want to come with us? Or—would you mind staying here and going over everything you found on the protections and bl—"—she nodded down at her hand—"with Headmistress Bloodgood?"

Ghoulia responded in Zombie, "I think the second plan is more my speed."

Draculaura hugged her again. "I couldn't have made it this far without your brains. Thank you." She turned to the headmistress and held out the sword.

Headmistress Bloodgood re-sheathed the weapon. "I don't boolieve I want to know what you ghouls will be up to."

"Probably not," agreed Draculaura.

Headmistress Bloodgood pressed her lips together but nodded. "Be scareful. And thank you—whatever you did—it saved us."

"Ghoulia will fill you in," Draculaura called from within the group hug that had engulfed her as soon as she stepped inside the main hall.

"Oh my claws, ghoul—you were amazing," said Clawdeen.

"I know it was hard, but you *did it*! Truly fintastic," added Lagoona, her words being smothered by arms and shoulders as the other ghouls jostled to squeeze her tighter and add their own praise.

Even Toralei had participated, before she pulled back and added, "So, that whole coming up with a plan to save Frankie part? Not going so well."

"Have there been any new videos?" Draculaura asked, then, based on their expressions, knew she didn't want to know.

"Just one," said Clawdeen. "That same Van dude, but that can't really be his name, since the Van Hellscream Society has been around for millennia and he's not *that* old. He held up a scalpel and said he was going to slice her stitches and see what color she 'oozed.'"

Draculaura inhaled slowly. She should've expected as much. Maybe even worse, knowing they had Poe's notebook. But if they hadn't cut her yet, then there was still time to prevent it. "What's the plan?"

"I'm saying we dress up as normies and go into their town and ask where the Van Hellscream group meets—then we use our disguises to sneak in. *Then* we drop them, scare the normies, and rescue her," said Clawdeen.

Draculaura winced. Yeah, they weren't doing that.

"And *I* say we use one of the artifacts from my Uncle Tut's collection. We can just curse them all with bad luck, bad posture, and bad skin. While they're all distracted, we free Frankie. Easy-queasy."

"Yeah, because your curses *never* backfire," said Clawdeen.

Cleo stepped forward, chin raised, "And *your* bad attitude never—"

"New plan," said Draculaura, moving between the glowering ghouls. "You follow *my* plan." She braced herself for their objections—but the ghouls just nodded and fell quiet.

Well, that was new. Apparently forcefully expelling dozens of humans with the power of your blood bought some reverence.

"What do you want us to do?" asked Lagoona when Draculaura had been stunned silent for a beat too long.

"Right, um." Draculaura took a deep breath. "I know where Frankie is being held. It's a warehouse on the edge of New Salem. We're going there and getting her back." She didn't tell them how she'd gotten that address; there was no way she could. There wasn't enough time to catch them up or explain Poe in a way that would make them trust him.

Instead, she kept explaining, going down the line of ghouls, pointing to each of them individually and telling them their assigned part of the plan. She selected their roles based on their freaky flaws—or scary strengths, as they really should be called. And the ghouls seemed to recognize that leaning into the things that made them unique was a better idea than rushing in and being loud.

"That's clawsome," said Clawdeen, and even Toralei purred her agreement before giving her ghoulfriend a quick smooch and heading off to enact *her* role in this plan.

Toralei would be staying behind and working with Spectra to spread the news that the school's power was back, that the protections were resealed, and that the safest place in the world for monsters was currently Monster High.

Draculaura had no doubt that the werecat was going to give her message some dramatic spin, but she couldn't worry about that now. They had the more dangerous part of the plan to enact.

They had Frankie to save.

She just hoped they weren't too late.

CHAPTER 24

Ghoulia had set the ghouls up with body cameras before they left—everyone but Draculaura. She'd declined, worried it would weigh her down or get in the way during the battier portions of her plan.

But the other three ghouls had the cameras strapped to their chests. Cleo complained that the gray color didn't suit her. Clawdeen said that if she'd had time, she could've designed a harness that didn't ruin the lines of her outfit. Lagoona had just said, "Cool" and slipped it over her head.

All three of those cameras were currently trained on the warehouse in front of them.

Cleo had bribed one of her ushabtis to drive them to the address from Poe's hext, but the jackal-headed servant had peeled rubber out of the far end of the parking lot before the ghouls could offer him double to stay and wait for their return.

So, how they'd get *back* to Monster High after they faced down the Van Hellscream Society and saved Frankie? That was a problem for future-Draculaura to figure out. Right now, she was a little busy. She had an enormous warehouse to break into and a beast friend to locate.

Draculaura had always seen well in the dark, but tonight's adrenaline had her precision cranked up to levels she'd never managed even on Mr. Hackington's microscopes. The building was made from steel panels. They'd been white, now they were dingy, spotted with mold and rust and other mystery stains. There was an immense set of gray double doors in the center of the side facing them. They'd been constructed from metal plates bolted together, each half large enough to load a long-haul truck. There was no way to open those discretely, so there was no way that was their entrance. A row of small square windows ringed the building, and an even smaller line of brick-sized ones striped the upper level close to the black metal roof.

A few of those upper windows were open—or maybe missing, having been broken during the years this warehouse had been empty. Clearly the Van Hellscream Society had decided they needed a building as creepy and nefarious as their intentions.

"There's our entry point," said Draculaura, pointing to the missing upper windows. "I can go batty and fit through there. Then I'll fly down and let you in"—she pointed again, this time to a door in the far corner of the building, barely visible from their hiding spot behind the dumpsters—"there. If that doesn't work, I'll hext you the new plan. Maybe one of the lower windows opens."

As the ghouls nodded and she took off into the sky, Draculaura wondered if Poe would recognize this version of her. No, not just the bat form—but *her* taking charge, making plans, leading. It felt unfamiliar but also *right*. Like shrugging on a jacket that fit perfectly. Dracula had always told her she had the ability to be a fangtastic leader—all she needed was the desire.

But maybe she'd just needed the right motivation.

Soon she was flapping her way through the window and inside the building. Luckily, the door she'd pointed out to the ghouls was in a dark corner behind a stack of mushy cardboard boxes. Draculaura did a quick, ceiling-level loop of the perimeter. She saw plenty of henchmen and henchwomen. Most of them were still dressed in their gray intruder apparel, though they'd ditched the masks. At least twenty of them clustered around computers and monitors set up on metal shelves and plugged into overloaded extension cords. The whole thing looked more firetrap than coordinated-evil, but she guessed it could be both.

She hadn't seen Frankie. Or Van, the man who'd threatened her in the videos.

Draculaura whispered all this to the ghouls as they squeezed in through the door, propping it open with a wedge of cardboard.

"Okay, Clawdeen, you're up," she whispered.

The ghoul stuck her nose in the air and inhaled dramatically. No one's smelling abilities matched a werewolf's. Clawdeen was always the first to know if someone changed perfumes or if the milk in the creepateria had gone murky. She could tell if Lagoona had snuck in swim practice during Study Howl—even if the ghoul showered afterward—by the trace of chlorine that clung to her skin. Hopefully that was enough to track down Frankie in this cavernous building.

"I smell"—the ghoul sniffed again—"dust, mildewing cardboard, soldering material on the new computers, someone down there stepped in dog poop and doesn't realize they're tracking it everywhere, someone else is wearing way too much cheap cologne, and there's at least three smokers. Many crimes of hair gel and body odor are being committed." She cringed and looked to the ghouls. "This is olfactory torture, just so you're aware."

"I'm sorry," said Draculaura. "But I know you can do this! Try again, please."

Clawdeen sighed, then inhaled again. "Stale coffee, some sort of pepper spray, more cologne, or that might be aftershave? Fabric softener—which, as a future fashion designer, I'm duty bound to tell you is actually really bad for—" She broke off and sniffed again, her face splitting into a wide grin. "Formaldehyde! I've got her."

Draculaura caught the moment where the other ghoul had to stifle her urge to let out a triumphant wolf howl—a sacrifice for which she was eternally grateful. Four ghouls versus dozens of humans? They *needed* the element of surprise on their side.

Lagoona patted her back, and Cleo fist pumped, but Draculaura just nodded and gestured for Clawdeen to lead the way.

They followed Clawdeen's nose to a metal ladder. Each ghoul turned to shush the one behind them as they tried their best to climb silently to the grated platform that ringed the warehouse below. Cleo was last in line, and Draculaura caught her annoyed expression as she realized there was no one behind her to shush.

She hadn't expected Cleo to come with them—she was still impressed the ghoul had stood up to Ramses and Nefera but hadn't fully known how to include her in their plans. Hadn't known if she *should*, for fear that Cleo would panic if this dark, enclosed space triggered her worst trapped-in-a-pyramid phobias. So far, she seemed steady. Disgusted by the dust, but steady. So far, that was enough.

By the time Draculaura and Cleo made it onto the platform, Lagoona and Clawdeen were racing ahead. Draculaura let Cleo pass her so the ghoul could have someone to shush as they speed-tip-toed to where the other ghouls had paused.

"Is that a mouse? I don't do mice," Clawdeen whisper-shrieked, going up on the toe of one shoe and practically scrambling onto Lagoona's back when the sea monster bent to look. "Where's Toralei when I need her?"

"That's no mouse, mate," Lagoona gasped out, trying to untangle herself from Clawdeen's chokehold. "I think—it *is*! That's Frankie's hand."

If a hand could cower, that's what those four fingers and a thumb were doing. Hiding in a corner beneath a layer of dust and cobwebs, too scared to care what the dingy concrete floor had done to their manicured nails.

"Oh. Right. I totally knew that." Clawdeen straightened and dusted off her skirt.

Cleo sniffed her disagreement, but Draculaura was pretty sure they were all relieved she didn't voice it. At least not while the peace between her and Clawdeen was so fragile and new.

"Where's Frankie?" she asked the appendage. It pointed: down, beyond the computer monitors, to a window-lined office. It had probably belonged to the boss, back when this building had been operational. But now it was a mess of cracked and missing windows, a door that hung crooked on its hinges.

Leaning against the metal railing, Draculaura squinted through the dark. She could make out a chair in its interior. A single exposed bulb hanging from the ceiling—turned off. On the far side of the room, a desk. There was a cell phone perched on top of a coil of rope. The rest of the desk was covered in weapons. A lethal collection of blades—varying in size and shape, but all so sharp it stole Draculaura's breath. Van was pacing behind the desk, a serrated knife in one gloved hand. He looked sweatier, less polished than he'd been in the first video. Draculaura's eyes flitted back to the chair. To the figure seated on it.

Frankie.

"I found her," she said. And she knew the ghouls were sharing a celebratory smile, but she didn't turn or join in. Finding Frankie wasn't the same as *saving* her. The hardest part still lay ahead.

She glanced over the railing again. Was Poe's father among the humans pacing the warehouse floor? The ones making themselves feel big and tough by making a small ghoul cower? The ones hiding behind computers and making threats—and the ones who'd feel inspired by others' big, tough talk to follow through on those threats with actual violent action? How many people had amassed at Monster High with the intention to attack it because of the words of these humans? And who among them had participated in the invasion and abduction?

Had Poe's father?

If so, she wasn't sure she'd be able to keep her promise not to hurt him.

A new thought made her pause, her hands tightening on the railing—she *had* just hurt his son. She'd just done the thing all these people feared most from her kind—she'd drunk from one of theirs . . . And she still didn't know how to handle that thought.

It was another topic to add to her mental coffin: *Was* she as evil as the humans feared? But she didn't have time to process it now. She needed to act. Any deep self-analysis or panic would have to be done later—likely with some heavy-lifting from her scare-apist—because this was a moment of transformation. Literally. And she was worried that if she stopped to think too much, she'd jinx her brand-new abilities.

Bat. Bat. Bat-bat-bat. Dracula had always told her to slow her breathing, to visualize the bat she wanted to be—picturing the details: the little bat ears, the tiny bat claws.

But Draculaura had barely visualized a snout before the change took hold—the ability coming at her with such speed and ease that it gave her a head rush as she shrank and grew wings, which were flapping to keep her hovering in place.

"I know I saw you do that outside, but still, that is *so* claw-some, D," said Clawdeen, who apparently didn't find bats as terrifying as mice, since she hurried over to hold up the tiny scroll they'd pre-written back at Monster High for just this purpose.

Draculaura grasped the scroll and flapped a wing in acknowledgment of the good-luck wishes of the other ghouls. She saw Lagoona scarefully place Frankie's hand in her backpack. Then she soared upward, circling the rafters once before swooping into the shadows and following them down to where Frankie was being kept.

She did a pass on silent wings, marking where Van stood in

the room (behind the desk, posing for social medea posts with all his knives) and gliding past to make sure Frankie saw her. Every emotion flitted across Frankie's face as she recognized her friend, then realized what Draculaura in bat-form must mean—since the last conversation between the two of them had been about Draculaura's decision to stay human.

As Frankie's expression crumpled, Draculaura wished she had a way to communicate that she was okay—that she'd still had a choice and had made a better one.

Instead she landed lightly on the bindings holding Frankie to the chair and began to gnaw. She pressed the scroll into the ghoul's hand as the ropes at her wrists gave way and she moved on to the ones at her ankles.

Don't move. Draculaura wasn't sure if vamp-powers of persuasion worked in bat form, but she sent this thought as hard as she could in Frankie's direction. *Don't move. Not yet.*

Not with Van so armed, so close. He was still wearing his invasion uniform—though his looked fancier than what the other normies wore, like he'd had it custom tailored. He propped the phone back on the desk, the camera now facing Frankie. Draculaura wasn't worried about appearing on video—she wouldn't, even in bat-form—but the man in the room would be able to see her. So she stayed concealed behind the chair legs as she gnawed the last rope. And she wasn't sure if it was persuasion, Frankie's common sense, or fear—but the ghoul stayed immobile as Van stalked closer. He'd traded his serrated knife for a bigger one, the blade glinting in the low light he'd flipped on when he started filming.

"What do you say we open you up? Rip those seams and take you back to pieces?"

"N-no. Please," blubbered Frankie. Behind the chair, Draculaura briefly nuzzled her snout against the ghoul's leg before resuming her bites on the cord binding her.

Lagoona was up next—and her part of the plan could commence any time now. As in, *now* would be a really creeptastic time for it to commence.

It started with a drip, then a trickle—then a blast, as the pipes above their heads burst. The water flowed away from Frankie's chair, aimed with striking precision in the face of the knife-wielding man.

Van gasped, sputtered, and ran out of the office. All around the warehouse, other pipes were doing similar things. Lagoona was controlling the water inside them, directing it at the people, at electronics.

And even though he'd run scared, Draculaura could hear Van yelling at the others, "This isn't supernatural, it's rust. Stop panicking like a bunch of babies."

Draculaura nudged Frankie's hand—the one still attached, the one containing their note—the other hand was, presumably, still in Lagoona's backpack. Frankie pulled it forward and quickly read the small scroll. She had a part to play in this plan too, and in a few strides, she was on it—off the chair, out of the room, directing her own powers at the pools of water collecting along the floor.

The first sign it was working—beyond the visible currents of electricity arcing from her bolts—was that the water in the closest pools started smoking. Then a few men standing in puddles jerked and jumped back as the jolts hit them.

And then—the real payoff—the computers, monitors, tablets, and anything electronic began to spark and sizzle.

Draculaura knew they hadn't taken the Van Hellscream Society offline permanently, but frying all their hard drives and devices would at least set them back a bit. Maybe it would buy the school and monster world a moment to regroup.

But speaking of regrouping—the normies were pulling it together faster than she'd anticipated. Apparently not even threats of drowning or electrocution could deter them from their hatred. They were closing in on Frankie from multiple sides.

Lagoona was trying her best to stop them with water, and Frankie was still shooting zaps, but both of their powers were flagging.

Mid-flap, Draculaura changed back into ghoul-form. She hovered slowly to the floor, purposely flashing her fangs as she descended.

The normies shrieked, some of them crying out prayers to gods that Draculaura knew would never condone their actions.

"Stop," she ordered them.

The normies froze, then looked at each other in confusion.

"Don't just stand there, get them," ordered Van.

"On it, Van," said a man in coveralls, who stepped forward holding a crowbar.

"Don't get us!" yelled Draculaura. "No one get us."

But it was too many people for her to concentrate on all of them. Vampiric hypnosis worked best when you could make eye contact with the person you were persuading. None of these humans was making eye contact with her—they were all too busy drawing their weapons.

She could hear Clawdeen howling from the upper landing, hear footsteps clattering down the ladder. But none of that helped them. Not when Van and his knife were only an arm's length in front of them. Not when there were other normies just as close behind, so that when Frankie and Draculaura jumped backward to avoid a knife thrust, they landed in the grasp of a pair of his henchmen, who twisted their arms behind their backs, smiling their perverse delight when Frankie gasped in pain.

"Take them back to my office," Van ordered. He tapped the flat of his knife beneath Draculaura's chin. She bared her fangs at him, but he just chuckled. "And don't even dream of trying anything else—unless you want to see your friend come apart in slices."

"Halt right there!"

Draculaura didn't even recognize her friend's voice until Cleo stepped forward from the shadows, one arm raised. "Woe on you humans. Woe. Those of you foolish enough to take on me—a princess of Egypt, daughter of the pharaoh, descendent of an ancient line. The power that runs beneath my bandages is as old as the sands in the desert, as unstoppable as the winds. It should make you quake and call for your mummy—"

If they hadn't been quaking already, they started to then, because Clawdeen and Lagoona must've found some sort of spotlight and fan to position at just the right angles. Switched on—the combination made Cleo look like she was lit up from within and controlling the air inside the warehouse.

Van had stepped backward to watch—his knife dangling by his side. His henchmen hadn't let go of Draculaura's or Frankie's arms—but they'd stopped marching them toward the office.

Cleo extended her other arm, showcasing something roughly double the size of her fist. It glittered golden in the spotlight, but Draculaura didn't recognize it.

"Behold!" said Cleo. "I hold the ancient relic of Snakestone—"

Draculaura and Frankie looked away from each other, Frankie biting into her shoulder and Draculaura covering a laugh with a cough. *Snakestone?* Due to Cleo's chronic over-sharing, the ghouls both knew that was Deuce's pet name for the, um, *obelisk* in his pants. But none of the normies knew that, and they were repeating it with terrified reverence.

"With this relic I can curse you—I can curse your families. No one from your line will ever again know peace."

"Don't do it!" cried a woman near a smoking computer.

"Please, don't!" said the man behind Frankie. He'd dropped her arms and was backing away. "I don't want to be snakestoned."

Cleo raised an eyebrow and gave a pointed look at the man still holding Draculaura.

He released her arms and ran.

As soon as the ghouls were free, Cleo let out a haughty cackle and smashed the golden object on the ground. Draculaura noticed that Clawdeen used that exact moment to drag her claws through a bag of unmixed concrete and tip it off the suspended platform.

It covered everyone below in gritty powder. The normies coughed and cried out about curses.

The ghouls coughed and ran.

Clawdeen was the first to reach the massive double doors and roll one open. There was no need for secret entrances or skulking now—the faster they could exit, the better.

Lagoona was following close behind, then Cleo. Frankie had just reached the door when Draculaura paused.

She saw it.

Poe's notebook. Clutched in the grasp of a man who was hard to look at, because he looked so much like the boy who'd just broken her heart. She recognized the same hurt in Mr. Beissen's eyes, only instead of being brave enough to face this world sad and vulnerable like his son, he'd turned his hurt into hatred. She wished she had the words to tell him how wrong he was, how much his actions were harming his son—and how worthy Poe was of a functional, present father.

She couldn't do any of that. She also couldn't erase the way her own actions had hurt Poe, but she could at least remove the guilt of this notebook from Poe's emotional burden.

She could eliminate the risk that spiral-bound disaster posed.

And if she scared the hex out of Mr. Beissen while doing that—well, that was a bonus.

She met the man's eyes and hardened her voice to deadly persuasion: "Poe deserves a better father than you've been."

"He does," he said with such conviction that she wondered

if it wasn't just her vampiric hypnosis at work here but his own beliefs as well.

"*Draculaura*," called Clawdeen from the doorway. "Get out here!"

She didn't break eye contact. "You will stop attending the Van Hellscream Society and be more present in his life. Listen to him before you lose him too."

The man nodded, but he was frowning now.

The ghouls' voices were louder, intrusive, wearing at her focus. "Give me the notebook."

Mr. Beissen looked down at it in confusion, but instead of relaxing, his fingers tightened. "This is Poe's."

"Give it to *me*!" Draculaura put so much desperate persuasive power in her voice that other Van Hellscream Society members picked up whatever was closest and held it out in her direction. Poe's father didn't—but he'd relaxed his fingers enough that she could tear the notebook from his grasp.

"Draculaura, hurry!" Frankie called from the door.

"What are you even doing?" demanded Cleo. "They're going to, you know"—she switched to Zombie, a fact that would make Ghoulia beam when Cleo repeated this part of the story later—"realize there's no curse."

With the notebook in her hands and Van Hellscream members starting to stir from their stupor, Draculaura turned and ran toward the door.

She snagged a rod of rebar from a shelf as she passed, and once she was through the doors, paused again.

"Ghoul, we've got to run," Clawdeen insisted.

"Not yet." Draculaura slid the rebar through the handles, but it wouldn't stay, not just balanced like that. Taking a deep breath, she gripped the ends of the steel rod and pulled.

She had a feeling these super-vamp skills were temporary. A result of being newly changed—maybe all baby vampires were super strong? Or maybe it was because this was her second transformation—this time she'd gotten all the powers and none of the nasty new vamp self-control and bloodlust distractions? Or maybe—maybe those images of her dad teaching her hadn't been memories or hallucinations. Maybe vampires didn't turn to dust and disappear. Maybe Dracula . . . maybe he was still with her. Maybe she'd always carry him with her.

The bar twisted in her grasp, bending into a knot that would take some time—and potentially someone with a hack-saw—to undo.

There were other exits that the normies would remember and use eventually, but right now the angry crowd inside was hammering on this one.

Draculaura slung an arm around Frankie, who was wiggling her reattached fingers and looking exhausted. She slumped against her and struggled through a sob. "I didn't think anyone would come in time. I thought I was . . ."

"We'll always come," she told Frankie. But right now there was a bigger problem: How would she get them out of here?

There was a skid of tires and a beep from their left. The ghouls' heads whipped around to see Deuce sitting behind the wheel of his neon green SUV. He called through the open window, "I saw the video stream and came in case you needed any stone-cold backup. But since you ghoul-bosses had it covered, does anyone want a ride home?"

Draculaura could've just about kissed him. But she didn't need to because Cleo already was. And claiming shotgun. The rest of them piled in the back, and Deuce had the gas pedal to the floorboard before their car doors were even fully shut.

Cleo leaned against his shoulder. "Did you see that? Did you see how freaky fierce I was? Those normies were quaking like sand in a windstorm."

"I saw it *all*, babe. You freaking rocked!"

Cleo preened and pressed a kiss to his cheek. It was, objectively, agoreable. Even Clawdeen was smiling as she rolled her eyes, but Draculaura couldn't watch. Not with Poe's notebook curled in her hands, the one that listed all her answers and all their canceled future plans. She couldn't join in their celebration. But she couldn't ruin it either.

"You know what," she said, lowering the window beside her. "There's not enough seat belts and I—I want to just go fly over the building one last time to see if they've gotten out or if anyone is following us. I'll—I'll meet you back at school."

She was sure they objected, had thrown all sorts of protests her way, but she hadn't stuck around to hear them. She'd transformed in a blink and taken to the sky.

CHAPTER 25

There was a crowd of monsters at the school when Draculaura arrived. Not just some students—*all* the students gathered on the front lawn, and parents and alumni too. Jackson Jekyll and Heath Burns were tearing down the sensors above the doors. Lagoona was in a huddle with her coach—smiling as they discussed some sort of training plan spreadsheet on a clipboard.

Abbey was sending showers of cooling flurries toward Manny, Slo Mo, Clawd, and the others who were clearing rocks, bricks, and other things the humans had thrown onto campus.

Frankie was sandwiched in a sparktacular hug between her parents, looking whole and happy.

And best of all—Draculaura had done a slow circle of the whole perimeter, and she hadn't seen evidence of a single lingering normie.

She transformed back and hovered slowly to the ground near where Medusa was tutting at her son and extending her palm as if he was a toddler who needed to hold her hand to cross the street. "Come on, Deucey, we are *leaving*. And you are in so much trouble, manster! I did not give you permission to—"

"Permission to *what*?" asked Cleo, stepping toward the duo and draping herself around Deuce's other arm. "Save the school? Save our afterlives? He's not a baby; he's a nearly grown manster with a mind of his own, and he's a creeperific chef and kisser. He was also a hero today. You should be *praising* him, not punishing him."

Medusa sputtered; her snakes hissed. "Well, I never."

"You never *what*?" asked Cleo calmly. "You never said he couldn't go to Monster High anymore? Because you certainly did do that. Talk about mixed messages. *You* are the one who's always yelling at him to take school more seriously—didn't he prove he does by, um, *saving Monster High*? Are you really going to be the one who stands between him and a deaducation?"

Medusa opened her mouth, closed it. Opened it again and said, "Fine. He can attend." She wrapped her shawl around her shoulders with a flourish, and added, "For now—" before marching off.

Deuce swept Cleo up into his arms. "That rocked. The last time I saw her speechless was when I was eight and accidentally stoned her."

Cleo giggled. "I was petrified, but you are worth it."

"And *you*, babe, are amazing."

Then they were kissing again—the type of kissing that deathinitely didn't belong in public around impressionable young monsters and ancient alumni. The type that normally Mr. Hackington would've dielighted in breaking up and assigning detention for. But it seemed like saving the school gave them a momentary free pass.

"I guess those two are back together," said Clawdeen.

Toralei gave her ghoulfriend a soft look. "Some things are just meant to be, I guess." Then, before she could be accused of being mushy, her grin sharpened and she added, "Besides, she's much more tolerable when he's around."

Draculaura felt her smile slipping. All the talk of *meant to be* made her think of what wasn't. Made her think of a boy she'd left in a graveyard. A boy whose mom was dead and dad was worthless—and now he'd lost her too.

"Excuse me, Cleo," said Headmistress Bloodgood, once she'd decided the PDA had gone on plenty long enough. "I have a question."

Deuce was wearing more lipstick than Cleo was when they broke apart and turned to face their headmistress.

"What was the 'Snakestone Relic'?" she asked from atop her horse. "I've never heard of it."

Draculaura was pretty sure she wasn't the only ghoul biting the inside of her cheek to keep from giggling while deliberately *not* looking at Deuce, who had to be ready to petrify himself. Well, maybe this would finally teach Cleo to keep private things private?

Except, nope, she was totally unperturbed, shrugging and answering, "Oh my Ra, I just broke the top off a trophy for something called *bowling*—I figured it was shiny and they wouldn't know any better. It worked."

"Bowling. Hmmm." Headmistress Bloodgood nodded. "Good thinking. And creeptastic work, all of you." She waved her hand to indicate the small group of them standing by the fountain, but also Frankie, Lagoona, and Ghoulia, who were walking over to join them.

While the first two were clearly in celebration mode, the zombie had something in her hands and headed straight for Draculaura.

"Ghoulia, I love you, but I think I'll be so much happier if you never thrust a book at me with some dire, life-changing news again."

Ghoulia rolled her eyes and pointed at the page, then lost patience with Draculaura's slow reading pace. (To be fair, it was written in Latin *and* fancy old-style calligraphy, plus, Ghoulia wasn't exactly holding the book steady). The ghoul sighed and gave a concise translation in Zombie: "The reason there had never been elections for school boards in the past is that the position of head is tied to the blood protections. Ipso facto, Draculaura's blood protects the school, so she's now head of the board."

Draculaura spluttered in protest. "I'm not—I've never—"

"You're a natural leader," interrupted Headmistress Blood-good. "And you have my full support." She held up a hand as Draculaura continued to shake her head. "But . . . we could hold an election, if that would make you feel comfortable?"

"I, um, guess?" squeaked Draculaura. Now that the shock was wearing off, the idea of holding her father's old position and feeling connected to him in that way sounded, well, fangtastic. "Could we make it so that students could vote too? It *is* their school board after all."

"You'd have my vote," barked Clawdeen.

"And mine," said Deuce, who was still wearing more of Cleo's gold lipgloss than she was.

"Purrhaps, I could be purrsuaded," said Toralei. But she winked as she said it.

The volume of people offering support surged to a roar, which Headmistress Bloodgood silenced with a wave of her hand. "Students voting is an intriguing idea. Let's meet after class tomorrow to discuss. Until then, go home, get some rest. All of you." She pointed at each of the ghouls before turning Nightmare to shoo the rest of the monsters gathered in the courtyard toward their homes.

Cleo watched the departing headmistress. She tapped a finger against her lips and *hmmm*'d.

Draculaura braced herself for an outburst in defense of Ramses. Beside her, she felt Frankie and Lagoona stiffen too.

Then Cleo turned and tore a poster of her father off a lamppost. "I guess we won't be needing these anymore."

Frankie chewed her lip. "Do you really think your dad will give up that easily?"

"Yes." Cleo's answer was immediate and firm. "Because if he doesn't, I'll go public about how *I* am voting for Draculaura . . . And I'll call his mummy and tell her about his bribery scheme. There's a reason he always goes on vacation when Grandmummy comes to visit—if you think *he's* bad, she's *worse*. He fled the school when it was in trouble; he doesn't get a say in how it's run." She ripped down a second poster, balled it up, and threw it at the ghouls. "Well, are you just going to stand there watching me ruin my manicure, or are you going to help?"

Toralei was first to jump to action, raking her claws down a flier hung on a statue, shredding the paper to ribbons. She grinned over her shoulder at Cleo. "Look at us, finally finding common ground."

"Oh my Ra," said Cleo, who, now that everyone else had spread out across the courtyard and was removing posters, was reclining against the fountain. "I'm going to be quite peeved if you sphinx this is the *only* thing we have in common."

Toralei eyed her skeptically. "You can think of something else?"

"Do you or do you not sphinx that ghoul over there is creeptacular? Because if you do *not*, then we have a major problem."

Clawdeen was tackling a poster-covered bench across the quad. Too far away to hear their conversation but very aware that they were talking and that Cleo was pointing at her. She shot Draculaura an apprehensive look as she called, "Everything okay over there?"

Draculaura laughed when Toralei and Cleo gave her simultaneous thumbs-up.

Clawdeen's frown deepened. "Why does that make me *more* nervous?"

And maybe Draculaura should be nervous too—not about Cleo and Toralei, who would happily bicker for the rest of their afterlives, but about this new role she'd likely be tackling, assuming the election went her way. Head of the school board? Her?

Except, for the first time all school year, everything at Monster High felt balanced. Safe. She could see it in the posture of the departing families, in the expressions on the creatures' faces. She could hear it in the laughter ringing out across the school grounds.

And she could feel it—a sense of rightness seeping out of the school's stones, singing in her blood.

CHAPTER 26

ater, Draculaura wouldn't have been able to explain why she went to the graveyard before school. Two weeks had passed since the showdown with the Van Hellscream Society. One week since the school board election she'd won in a landslide.

There'd been no word from the monster hunters. Draculaura wasn't naïve enough to think they'd gone away for good; they'd simply gone underground.

They'd lick their wounds and grow their numbers and wait for the public sentiment to change, because videos had emerged of them attacking a school of unarmed teens, and monsters or not, it was not a good look. There were normie protests all over the place rallying against what the monster hunters had done. Draculaura searched every news article and photograph for sad eyes and chaos curls. She hadn't found him yet, but she knew Poe had attended—he'd promised he would.

Eventually, though, she knew the protests would fade and the Van Hellscream Society would reemerge, angrier than ever.

But at least they didn't have Poe's notebook to use as ammunition for their hate. She'd burnt it and buried the ashes.

It was so hard to boolieve two weeks had passed since she'd spilled her blood on the school's bricks. Since Poe had shared his blood with her.

True to Poe's promise, she hadn't heard from him. On the same day his dad had betrayed him, she had too. He'd lost them both. She hoped he had other people in his life who loved him—other people he loved.

True to Ghoulia's research, the school had been a sanctuary since then. There'd been no additional attacks. Not internal or external. She hadn't heard any more talk of students transferring.

But that morning, Draculaura had woken up early with a sudden conviction that she needed to go to the cemetery. It didn't make any sense. She'd never met Poe in the morning, and she had no way of knowing if he'd be there.

Except she *did* know. She could feel it in her bones, in the anxious knot at the base of her throat that only pulled tighter when she caught that first glimpse of him halfway across the cemetery in the misty morning air. His chaos of curls weren't all that different than the whisps of fog spiraling off the ground, and if she didn't know how very, very human he was, she might have convinced herself he was a phantom or specter.

He was certainly a professional at haunting her thoughts.

Poe stood at the edge of his mother's gravesite; his sneakers darkened damp with dew. Was his face wet too? She couldn't tell from her place, hidden among the trees and shadows. Hers was.

She swiped a hand beneath her eyes, the tear leaving a watery red streak on her fingers.

She couldn't let him see her.

She was certain of that. More certain when he turned his head and revealed the bandage on his neck.

Technically she was breaking her promise just by being here, just by watching him. But this—crouching in the shadows—this couldn't endanger him, right?

She'd given up too much to keep Monster High safe. She couldn't risk exposing it now. Also, the last time he'd looked at her had been with love. Draculaura couldn't bear it if he rejected her. Or, worse . . . feared her.

He was talking. To his mom, presumably, but she was too far away to hear what he was saying. He absently traced the edge of the bandage with a finger, the same way she unconsciously ran her tongue across her fangs. Was he telling his mom about *her*?

Draculaura hadn't told the ghouls about Poe, and at this point it didn't make sense. She didn't know how. She couldn't explain who he was, who he'd been to her this past month. How he'd saved her from grief, from loneliness, from herself.

How his blood had literally saved *her*—and saved the school.

And how he'd said *I love you* before they said *goodbye*.

She had the picture, though. The one from their last good night, when she thought they'd have a future. It was likely the only picture she'd ever appear in, so she was glad it'd turned out well. She was relieved to have proof that he was *real*, they had happened, it hadn't all been in her head.

The picture would have to be enough. She knew, even as she swore there was no harm in this—that she wouldn't come back here, wouldn't spy on him again.

She lifted her hand, pressed it to her lips and then the air, and whispered, "Goodbye, Poe."

CHAPTER 27

It had become Draculaura's new ritual to end every school day in her new office. It still felt like her dad's, partly because when Ramses had ordered his servants to return the room to the way they'd found it, they'd followed that command to the letter. Right down to the pens Draculaura had scattered on the desktop back in June.

These she'd hastily crammed into their cup and stowed in a drawer.

Maybe in another week or two she'd be ready to emotionally and physically sort that out—but right now, it just needed to be out of sight.

When Headmistress Bloodgood had first met with her about the position of head of the board after the election a week ago, Draculaura had expected to be told the role would be mostly ceremonial. It wasn't.

There were papers to sign, proposals to read. Budgets and policies to approve. Meetings to *lead*. Thankfully the other board members were warmly welcoming. They were excited about having a student's perspective on the board and willing to lend a hand (or three hands, for certain members of the board) with whatever she needed.

The true test would be their first meeting next week. They'd had to move the time so it wouldn't conflict with fearleading practice . . . though, if she didn't get started on the makeup schoolwork from all the times she'd played hooky to hang out with Poe, she was going to get kicked off the team. Luckily, Ghoulia had already volunteered to help catch her up.

Draculaura straightened her dad's garlic-shaped stress ball and a picture frame. She was a very different ghoul than the one who'd whimsically sat on this desk back in June, swinging her legs and making a mess.

What would her mom think of the choices she'd made this year? What would her dad? And would there ever be a crossroads in her life when she didn't wish they could be beside her, giving her advice or encouragement? And sometimes, in her darkest, most sleepless midnights, she lay in her casket and let questions and conspiracies unspool in her mind. She'd only seen ashes . . . was her dad truly gone? But if he wasn't, where was he? And the pharmacy—could they truly make such a dire mistake *by accident,* or had darker forces been at play?

Draculaura had told Headmistress Bloodgood that she'd changed her mind; she would like to talk to the inspectors working on her father's case after all. No matter what they told her, it would be answers. She could close the casket on her doubts, bury her questions. Move on.

And no matter what those answers were, after everything she'd made it through this year, she was confident she could face whatever lay ahead too.

There were deathinitely some challenges coming her way. Even if you ignored the Van Hellscream Society and their fringe group of haters, the threats to Monster High from the wider world weren't over. People now knew they existed. Humans' reactions to that fact were as diverse as monsterkind itself, but the werecat was out of the bag, so to speak. There'd be consequences for that.

"What's that serious face about? You're going to give yourself wrinkles." Cleo had never fully grasped the concept of knocking. "Besides, it's time for ghouls' night. All this school board yuck can wait until Monday."

She had—of all things—feather boas in her hands. She draped a neon pink one around Draculaura. The other ghouls were waiting behind her in the doorway, already festooned with feathers that matched their outfits.

"You almost ready?" asked Frankie. "And for real, if you need a school board secretary, I'm always ready to lend a hand."

Draculaura closed the file of documents she'd been working on and stowed it in a desk drawer until Monday. "I'm going to take you up on that," she said. And she would. She was done keeping her friends at a distance. "I'll take all the help I can get."

"In that case"—Cleo paused in the center of the office and looked around, tapping her lip—"you desperately need some help with your interior design. First, you need more lighting—where do you land on the spectrum of chandeliers versus candelabra? Second, how do you feel about gold? If not everywhere, at least as an accent color."

Draculaura pushed her chair back and stood quickly. "I feel a lot better about pizza."

"Did someone say *pizza*?" Deuce appeared behind the others holding a huge stack of boxes. "I gotchu covered."

"Oh, I'm sorry, babe, but it's *ghouls'* night." Cleo pouted. "But I'll make it up to—"

"Yeah, I know," Deuce interrupted, ducking so Frankie could wrap a bright green boa around his neck. "And I've got this killer new recipe for a face mask that I cooked up in Home Eek. Avocado, yogurt, tomb-eric, and honey." He turned to Lagoona, Frankie, and Clawdeen. "I can't wait for you ghouls to try it. These guys love it." He juggled the pizza boxes so he'd have a hand free to point up at his snakes. They all rattled their approval.

"I've heard good things about tomb-eric," said Lagoona. "My coach says it's a fintastic antioxidant."

"Wait. You ghouls are okay with Deuce coming?" Cleo was clearly torn between kicking him out or holding his hand. Draculaura hoped that if he did get the boot, they still got to keep the pizza and face masks.

"Uh, yeah," said Clawdeen. "As long as he promises not to blubber so loudly we can't hear the movie this time. That was our deal, right, big guy?"

"Then don't make me watch *To All the Boys I've Bled Be Gore*. I don't even *have* sisters, but those ghouls—the way they love each other—it just gets to me."

Cleo looked from Deuce, who was wiping his face with the boa (which made one of his snakes sneeze), to Clawdeen and

Frankie, who were nodding agreement. To Lagoona, who was still taking about tomb-eric. To Draculaura, who shrugged and said, "I guess you had to be there?"

"So, are we getting this ghouls' night started or what?" asked Toralei as she pushed her way through the crowded doorway to stand by Clawdeen. "Wait, it's not happening in *here*, is it? If so, I'm out. I already spend too much time at this school."

Clawdeen caught her ghoulfriend's hand before she could exit. "We were just leaving. Right, ghouls?"

"Right," they chorused. At least everyone but Cleo did. She was busy looking at her reflection in Deuce's sunglasses and fussing with her boa. When she realized she'd missed the cue, she added a belated, "Yes, right. Or, well, you know what I always say about ghouls' night," Cleo paused for dramatic effect and added, "The party never dies."

"You've literally never said that," said Clawdeen. "Not one time. I don't ever remember her saying that, do you?"

Frankie held up her hands and backed out of the office. "I'm staying out of this."

Lagoona snagged a piece of pizza from one of Deuce's boxes and shoved it in her mouth. She then pointed and mumbled something like, "Cambt twak. Chuwbing."

"You're all the worst," said Clawdeen with a grin.

"Nope. We're freaky, chic, and fly," said Draculaura as she spun her chair back under her desk and herded them all into the hall, locking the door behind her. "C'mon, let's get out of here. Monster High isn't going anywhere, and I could use some time with my beast ghouls." A throat cleared, so she added, "And Deuce."

"Awww." Frankie corralled them into a walking group hug—managing to shock them all in the process. "Lucky for you, we're not going anywhere either."

As they chattered, bickered, and danced down the hallway, Draculaura gave one final glance over her shoulder at the office door. She wasn't the same monster she'd been just months ago. Who knew who she'd be a few more months from now.

But with these ghouls by her side, she couldn't wait to figure it out.

ACKNOWLEDGMENTS

Like so many in the Monster High fandom, my favorite part of this world is the friendships between the ghouls. Getting the chance write new interactions between these characters was such a pure joy. Also, the puns and portmanteaus—those were fangtastically fun to write too.

Draculaura may have the Ghoul Squad backing her up, but I've got something just as amazing: the clawsome teams at Abrams and Mattel! Huge thank-yous to Brann Garvey, Ashley Albert, Maggie Moore, Andrew Smith, and Elaine Gant. Cristiano Spadoni, your artwork on the cover is beyond creeptacular. As for Anne Heltzel, any author would be lucky to work on a single book with you—I can't boolieve this is our *sixth* book together! Thank you!

Kate Testerman, you are the ghoul boss of agents! Merci boocoup for all you do!

In the words of the "Fright Song"—these are my boos, my skeleton crew—and I couldn't have written this book without them: Lauren Magaziner, Lauren Morrill, Jessica Spotswood, Miranda Kenneally, Sarvenaz Tash, Rebecca Behrens, Jackson Pearce, Courtney Summers, and Emily Hainsworth.

Haley and Jen Zelesko—from Fangsylvania to Bitealy—thank you for helping me brainstorm across continents and time zones.

Much like Frankie, I'd fall to pieces without the family and friends who help stitch me back together: St. Matt, Shannon, Anne, Libby, Heather, Nancy, Jena, Kira, and of corpse, my Schmidlets and Theodosia.

And finally, to the Monster High fans—those who've been watching from the original webisodes and those of you who made your first trip into the school in these pages—thanks for sharing your enthusiasm for these characters and this world with me. Thanks for joining me on this spooktacular adventure. As long as you love Monster High, the party truly, truly never dies.

ABOUT THE AUTHOR

Tiffany Schmidt is the author of *Once Bitten, Twice Dead* in addition to nine other acclaimed young adult novels, including *I'm Dreaming of a Wyatt Christmas* and the Bookish Boyfriends series. A former sixth-grade teacher, Tiffany is the wife of a saint, mother of three impish boys, and owner of two mischievous pups. She lives and writes in Doylestown, Pennsylvania.